THE URUGUAY AMETHYST

An Ainsley Walker Gemstone Travel Mystery

J.A. JERNAY

ISBN (electronic): 978-0-9836852-1-0

ISBN (print): 978-1-960936-16-5

CHAPTER ONE

Ainsley Walker knew a lot about gemstones, but she was stumped by question number forty-three.

Hunched over a small worktable, she clutched the sides of her head, twisting her hair in her palms. Staring hard enough at the paper to make it burst into flames.

43. Which one of the following types of quartz does NOT possess a cryptocrystalline structure?
A) Jasper
B) Carnelian
C) Sardonyx
D) Agate
E) Citrine

Ainsley loved gemstones, but the chemistry was beyond her. She didn't have a degree in gemology. Or wanted one.

She leaned back and stretched her arms to the ceiling. Parked on a chair in the outer office of Associated Industries, Ainsley knew nothing about this company. The day before, she'd been trying to hock her engagement ring when the jeweler, impressed by her knowledge of gemstones, had referred her here.

And the first thing they'd done was hand her this bleeping test.

The manager, a woman named Martina, waited behind her. She had her legs crossed and wore a severe gray suit with an updo held in place by bobby pins. Ainsley could feel her eyes burning a hole in the back of her neck.

"Finished?" said Martina. Her accent, while Latin, was unusually soft.

Ainsley shook her head. "Just one left."

"Number forty-three?"

"Yes."

"Don't worry about it," the woman replied, taking the test. "Agate is a nontechnical term. The question should be disqualified."

She began marking the answers. Ainsley noticed a heavily bolted door with a security pad behind her. She guessed that the real business of Associated Industries, whatever that may be, occurred beyond.

"You scored forty-seven of fifty," the woman said.

"Sorry. That was really tough."

"Of course. It's from GIA."

The Gemological Institute of America. Ainsley was surprised that she'd done so well.

"Will that be enough?"

The woman smiled. "I think so. But it really depends on her mood."

"Whose mood?"

"My boss." She stood up and smoothed her outfit. "I need to speak to her. Excuse me."

Martina walked to the heavy door and keyed in a seven-digit code. The green security light flashed on. She went through and shut the door behind her.

Ainsley was left alone in the lobby. She strolled in a circle, pretending to be interested in the paintings along the walls. A pastel sunset over a harbor. A windmill draped in ivy. In the corner was a potted ficus. Gray carpet covered the floor.

So far, nothing here indicated that Associated Industries had either money or taste. She wondered what type of job they were considering her for.

Then the security door opened again, and Martina was back. In her hand was a manila envelope.

"Miss Walker," she said, "my boss would like to offer you a temporary contract position with our company. Congratulations."

Ainsley felt a thrill shoot down her spine and into her legs. But she needed to play it cool.

"What is the position?" she said.

"That I cannot tell you," said Martina.

Ainsley was taken aback. "Why not?"

"Because our business is very sensitive. Here." She handed Ainsley the manila envelope. "Inside is your contract. Please take it home and read over it. We cannot answer any further questions until you have signed it."

Stunned, Ainsley accepted the manila envelope. She was tongue tied. This wasn't how jobs were typically offered.

"When do you want my answer?"

"As soon as possible. We are hoping to start you immediately."

Martina smiled for the first time. Two rows of white teeth shone like bits of valuable ivory.

"Then I'll call you when I've made my decision," Ainsley said.

"Good. I'm looking forward to it."

They shook hands, and Martina held the outside door open. As Ainsley walked across the parking lot towards her car, she was already pulling out her phone.

She needed to talk to David.

CHAPTER TWO

Except for the forty-degree chill in the air, Ainsley could've been at the beach.

She was laying on her back in groomed sand. She was wearing tiny shorts and a tank top. She was gazing at the enormously blue sky. It felt good here.

But Ainsley Walker wasn't at the beach. She was in a long jump pit. And next to her was David Madradis, a lawyer, marking her leap with a measuring tape.

"You were a silver medalist in high school? Seriously?" He shook his head. "I could've thrown a kid in a wheelchair further than that."

"It's not even six in the morning," she said. "And I haven't done this in years."

"No excuses, Walker."

Ainsley started to pull herself up. "No, stay there," he said, walking to the top of the runway. "I'll toss bonbons into your mouth as I sail over you."

She laughed as she rolled out of the pit. David was such a cocky bastard.

Ainsley brushed the sand from her arms and watched his

attempt. He started a fast approach, abruptly shortened his last two strides, and executed a perfect takeoff. His skinny arms and legs cycled through the air until he hit the dirt and fell forward.

"Nice technique," she said.

He brushed sand off his legs and stumbled out of the pit. "What's the damage?"

Ainsley checked the tape. "Six point four meters."

"I'm off today," he said. "Your fault, Walker."

"Whatever. Just read the document while I try again."

Ainsley smiled as she walked to the top of the runway. Behind David's taunts lay a brilliant mind. He'd graduated at the top of his law school class, along with the Legal Weasel, Ainsley's disappeared husband. Now David had been hired as junior associate at a prestigious law firm. And despite his aggressive teasing, she knew that he felt sorry for the way her husband had mercilessly left her.

She cracked her neck. Did a deep knee bend. Then visualized the steps. Fast sprint as possible, two short steps, and launch. She'd been good at this, once upon a time.

A few seconds later, she found herself facefirst in the dirt.

"What the hell happened?" she said.

"Congratulations," David said from a nearby bench, "not many people can trip on flat ground."

Ainsley brushed herself off and joined him on the bench. Her knees were scraped. "I'm done," she said. "Kill me now."

"Mm."

She watched him reading the contract intently. "What do you think?"

"They've got good counsel," he said. "It's airtight. Look. They are responsible for nothing. Not injuries, not illnesses, not even future loss of income. You even pay for airfare."

She knew all that.

"Here's my favorite part," he said. "A non-compete clause.

Seriously? For an unknown position? They could be forbidding you from ever making money, doing anything, ever again."

"What would be the point of that?"

"There probably isn't one. I'm just being paranoid." He swung his lawyerly gaze upon her. "That's how I make the big bucks."

"So give me the good news," she said.

"You're being paid to travel somewhere, which is exciting. Also they're providing some kind of training, though that could be anything."

"Like pole-dancing."

"Or how to torture cute little indigenous rebels. Plus they pay half up front, the other half on delivery. Nice amount too."

Ainsley hadn't been able to stop thinking about that: fifteen thousand dollars. Seven thousand five hundred dollars dropped into her bank account immediately. That would take care of her financial problems for a good while.

"But delivery of what?"

"You tell me," David said.

The unspoken hung between them. Martina didn't *seem* shady. She was too prim to be a madam. Ainsley couldn't imagine her acting as a conduit for drugs either. And weapons dealers generally avoided pastel art and potted plants.

She thought back to the GIA test that had been part of her application. It was no red herring. They really must be dealing in gemstones.

Ainsley would *totally* be onboard with that.

David put the contract back inside the manila envelope and handed it to her. "I think you should take it. Of course, that's coming from someone who's mortgaged his entire future to the inside of a law firm."

"Oh, come on."

"No, really," he said. "Why do you think I run on this track every morning? It's the most excitement I see all day."

She understood his point. This contract represented everything that was missing from her life. Travel, gemstones, glamour, uncertainty, maybe even danger.

David stood up and toweled off his face. "You want to do wind sprints tomorrow morning?"

"Sorry," replied Ainsley, "but I think I'm going to be at my new job."

CHAPTER THREE

Ainsley laid awake all night, staring at the red digits on her bedside clock radio. At six a.m., she showered and chose her favorite coral silk camisole. She added slim fit jeans, a wide loopy belt, and a pair of suede boots.

She arrived at the offices of Associated Industries at eight a.m. It was too early. The door was locked, the lights off. Instead, Ainsley walked across the street to a coffee shop and parked herself at a table with a clear view of the office front door.

At nine a.m. the lights flipped on. She left her cappuccino on the table and ran back to the door.

Martina answered. "Hello, my dear," she said.

"I'm ready to accept," said Ainsley. "Can I use the table to sign?"

"Of course. Do you need a pen?"

"I've got one."

Martina murmured approval. It was apparently a sign of preparedness to carry a pen. Ainsley sat at the desk and whipped her signature onto the various forms.

She handed them over. "Excellent," the woman said. "I'll

give you copies in a moment. Let's go in the back and meet everybody."

She punched the seven-digit code into the security pad, and the heavy bolted door swung open. Ainsley stayed back.

"Are you coming?" she said.

She fought down her nerves. "It's kind of a big moment for me."

Martina frowned. "You have a bigger one coming up," she said. "You're going to meet Gugina."

"Is she the boss?"

Martina nodded. "If she doesn't like you..." She jerked a thumb back towards the outside. "One more thing. I need your phone."

Ainsley stopped. "Why?"

"Security."

Fine. She shrugged, handed the woman her phone, and stepped through the door.

Ainsley found herself in a small, clean, brightly lit facility. It was a small warehouse, really, lined with several rows of glass cabinets. Inside were geodes, crystals, vases, necklaces, pendants, goblets, precious objects of all types, all colors. Each was labeled and brightly lit. Paperwork hung inside plastic sheets tacked beneath each door.

Ainsley stifled a squeal. It was like walking into an adult version of Candyland. She struggled to keep a straight face, but her knees knocked back and forth, always the surest sign of her excitement.

"This is our business," said Martina.

"How many people work here?"

"Just three. Here is our youngest."

Ainsley swiveled. Behind her, a tiny girl, dressed in a blue sequined tank and white miniskirt, dropped a phone into its cradle. She had a gorgeous mass of black hair. She was teetering in a pair of five-inch Louboutins.

"Ainsley," she said, "*so* nice to meet you. My name's Viviana." They shook hands. Hers felt thin and cold. "Your resume looks incredible. You are going to do an awesome job."

Odd: Ainsley hadn't submitted a resume. But she was grateful for the welcome nonetheless.

Then Viviana looked down at Ainsley's legs. "Those are *fantastic* boots. Where did you get them?"

Ainsley had bought them for eighty percent off during a Labor Day sale at an outlet center on an interstate forty miles outside of town. But she didn't want to reveal that, because this girl looked like a high roller.

"I'll give you one guess," Ainsley said.

"Barney's."

"Are you kidding?"

"Saks?"

"Much better."

Viviana smiled. "We're going to be best friends. I *know* it."

Ainsley kept her guard up. This girl might turn out to be a snob, but at least she was making the effort to be welcoming.

"Thank you. I have to go. Martina wants me to interview with her boss."

Viviana grew cold. "That would be my grandmother. Don't mess up." She threw Ainsley a significant warning glance.

Feeling more alarmed, Ainsley followed Martina down one of the aisles lined with glass cabinets. Sparkling jewelry flashed past Ainsley's eyes. She felt her heart racing. She was embarrassed that she had doubted these women's taste or wealth. They had some serious dough.

And now she was about to meet the owner.

They came to a door made of what appeared to be solid mahogany. Martina rested her hand on the knob, which was shaped like a dragon's head. It looked terrifying.

"When we enter," said the woman, "I will introduce you first. Don't shake her hand. Don't make small talk. Just sit down and answer her questions."

"Is there anything I should say?"

Martina thought. "It is better to know what *not* to say. Let's go inside."

CHAPTER FOUR

The room felt ancient. Heavy red woven shades had been drawn against the morning light. There was an old settée at one end of the room, and a very heavy vanity edged in gold. Ainsley smelled unfamiliar creams and powders.

At the other end of the room was an elegant golden armchair.

In the chair was an elderly woman.

Her silver hair had been sprayed up until it resembled a wreath of smoke. Her wrists were a mass of delicate green veins. Her shirt was laden with sequins that glittered like reptilian scales. A heavy blanket had been tucked around her legs.

And inside the woman's face were a pair of black eyes, which were fixed upon Ainsley.

Watching.

Martina led the guest across the room. "Gugina, *tengo Ainsley*. Ainsley, this is Señora Gugina Carlotti."

"A pleasure meeting you," Ainsley said.

The old woman angled her head as her black eyes roved up and down the visitor. Ainsley stood uncomfortably.

Then her black eyes found Ainsley's purse. "Who gave you that?" she asked. Her voice carried the same soft Latin accent.

"I bought it."

The old woman made a face. "It's ugly."

Ainsley didn't feel offended. This woman had the peculiar talent of making even the baldest insults sound like matters of fact. She could tell you that you were the bastard daughter of a truck stop whore, that your toes looked uglier than moldy pieces of fried tofu, and you would find yourself nodding in agreement.

"It's not my favorite purse either," said Ainsley.

"Why don't you bring your best today?"

"Because it doesn't match this outfit."

Gugina coughed, her small frame doubling up. Ainsley handed her a box of tissues. The old woman swatted it away. "My nurse will be here soon. Sit down."

She pointed at the matching chair next to her. Ainsley obeyed and perched on the edge of the cushion. The seat felt firm and unforgiving.

Gugina cleared her throat. "Something I have learned is that many Americans are afraid to travel. They are satisfied with their own lives."

"Not me."

"I have been to almost every country in the world," she finally said. "I have seen how many people live."

"I'm jealous."

"Have you ever travelled?"

"Yes."

"To where?"

Ainsley thought back to her father. He'd taken her on a vacation each of the first eight years of her life. She still had the foot photos to prove it. He'd snapped pictures of their four bare feet overlooking a cypress swamp in South

Carolina, a canyon in New Mexico, a snowy mountain range in Alaska, a pine forest in Michigan.

Then the little carcinogenic masses had formed in his liver, hospice had appeared in the living room, and one morning there had been a trip to a nearby lake with a ceramic urn. The travelling had finished. But Ainsley still kept those foot photos, had stared at them for years until she'd forgotten his face but memorized every detail of the tops of his feet.

"Mostly around America," she said, "but I'm open to wherever."

The old lady didn't acknowledge the answer. Ainsley wasn't sure how the interview was going. Pleasing Gugina felt like practicing blindfolded archery.

The old woman's hand lifted a cup of water to her mouth. Ainsley watched her thin lips suck greedily from the rim.

When she was finished, Gugina set the cup down. She seemed refreshed. "You have a husband, Miss Ainsley?"

"No. He dumped me and moved out."

"Do you have children?"

Ainsley smirked. "Please."

A look of impatience flashed across Gugina's face. "Why *please*? I'm not a waitress. I can't bring you children like a pile of beans on a plate."

"I mean that I don't have any."

"That's very wise." The old lady fixed her eyes on the ceiling, as if her next words were etched in the woodwork. "There are too many people on the earth. And people are terrible anyways. I don't like them."

"I don't care about saving the earth," Ainsley said. "I just don't want kids."

Gugina's black eyes suddenly lit up. "Do you know Spanish?"

"Some."

"How much?"

"I studied for three years in school."

"And do you speak it?"

Ainsley swallowed hard. She hadn't for several years, except to talk to the maintenance men coming into her apartment to fix her shower. There'd been one long-ago boyfriend, a Venezuelan, who'd been a native speaker. But they hadn't really talked much at all, which is probably why the relationship had ended.

But she said, "Of course."

The old woman barked something to Martina, who quickly brought over a plate of fruit, placing it on the low coffee table.

Gugina pointed at a peach. "What is that called?"

"A peach."

"How do you say that in Spanish?"

Ainsley squinted at the fruit and thought hard. "*Melocotón*."

Gugina frowned and shook her head. "No, no. Let's try another. When you squeeze a peach, what do you get?"

"Juice."

"How do you say 'juice' in Spanish?"

She though back to her high school Spanish teacher. He'd been from Madrid. "*Zumo*," she said.

The old woman was angry now, but Ainsley didn't know why. "What is the Spanish word for 'street'?" she said.

Finally, an easy question. "*Calle*," replied Ainsley.

To her surprise, Gugina threw her arms into the air roared. She turned and breathed fiery bursts of rapid Spanish at Martina, who answered politely but with obvious frustration. It was clear they were arguing about her.

"Ainsley, can you excuse us for a moment?" said Martina.

She nodded, happy for the break from this testy old woman. Ainsley went back into the small warehouse and exhaled. Where were these women *from*? With their soft Spanish accents, Italian names, and white skin?

She roamed the aisle, hands clasped tightly behind her back, until she spotted a chalice, studded with blue stones, glittering in a cabinet under the light. It looked like chalcedony. Ainsley had just picked up the informational tag when Martina's voice cut across the floor.

"Please *don't* touch that."

She was standing in the doorway of Gugina's den, and the tone of her voice meant business.

Ainsley dropped the tag and backed away. "I was just curious."

"We are ready for you again."

The heavy scents enveloped Ainsley as she stepped inside the lair again. The old woman was still in her golden armchair, but now Martina sat beside her.

With no place to sit, Ainsley stood before them, trying to keep her knees still. This was an audition, these women her judges.

"We want to welcome you to Associated Industries," said Martina.

"I'm excited to be here," replied Ainsley.

"You're aware that this position involves travel."

"Yes."

"Would you like to know the location of your assignment?"

"Yes."

Martina paused. "You will be travelling to Uruguay."

Ainsley didn't know what to say.

"Do you know about Uruguay?"

Ainsley was drawing a blank. Try as she might, she couldn't think of *anything* she knew about Uruguay. She'd always confused it with Paraguay. And one of them had two capitals. Or was that Bolivia?

"No," she confessed. "Tell me."

She wondered if this would be the end of her employment. But her judges just smiled. "Good," hissed Gugina. "It is better that way."

"What will I be doing?"

Martina shook her head sadly. "We cannot tell you that yet. You must do something else first."

"What?"

"Learn Spanish."

"I already know—"

Martina silenced her. "No, you know Castellano. You don't know Rioplatense. That's the Spanish we speak in Uruguay."

So that's why Gugina had been testing her. And apparently she'd been answering wrong.

"How am I supposed to learn it?" asked Ainsley.

"We are going to send you to a private tutor. We will give you four weeks to learn from him. If you pass his tests, we will give you the mission. Is this clear?"

Ainsley nodded. "One problem."

"What?"

"I need to pay my rent."

The old woman sneered. Ainsley thought she glimpsed actual steam curling out of her nostrils.

"When you pass his test," said Martina, "we will deliver the first half of your money into your bank account. The speed of the learning is up to you."

Ainsley was floored. It was the nineteenth of the month. She didn't have four weeks to learn Rioplatense.

If she wanted to avoid eviction, she only had eleven days.

CHAPTER FIVE

Ainsley buried her head between her arms.

She'd been trying to use the subjunctive voice. That was hard enough. But she was trying to use subjunctive in *rioplatense*, the local dialect of Uruguay and Argentina.

It wasn't working.

She was sitting in a study room at a local library with the private tutor, Marco, an *uruguayo* who was a graduate student in linguistics at a nearby university. He had a long face with droopy eyelids that gave him the air of constantly being unimpressed with the world.

"No," he said, "the situation doesn't exist yet. You have to change your conjugations."

"I thought I did."

"Try again. Here's another situation." He thought for a moment. "Describe the party you *might* go to tonight."

Ainsley took a deep breath. Today was the thirtieth of the month. She had been studying with him four hours a day for the last eleven days. Today was her last chance to prove her semi-fluency in the Uruguayan dialect.

It'd been a very intense week and a half. On the first day,

she'd relearned basic Spanish vocabulary. A skirt wasn't a *falda*, it was a *pollera*. A suitcase wasn't a *maleta*, it was a *valija*. A peach was a *durazno* and juice was *jugo*.

Second day: pronunciation. Ainsley had felt embarrassed because she hadn't known that Rioplatense speakers say the *ll* sound differently from the rest of the Latin world. The word *calle*, she learned, has a *zhe* sound like the word 'measure'. And the 's' is dropped before 'p', so that *espejo*, or mirror, is pronounced 'epejo'.

Third day: verbs. Marco taught her to drop the present perfect, to say *vos* instead of *tú*. Then he gave her a hundred idioms to learn by the next morning.

Fourth day: total breakdown. Ainsley spent the day in a fetal position under her covers.

It'd grown slightly easier after that. During smoke breaks outside, Marco had complained to Ainsley about his Mexican girlfriend whose parents had a problem with her dating such a *blanco*-looking Latino. He said the world was upside down.

Ainsley didn't know what to tell him. She had her own problems, not the least of which was her secret but growing obsession with his homeland. Every night, when she couldn't study any more vocabulary, she read voraciously about Uruguay.

It was a fascinating country.

Eighty years ago, little Uruguay had been the pride of the continent. Part was sheer geographic luck. It had avoided the systematic rape of its resources by the Spanish *conquistadores*. No shiny silver (poor Bolivia), no tasty dunes of sugar (poor Brazil). Just good land and pretty pink sunsets.

And a port. The capital, Montevideo.

This little postage stamp of soil became a beacon for immigrants in the nineteenth century. Two million sailed over, poor Italian farmers, poor Spanish farmers.

A few aristocratic families took control of the rolling

fields. They raised cattle, sold beef to the trading families in the city, who packaged and shipped. Slabs of beef, bags of wool shipped out; stacks of money rolled in. The homes in Montevideo grew more stately. The standards of workmanship grew higher, the walls thicker, the front doors more ornate. Their cars grew heavy and large. The latest Fords, the best Mercedes.

They won the very first World Cup in 1930. Then they won another in 1950, this time against mighty Brazil, in a packed stadium in Rio de Janeiro.

All of this surprised Ainsley. This small country, the so-called Switzerland of South America, used to be really famous. She learned that Uruguayans call this the time of the *vacas gordas*, or fat cows.

What happened?

There are a thousand responses to that question. They all lead to the same answer: Uruguay has become the forgotten jewel of southern South America. Go to a party today, say that you are from Uruguay, and dare somebody to pick it out on a map.

But here, in the tutoring session, Ainsley was struggling to describe an imaginary party that she may or may not attend depending on the weather. It felt so fake, so forced. She wasn't attending any parties, no matter what the weather.

Marco stopped her.

"I don't feel your heart in your words," he said. "You are too much in your head. Where is the passion?"

"You have no idea how hard this is," she said.

"Yes, I do," he replied. "I had to learn your language. Don't get me started on your prepositions." A sly look came over his face. "I have another idea."

"What?"

"You said your husband left you."

"Yes."

"With no explanation."

"None."

"Tell me what you *would* ask him *if* he were here right now."

She sat back. That was wicked. She would have to use conditional verbs. And boy could she ever get into *that* subject.

The words started to flow. Ainsley talked for ten minutes, uninterrupted. What he'd done wrong, how empty her life had become. She even launched into a vicious revenge fantasy involving a cutting board and sauté pan. She didn't know that she remembered the Spanish for those words.

Then she heard Marco laughing. She stopped the story.

"What's wrong?"

"Nothing," Marco replied. "That was really good."

"Perfect?"

"No, but good enough." He stuck his hand across the desk. "Just find your passion. You'll get along fine."

She shook his hand. "Am I done?"

He nodded. "I'll call Martina. Congratulations, *paisana*."

Ainsley grinned at this friendly term. As she left the library, dazed, she got the very strange feeling that a new identity was waiting for her, far away, on the other side of the world.

In Uruguay.

CHAPTER SIX

Ainsley followed Gugina across the floor of the small warehouse. The old woman was headed towards the library of Associated Industries, where they stored their valuable information.

There, Ainsley would be given her Uruguay assignment. She felt nervous, as though she were climbing atop a giant missile, wrapping her legs around it, and waiting for launch.

"I need water," said Gugina.

"Martina has some," replied Ainsley.

"How do you know?"

"Because I saw it in her hand."

The other woman had gone ahead, leaving Ainsley to escort the elderly woman. Suddenly Gugina stopped. She lowered her head and coughed. It sounded like an old but powerful airplane engine sputtering to death.

Ainsley wanted to help but was pretty sure that the old woman wouldn't want to be touched.

At last they arrived in the small library. Martina helped her get settled on a chair and passed her a cup of tea.

Meanwhile, Ainsley admired the décor. Cordovan leather

furniture, baize carpeting, an old-fashioned globe. But mostly the room was filled with drawers, racks, and shelves of books, all stuffed with yellowing scraps of paper. In this room lay a wealth of information about precious gems.

Everything here predated computer systems. Ainsley suspected that a fire would devastate their business.

Martina turned on a single desk lamp, then checked on Gugina. As she sipped on the tea, the old woman's thin lips were pulled back and she was showing her perfect white teeth. This room seemed to invigorate her.

"So," said Gugina, "your assignment."

"Yes."

She nodded towards a single wooden cabinet, set against the back wall. Ainsley thought that it looked different from a typical china cabinet. Martina wrenched open its doors with an enormous effort. Inside was a very modern-looking safe.

"Something was taken from me a long time ago," said the old woman.

"What is that?"

"A very precious object."

Martina had dialed the lock on the safe and swung open the door. From the inside she removed a yellowed newspaper article. She handed it to Ainsley.

"Look."

It was from *El Pais*, which Ainsley assumed was a Uruguayan publication. They paper was dated *21 septiembre 1965*. The headline read *El Árbol Negro*. There was a picture of some men loading a crate into a truck as a crowd watched.

Gugina watched her. "Uruguay was my homeland. I spent my first forty years there. Uruguay has the best amethyst in the world." She pointed to the picture. "And this is the most famous amethyst we ever produced."

Ainsley peered closely at the gemstone. "It looks like a really dark tree."

"Of course, stupid," said Gugina. "That is why it's called El Árbol Negro."

Ainsley rolled those three words around her tongue. *El Árbol Negro*. The Black Tree.

"But why is this one so valuable?" she said. Amethyst was a semiprecious stone. You could buy it for about the same price as a garnet or a topaz. It sure as hell wasn't worth flying around the world for.

"It is from La Purisima."

The old woman sat back smugly. As though name-dropping La Purisima was supposed to impress Ainsley.

"So?"

The old woman's nostrils flared. Martina quickly draped a blanket over her elderly boss' shoulders. "I know what Ainsley is thinking. Amethyst isn't black. But Uruguayan amethyst is deep violet, the most valuable kind. La Purisima mine yielded the darkest of the violet. And El Árbol Negro was the darkest of La Purisima. It was nearly black. There is nothing else like it in the world."

"Thus the name," said Ainsley.

"Correct. It was discovered by Tarasconi. He found the geode, opened it, and did nothing to change it. Nature created the perfect amethyst tree."

"That probably adds to its value," said Ainsley.

"Yes."

"So what am I supposed to do?"

Gugina' burning eyes flashed to life. "*Buy it*."

The old woman's stare was so intense that Ainsley felt uncomfortable.

"They stole it from me," she said. "Years ago. Now it has reappeared. The thieves think I have died or forgotten." She barked a vicious laugh. "I haven't."

"It will be going on sale at an auction. We want you to buy it." The old woman's bony fingers wrapped around

Ainsley's arm. "You must believe me. They *stole* it. From *me*."

"I believe you," said Ainsley. "But who?"

She started to read the article, but Martina leaned over and snatched the old newspaper from her hands. "Gugina has said too much. You don't need to know any more history than that. We just want you to buy El Árbol Negro and ship it back to us."

"Why don't you find someone in Uruguay?"

Martina shook her head. "We can't trust anybody there. Why do you think we moved here?" She returned the article to the safe and locked the door. "Anyways, don't worry about the why. We are hiring you for the *how*. Just buy the amethyst and ship it back to us."

It seemed simple enough. "Who is selling it?"

"An auction house in Montevideo."

"When?"

Martina smiled. "Next Tuesday."

"That means I have to leave—"

"Tomorrow night. I already bought the ticket and deducted it from your upfront retainer. You return five days later."

She handed Ainsley another manila envelope. "Everything you need to know or possess is in here." She paused. "We expect daily updates. And don't think about running off."

"I wouldn't do that."

"Of course not. But we have your home address, and bank account number with the routing number. We can take back the money if you forfeit the mission."

That was true. But Ainsley had no intention of gypping these women. Finding a valuable amethyst was the purpose she needed.

"Can I call you tomorrow? With any questions?"

But Martina was already pushing her out of the room. "Of course. But Gugina is very tired now. Have a good trip."

And just like that, Ainsley was left standing outside the library, in the warehouse.

The girl with the fabulous hair, Viviana, was watching her from her desk. "Did they give you the Uruguay assignment?"

"Yes."

"That'll be an adventure." She twirled a piece of hair. "I might be going there next week too."

"Really?" Ainsley felt excited. "Why?"

"My grandmother gets a weeklong rental in Punta del Este every year. If we don't use it, we get taken off the list."

Punta del Este. Marco had talked about that place. It was a glamorous beach resort, supposedly the Riviera of South America. The wealthy, the famous, the beautiful all spent their summers there.

"That'll be fun."

"No, it'll be a total nightmare. Nobody goes this time of year."

Ainsley couldn't tell if she was serious. "Well, I'm leaving tomorrow night."

"Maybe we can hook up. But you'll probably be too busy chasing the amethyst to think about me."

Ainsley smiled. She couldn't believe how accommodating this girl was acting. Maybe they could even end up as friends.

She drove home with excitement fluttering in her stomach. Her life was about to change.

CHAPTER SEVEN

Ainsley Walker was facing the age-old dilemma of travelers everywhere: she couldn't decide what clothes to bring.

Looking in her closet, Ainsley pointed her left toe girlishly inward, one finger touching the side of her cheek. She loved making these types of decisions. The clothes needed to be flexible, appropriate for all situations, warm, cold, wet, dry, formal, lowdown, touristy, local. The clothes needed to travel well without wrinkling. And they couldn't be flashy. She'd been warned that Uruguayans dressed conservatively, in muted colors.

She threw fifteen finalists onto her bed. First, she ruled out anything too expensive. Second, any pieces that were too bright or ostentatious. Third, anything that reminded her too strongly of her present life.

Only four winners remained.

One: a pair of easy jeans with appliqué on each back pocket. She could dress them down with a t-shirt, or dress them up with heels and a shimmery top. Also, they were just beat-up enough that they wouldn't draw attention. She wouldn't be heartbroken if she had to lose them somewhere.

Two: a fitted, gray collared shirt. It had three-quarter-length sleeves and small epaulets. It was Ainsley's favorite go-to shirt. It could be worn anywhere.

Three: a white camisole top. Not silk, that would be too sexy for this job, but cotton. It was the fashion equivalent of a slice of bread.

Four: her beloved purse. It was pure white with killer hardware and gorgeous details. She would rather have left a kidney at home than part with that.

Half an hour later, with the satellite pieces chosen, her suitcase was neatly packed. She could build at least twelve different outfits with her choices.

She sipped a glass of red wine to steady her nerves. Ainsley had managed to keep her big secret from her new employers: That she'd never left America, ever. The idea frightened and exhilarated her.

She opened Associated Industries' envelope and reread its contents for the fourteenth time.

Martina had provided her with a photo of El Árbol Negro, maps of the city, instructions for finding the auction house and the Western Union branch. A sheet explaining how to buy a phone with prepaid minutes. Another sheet with the number of the jeweler who would verify the treasure. The number of the shipper.

And her fake name.

As soon as she passed through customs, Ainsley Walker was supposed to change her identity. She would be using the name Elizabeth Vargas with hotels, restaurants, strangers. They'd also forbidden her to use her personal credit cards, which'd made Ainsley laugh. Clearly they hadn't seen her credit balances. She didn't have enough open credit to charge a lollipop.

Why the precautions? Why would she need a phony identity in this tiny country halfway around the world? She was just buying a piece of amethyst. It wasn't supposed to be that difficult. This was all feeling a bit too unrealistic.

She dialed Associated Industries again. It went to voice-mail after four rings. These women hadn't answered the phone all day. And Ainsley had especially wanted to get Viviana's phone number.

Ainsley turned to her laptop, opened her web browser, and searched for Associated Industries again. She'd tried several online databases of art dealers, but she couldn't find any mention of them.

And yet...

She checked her bank account again. There it was. Six thousand two hundred and thirteen dollars pending.

She clicked over to her landlord's website and paid her rent for the next two months. Then she did the same for all the other bills that had been stacked in the background of her life.

When she finished, Ainsley sat back. She was free to leave. Nobody would want anything from her for at least a month.

Darkness had settled across her lonely apartment. There were no sounds except the tiny knocking of her wall-unit air conditioner.

Out of habit, she picked up her phone and started to scroll through her contacts. Then she paused.

Who really needed to know that she was leaving? She'd told David, the lawyer, just in case anything went wrong, but since he'd reviewed the contract, he was already in the loop. Other than him, she couldn't think of anybody, not one friend, who wasn't wrapped up in herself and building a family.

She didn't feel that she owed anybody any explanations.

Her thumb powered off the phone, and Ainsley dropped it into her carry-on bag. Martina had instructed her to leave the phone at home, but Ainsley was bringing this one. Just in case.

She looked at her love seat. What a depressing term. There was no love happening upon those cushions, hadn't been for months, years. She didn't have much appetite for it after the Legal Weasel's disappearing act.

This trip wasn't promising any great changes in that department. It wasn't a steamy sex vacation in Rio. It was just work.

Ainsley finished the wine and sat down on the edge of her bed. The apartment surrounded her, encasing her in silence and darkness.

Still dressed, she slumped over the bed, and hugged her suitcase to her body. Waiting for morning to come.

CHAPTER EIGHT

Fructuoso Rivera. His name had been *Fructuoso*.

When she read the name of the first president of Uruguay, Ainsley laughed out loud.

It was her thirteenth hour of air travel, and she was feeling a little punchy. *High-fructuoso corn syrup.* Hunkered down in seat 14-A, sealed in by a large pair of husband-and-wife cows occupying the middle and aisle seats, Ainsley was imprisoned in her window seat.

So she'd been reading. In her hands was a mildly interesting history of Uruguay. She'd learned some good background.

The short version: Uruguay was first settled by the Portuguese, then stolen from them by the Spanish, who slaughtered natives for fun. Then the residents fought off jealous attacks by Brazil and Argentina. Later, in the 1800s, they'd led an uprising against their Spanish masters, led by the sweet Fructuoso, and become independent. That was followed by a hundred years of stable democracy.

Until 1973.

A military junta appeared in that year, almost without

explanation, and dismantled itself just as mysteriously twelve years later. People were imprisoned, tortured.

Since 1985, Uruguay has had peaceful democracy once more. It's legalized gay marriage and marijuana. Crime is basically nonexistent. Renewable energy powers most of the country. Even Harvard Business School established its only Latin America research center there.

The humming sound of landing gear vibrated the floor beneath her feet. She closed the book and peered out the window of the Aerolineas Argentinas 747.

It was a gray day, and the airplane had just descended from the heavy cloud cover. She saw a vast stretch of green hills, snaked with brown veins of dirt and blue arteries of water. It looked lovely and pristine.

Her first glimpse of South America.

Ainsley's heartbeat quickened. This was feeling bigger and more intimidating than she'd imagined.

She leafed through the packet once more, mostly for reassurance. The information on amethyst was most interesting. How it turned yellow when heated, how purple is more valuable than pink, and how Zambia produces the world's cheapest.

Ainsley shut her eyes and swallowed hard, trying to keep her ears from popping.

When the plane's front wheels touched down on the soil, Ainsley felt the adrenaline rush.

And the pressure of the assignment. This would be a short, busy trip. Two days to learn the city, one day to outbid the opponents at auction, another day to crate and ship the tree.

Then she would leave. She fingered the return ticket that guaranteed it. Her flight was already booked. Five days from now.

In six days, she'd be back in the United States—and

fifteen thousand dollars richer. She'd be back job-hunting. Back to figuring everything out.

But there was one thing she hadn't counted on. An old saying.

The best way to make God laugh is to make plans.

MONTEVIDEO

CHAPTER NINE

All she wanted was to order a *torta* and a glass of *clerico*, but Ainsley couldn't catch the waiter's attention.

Any sandwich would do, but she really needed the drink. It was one of Uruguay's favorites, a mixture of white wine and fruit juice, named for the eighteenth-century priests who'd drunk it, sold it, maybe even killed the natives with it.

That would take the edge off the sixteen-hour flight.

Ainsley had arrived in the city without incident. At the airport, she'd flagged a black mini taxi, loaded her suitcase into the trunk, then clutched the arm rest as the driver barreled the car through the old streets. He'd rolled a toothpick around his mouth and cursed theatrically at other drivers.

In the back, Ainsley had watched the dilapidated brown mansions from Uruguay's long-gone golden years flashing past the windows, their ornamentation crusted with years of accumulated darkness. She'd seen children playing on stoops, kicking soccer balls down city sidewalks.

This wasn't what South America was supposed to look

like. Ainsley had imagined shantytowns, mud, electrical shortages, lonely burros.

But not Montevideo. This city was early twentieth-century *urban*. It looked like Brooklyn Heights.

Martina had booked her at the Hotel Real. Ainsley had been hoping that it would live up to its translation and would be fit for royalty.

What a laugh.

When she'd stepped out of the taxi, she'd been greeted by a grimy four-story brownstone. A blue tarp had been nailed across one window. An empty construction pit yawned next door.

Good. She'd been starting to like the look of the city. This hotel would be more reason to leave quickly.

The place had evidently once been a mansion. An old chandelier still hung in the entryway. The front desk clerk was squeezed into what had been a hallway closet. She'd checked in under the name Elizabeth Vargas. He'd thumbed through a pile of cards, then handed her a skeleton key marked 217, on the third floor, facing the street.

After dragging her luggage up three flights of stairs, Ainsley entered the tackiest hotel room she'd ever seen. It appeared to have been furnished from forty different estate sales. Wicker headboard, red flannel sheets, a Queen Anne chair, a Turkish rug, a checkerboard tile floor.

Ainsley'd dropped her things and sat down on the bed, sending a plume of dust shooting up from the other side of the mattress.

She'd dropped her head between her hands. This was Uruguay.

Ainsley was in *Uruguay*.

Twenty minutes and a change of clothing later, Ainsley had emerged on foot from the hotel, her city map stowed in her inner pocket. She needed water, food, and alcohol. In any order.

She would walk until she found all three.

Not as easy as it would seem. The sidewalk was a mess, a jumble of mounds, craters, gray cement, red stone, metal grates, chunks of concrete, nubbly bits, and dirt.

Ainsley minced her way carefully down the street. Wandering the Ciudad Vieja, she'd admired the dilapidated but stately old buildings. The neighborhood had good bones and the attention to detail that told stories of long-ago wealth: French balconies, mansard roofs, street-level Roman arches in bas-relief, door knockers carved in the shape of animals.

She passed block upon block of these ghostly beauties, a few restored, most crumbling. Ainsley thought the city could use some international investment money.

Soon she'd found her way to this café on Plaza Independencia, in the very heart of everything. And now she sat at a sharp café, admiring the burgundy tablecloths, sparkling glassware, elegantly folded white napkins.

A young waiter in a formal white tuxedo shirt was watching a soccer match on the television at the bar. He was tamping a pack of cigarettes against his palm.

Ainsley felt frustrated. This guy was young and fairly attractive. She was young and fairly attractive. At minimum, there should be certain benefits that went along with that. Such as a menu. Or a basket of bread.

For him, though, life went on here the way it always had, whether or not this American had just flown halfway around the world to sit at his table.

The soccer match broke just before her patience did, and the waiter finally sauntered over with a menu. Ainsley pushed it aside. In Rioplatense, Ainsley told him that she wanted a *milanesa* sandwich and a glass of *clerico*. He nodded and left. Her Spanish couldn't be that awful.

A moment later the waiter brought a half-carafe of the mulled white wine and poured it with extreme care into her wine glass. Ainsley began to feel a little better.

"Where are you from?" he asked in Spanish.

"United States."

"I knew you were American."

"How?"

"You seem like you are in a hurry."

"Really? I'm ready to relax."

To prove it, she lifted her drink and kicked her feet onto a nearby chair. The waiter laughed. "See, only an American could try to win the game of relaxation."

He disappeared back to the television. She thought about that comment as she sipped the tart spirit and rolled it across her tongue. A thin breeze flapped the edges of the tablecloth. Next door, the Palacio Salvo, the country's only skyscraper, an extraordinary art deco spaceship, cast its long afternoon shadow across the plaza.

Every minute or so, when the traffic light changed, a stream of small cars tore around the peripheral road a few feet from her table: new Mercedes, classic Volkswagens, even a perfectly preserved Ford Model A. It was a beautiful parade of automotive history.

At this moment, life in Montevideo felt good.

Her *milanesa* arrived, a breaded chicken cutlet with a side of potato salad. She tucked into the plate hungrily. It'd been at least seven hours since her last meal, a pathetic enchilada scarfed down while hunched over her fold-down tray on the plane.

Ainsley left a few hundred pesos on the table when she was finished and strolled down the sloping street towards the water. On the way, she watched a taciturn man hop out of his horse-drawn cart and empty a public trash can into his wagon. Ainsley had heard about these men from her tutor. Called *burgadores*, they were now the primary method of trash collection in this place, the capital city.

How far Uruguay had fallen.

And yet, a block later, she encountered the Teatro Solis, a gargantuan Romanesque theater that could've been at home in the Piazza del Fiore in Rome.

At last she crossed the large boulevard and set foot on La Rambla, the famous *peatonal*, a long ribbon of sidewalk that looped for twenty miles around the edge of the Montevidean peninsula.

Romantic couples walked hand-in-hand past her. A jogger with earbuds beat a heavy path on the concrete. Behind her were the ghostly brown mansions of the Ciudad Vieja.

Straight ahead was the red sunset. Below that were the tea-colored waters of the Rio de la Plata estuary, so wide at this point that it looked like the open ocean. The waves chopped and slapped against the retaining wall.

Ainsley put a hank of hair behind her ear and stared out to sea. She indulged in a moment of loneliness, the type of soul-deep longing that only being alone in a foreign country can bring.

Thus far, Montevideo had turned out to be far more attractive than she'd expected. Charming, historic. She could feel the elegant whoosh of history floating through the streets.

It would be easy to forget that she had promised to perform a job here. Especially if she allowed herself to meet a man.

She hadn't wanted to walk down that road. But a new man might put another layer of experience between her and the Legal Weasel.

She heard the unknown whispering into her ear.

Abruptly she pushed the idea out of her mind. She couldn't become a tourist of *any* kind, not historical, not culinary, and definitely not sexual. She had a job to do. Her livelihood depended upon finding and buying El Árbol Negro.

Then again, who was she kidding? Ainsley didn't really have a livelihood. She just struggled from one gig to another, barely making her credit card payments and rent payments and college loan payments. She had precious little dough left over for anything except for a very occasional spa treatment or cocktail session with girlfriends who were already moving on with their lives.

But those problems felt very distant now, an entire continent away. Ainsley started to yawn.

Her problems could wait until morning.

CHAPTER TEN

Ainsley spent the night in a restless jet-lagged semi-sleep. Her mattress was thin and hard. Five times she'd awoken to strange creaks and slammed doors in some distant part of the building. The mismatched furniture bothered her too, even in the dark.

At a quarter to eight, Ainsley staggered into the bathroom and clawed for the light switch. Then she dropped her underwear to her ankles and sat down on the shaky pink toilet. Then she noticed it.

There was no shower.

She glanced up. The showerhead was pointing directly down on the toilet. She looked around.

There was no stall. No tub. No curtain.

This was truly bizarre. She flushed and closed the lid. Then straddled the toilet as she turned on the handle.

A pathetic dribble of ice-cold water emerged. Ainsley turned it further and got blasted in the face with four jets of the same. She shrieked.

Two painful minutes later, she burst from the bathroom

with towels around her torso and head. Next mission: hairdryer.

She looked inside the Chinese armoire, underneath the rug, behind the door. Nowhere.

"Son of a bitch," she said. What was she supposed to do with wet hair all day?

She unpacked her clothing and hung it on dusty wire hangers in the Chinese armoire. Her skirts and pants had travelled well: she'd chosen wrinkle free items, mostly rayon and polyester.

Ainsley chose an emerald camisole top, black slacks, and the same pair of sturdy but attractive black wedges that she'd worn yesterday. Then she did her makeup quickly but demurely, just a touch of mascara, and light blush. No sense in attracting the wrong type of attention.

Then she selected her favorite coat: a burgundy fitted leather number with an asymmetrical zipper and banded collar. It was vaguely motorcyclist. It was also one of the few thrift-store purchases she'd ever made.

Next came her hair. She unwrapped the towel and watched the wet ropes fall and slap against her face and shoulders. Airdrying would make it flat and weird by noon. She wanted her hair to have a bit of bounce on her first full day in Uruguay.

She picked up the room's antique phone to call the front desk. Silence greeted her ear. Of course the phone didn't work. She tossed the receiver back on its cradle and left the room with her purse.

Downstairs, a new clerk was squished into the front-desk closet. He was middle-aged, balding, and had an air of casual indifference.

"I need a hairdryer," she said in Spanish.

"Me too," he said. "Look at this head. Like a field of wheat."

"I'm a guest here. I can't go out like this."

"You look beautiful."

He hadn't even glanced at her yet. "So you don't have a hairdryer that I can use?" she said.

He exhaled, an exasperated sigh. "Okay, *americana*, I will tell you how to dry your hair. Get into a taxicab and roll the window down. Put your head outside and sniff like a dog. Your hair will be dried in two minutes." Then he looked up. "Woof woof."

He smiled at her, like they'd just shared some great moment of intimate connection. Ainsley could feel her temper rising. This guy was one of those assholes who saw no difference between insults and flirtation. She wanted to reply with the worst Spanish insult she knew, *hijo de puta*, but that seemed too strong for this situation.

Instead, she pitched the heavy room key at him. She didn't decide to do it. The throw just happened. Ainsley had always possessed the deadly aim of a major league pitcher. Her older brother had always called her The Sniper, after her habit of waiting patiently for hours on the rooftop to assault him with eggs, always in revenge for some enormously trivial sibling disagreement.

Those skills, Ainsley discovered, had sharpened with age. The heavy key connected square on the crown of the clerk's bald head. He dove off his chair and hit the ground, moaning.

"Now we both have a problem," she spat.

Ainsley straight-armed the door and flounced out into the street. Over the years, she'd learned to keep her epic temper in check, but this fourth-rate flirt hadn't even made a pretense of caring about her needs. She thought about the apathetic waiter last night. Was decent customer service only a given back in the States? She felt a quick stab of home-sickness.

It was a crisp, cold morning, the air brisk enough to chill

beef, and the edges of her nostrils went numb as she walked down the street, past *lavanderias*, *panaderías, empanaderías*, electronics stores, past the women and men and children who moved at a surprisingly quick tempo. This wasn't a sun-dazed beach town or lazy backwater; it was a port city of almost two million. People had things to do.

As she strode down the narrow sidewalk, something else occurred to her. How had the hotel clerk known that she was from the United States? He hadn't been there last night. Of course it was possible that he had gone over the guest list, but considering his shitty attitude towards the task of procuring a simple hairdryer, she considered that unlikely.

That's when it happened. Her ankle twisted, her body crumpled, and the stones rushed up towards her face. Her right knee and the palm of her right hand crashed into the sidewalk, and she fell over on her side, gasping more from surprise than from pain.

She'd fallen. Spectacularly.

On her very first morning.

CHAPTER ELEVEN

An old man in a puffy gray winter coat was trying to help Ainsley up. She pushed him away. She didn't need anybody's help.

Ainsley inspected the damage. Her knee was bleeding and her hand was scraped. And her hair was freezing into heavy foot-long icicles. She knew she looked like a wreck. She felt herself starting to cry. She hated herself for it.

A female voice cried out: "*Aye, pobrecita*!" A young hair stylist, short and well dressed, was standing in the doorway of a hair salon.

Ainsley waved her off. She was in no mood.

"*Ven aqui*," the girl ordered. Then she switched to English. "Come here. No excuses." She waved a hairdryer.

That was tempting. Ainsley pulled herself up and teetered over to the door. The girl stood to the side and gestured towards a chair.

The salon was painted yellow, with plants on all horizontal surfaces. Black-and-white glamour photos hung on the walls in simple frames. Low music sounded from speakers hidden behind a potted ficus.

The hair stylist guided Ainsley to a chair.

"Do you have Spanish?" she asked.

"*Claro que sí*," Ainsley replied.

"Good," she said in Spanish. "Now you should learn to walk in Latin countries."

"Your country should learn how to put down a decent sidewalk."

The girl laughed and poured her a small cup of coffee. Ainsley sipped the beverage; it tasted fresh on her tongue. The stylist threw a ruby-colored salon cape over her shoulders and studied Ainsley in the mirror. "Now, I am going to take care of you."

"How much do you charge?"

She waved the question away. "It's nothing. It's early and this salon looks like a cemetery."

"Are you sure?" Ainsley said.

"Of course. This is good for me too. People need to see that I am busy or they don't come in."

The stylist used a damp washcloth to clean her palm and knee and patted it with disinfectant. Then she turned the hairdryer on, and Ainsley felt the sweet blast of hot air hit her scalp. She felt a small trickle of water running out down her ears and shoulders.

When she was finished, Sofia switched the hairdryer off. "Much better. But we are not finished." She pulled out a brush and ran it through Ainsley's hair.

"How are you called?" said Ainsley.

"Sofia," said the stylist. "It was my grandmother's name. This was her salon until last year when she died. Some people don't know she is dead yet. It doesn't help that I live in her old apartment upstairs, either."

"This salon is lovely."

The girl nodded at her in the mirror. "So is your jacket."

"Thank you."

"Did you buy it in the States?"

There, again. People instantly knew she was American. How? The cut of her clothing? The confidence of her walk? Ainsley'd never realized how much of her country was worn on her sleeve until this trip.

"Yes."

"You're here for vacation?"

Ainsley shook her head. "Work."

"What do you do?"

Ainsley thought hard. What was Spanish for *international errand girl*? Instead, she just said, "I'm a detective." It was close to the truth.

Sofia's eyes lit up. "How exciting! Who are you searching for? A cheating husband? An escaped convict?"

"I'm here to buy a gemstone."

Now the stylist's eyes were really shining. "What type?"

How much should Ainsley reveal? This hair stylist was an utter stranger. But there was no conceivable way that such a stranger could blow her plans.

"Amethyst," she said.

To her surprise, Sofia scoffed. "Amethyst is everywhere in this country. My grandmother used a piece as a doorstop."

"This is a special one. It's very dark, in the shape of a tree."

Sofia stopped brushing. "El Árbol Negro?"

"That's it."

"The one that has been lost for fifty years?"

"It's been found, and it's up for auction."

She made a long, low whistle. "My grandmother used to tell me about it. She said it was hidden during the junta."

That wasn't what Ainsley had been told. The junta had been in the seventies, but Gugina had said that it had been hidden since the sixties.

Sofia put the blowdryer aside and commenced brushing her hair. Her hands yanked roughly, and Ainsley winced.

Finally she pulled Ainsley's hair back and secured it using a beautiful bobby pin. It was a pink agate.

"This pin belonged to my grandmother."

"You talk about your grandmother a lot."

"Yes, because she gave me everything in my life, and the whole world adored her."

The whole world adored her. Ainsley smiled. She was starting to understand Latin exaggeration. It felt better than the grim Puritan heritage she'd been saddled with. A stepfather who had never offered more than a handshake. A Methodist aunt who spent an hour every morning in sober Bible study. A cousin so straight edge that he turned his nose up at beer-battered fish tacos.

"So she was important to you."

"Oh yes," the stylist said. "And now that you know its importance, this agate guarantees that you come back every morning for hair drying. Return it to me on your last day here."

"I want to pay you."

Sofia waved her off, as if she'd suggested a disgusting idea. "No. You're good for business."

"But nobody's come in."

"They will. Women in Montevideo notice these things."

She flung the cape off Ainsley's shoulders. Her hair did look good, especially with an agate decorating the back of her head. It was antique but didn't feel too heavy.

Ainsley nodded. "I will see you tomorrow."

"Of course you will."

Sofia hugged her. Nothing special, just a casual goodbye. But the naturalness of the gesture surprised Ainsley. It made her feel at home.

As she stepped out into the street, Ainsley noticed that Montevideo felt warmer, more human. She lifted her arm to hail a taxi.

She was going to scout the auction house.

CHAPTER TWELVE

The auction house was called a *remate*.

The auctioneering didn't take place until tomorrow, so today was just a preliminary visit. Ainsley would check that El Árbol Negro was on the premises, confirm the time of the auction the next day, then head to the nearby Western Union office to await the transfer of funds from the States.

The taxi driver had looked thrilled to get a fare to Ferrocarril, the far-flung barrio where the *remate* was located. Along with their white socks and clueless egotism, Americans were known for their generous tipping.

The taxi zipped along through neighborhoods that grew uglier with every passing block. Prado, Belvedere, Sayago. Ainsley felt saddened by the gray concrete block houses defaced with graffiti, the creaky old men perched on folding chairs on street corners waving at passing cars, the shirtless young bucks gathered around a fire in a metal trash can.

There was poverty in Montevideo, but it was hidden away here, in the swampy suburbs.

At last the car pulled up to a gray concrete warehouse,

one of many long walls that served no apparent purpose, interspersed with empty weed-strewn parking lots. On the ground around the entrance were packing crates and wooden pallets. The sun hung low in the sky like the head of a tired laborer.

"This is the *remate?*" she asked.

"*Sí,*" he said, then checked his meter. "*Novecientos y cincuenta.*"

She paid up and then tipped him generously. She hoped this wasn't a scam, that he hadn't dropped her off at some kind of horrific torture facility where she would be rendered into tourist lard. Ainsley sometimes had a hyperactive imagination, and Sotheby's this sure as hell was not.

Exiting the taxi, she picked her way across the raggedy front yard, avoiding chunks of Styrofoam, towards the dusty front door, and pushed it open.

She was standing at the entrance of an enormous warehouse packed from the floor to the ceiling with towering piles of antique furniture. So many stacked upon each other that the harsh sodium lights overhead couldn't even penetrate all the way to the cement floor.

She strolled in the shadows between towering rosewood armoires, gaped at cherrywood sideboys, marveled at the leftovers from old Montevideo estates. All of them were as heavy, rooted, and implacable as the trunks of rubber trees. The chandeliers formed a rich canopy overhead.

Soon Ainsley became lost in the smell of the vintage woodwork. The outside of the *remate* hadn't hinted at anything like this.

Twenty minutes passed. She'd lost sight of any walls. The objects had started to blur. Finding El Árbol Negro in this jungle of antiques would be impossible.

She needed help. A skinny kid in stonewashed black jeans

scampered down a nearby aisle, pushing an antique coat rack on a wheeled pallet.

"*Señor*," she shouted.

He looked back with surprise. Maybe nobody had ever called him that before. He did look young, especially in a country where even the young people looked a little old.

"Yes?"

"Do you work here?"

He shook his head no and continued on his way. The brushoff didn't hurt so much as last night's at the restaurant. Ainsley realized that she was becoming accustomed to Uruguayan customer service.

Instead, Ainsley spent the next hour discovering the used treasures of this forgotten city. She wandered into a wonderland of antique rugs and vintage kitchen appliances. She even blundered into the agricultural equipment section, admiring the old tractors and backhoes.

At last she spotted the skinny kid again. This time he was standing in an open room at the far end of the warehouse. There was nothing in it except a podium and a couple of tables lining the walls. A chalkboard alongside one wall. She recognized it as the auction room. He was sipping from a silver straw in a large gourd.

"*Señor*," she shouted again. He immediately pretended not to see her.

"I'm taking my tea break," he said. "Take yourself away."

"I need your help," she said. "Can you tell me if El Árbol Negro is on the premises?"

He set down the gourd and looked at her. "Of course we have it. No, you can't see it."

"Please, I need to."

"No. Anyways, your Spanish is terrible."

What a cad. Still, something needed to be done. In a second, Ainsley had settled on a solution. The clichéd answer.

She started to languidly saunter towards him across the empty floor, one hand placed on her hip. His narrow eyes embarked on a long southward journey down her body, from the agate in her hair down to her toes. She plunged a thumb into her right pocket. She knew she was trying too hard. More sophisticated men might've chuckled. But he was a kid.

She found the folded currency in her pocket. Best she could remember, it was about fifteen hundred pesos, or eighty bucks. She peeled off half the bills and pressed them into his palm.

"This is for verification."

The silver *bombilla* fell out of his mouth and clattered in the gourd.

"Of course," he said. "I am called Diego. Let's go this way."

She followed him back into the jungle of antiques. He led her towards an unmarked hallway with an employees' door at the very end. Next to the door sat a fat man on a shabby chair, smoking a cigarillo, working a crossword. An old radio played tinny dance music. He ignored her completely as Diego used a key from his belt to unlock the door.

It was a small room, plaster walls, blue carpet, bare-bones industrial office. There were only two objects within. One was a small Chinese vase with a paper tag hanging from the rim.

The other was El Árbol Negro.

Ainsley immediately felt all the air sucked from her lungs. The pictures hadn't done it justice.

The entire gemstone, from its roots up to its branches, was colored a blackish purple, as rich and inky as a glass of port. She'd never seen any gemstone like this. She wanted to inspect it.

"What time is the auction tomorrow?" she asked him.

"Of this?"

"Yes."

"It's not tomorrow. It's today."

"No," Ainsley said, "I was told that the auction was tomorrow."

"The boss changed it yesterday. The auction is at two o'clock. This is a special item so it goes on last."

"At what time?"

He shrugged. "Maybe four o'clock?"

Ainsley heard suspicious alarm bells clanging in her head. Gugina and Martina hadn't been on top of any of this. But then again, they were elderly women, living seven thousand miles away, trying to stay up to speed on events in a country that they'd left behind four decades earlier.

"*Señorita*," said a deep voice.

The fat man was standing in the doorway. His body was held perfectly still. She noticed the hardness in his eyes, the serious set of his meaty lips.

"This room is only available to members of our staff. Please."

He motioned to the hallway. His cement eyes bore deep into Diego, who had shrunk back against the wall.

"Can I—"

He cut her off. "You must leave now. Diego, you ass, show her out."

The kid obligingly steered Ainsley by her elbow out of the room.

"Outside," the fat man shouted at them. "All the way."

Diego apologized all the way to the front door. "I'm sorry. He's usually not like this. Please, come back this afternoon to auction."

Ainsley nodded. She was upset because she hadn't had the chance to inspect El Árbol Negro's branches. The way Martina and Gugina had insisted.

Now she needed to speed up the timeline.

"Four o'clock?" she said.

"Yes."

She found another taxi. Diego stood with his hand shading his eyes, watching her as she pulled away.

CHAPTER THIRTEEN

In her entire twenty-nine years, Ainsley had never carried this much cash on her person before.

She was walking out of a Western Union with two bricks in her purse. Each one amounted to about 200,000 Uruguayan pesos. Together they were valued at about ten thousand dollars: the legal limit that can be internationally transferred without being reported to governmental authority.

The clerk had tried to contain his curiosity as he'd counted out the bills. Ainsley had ignored his questions and left.

Now the two cash-bricks were at the bottom of her purse, wrapped together in a paper envelope and taped shut. Associated Industries had thought that ten thousand would be enough for a down payment on the amethyst tree, no matter what the price.

Regardless, Ainsley hoped that there weren't any clairvoyant muggers in Montevideo.

Her watch read three twenty. She had only forty minutes until the auction of El Árbol Negro began. Ainsley hailed another taxicab and clutched her purse to her chest in the backseat. Her stomach was growling but she didn't have time to stop for lunch.

Now the driver, having learned that Ainsley was an American *turista*, had decided to act as a tour guide. His arm was hanging out the window, pointing at utterly forgettable landmarks. The first armory in the country. The first sewage plant. The second armory. The second sewage plant. Ainsley stopped listening. She knew they were headed in the right direction.

By the time they arrived at the *remate*, her watch said four o'clock exactly. She handed the driver more than enough pesos for the cab ride and ran into the warehouse.

She raced through the labyrinth of antiques, first left, then right, wait, that was the wrong way, where was it? She retraced her steps, peered around some farm equipment.

There.

The auction room was straight ahead. She dashed towards it, holding her purse to her side.

Inside, a crowd of two hundred people had assembled around a small dais. The auction had already started.

On the dais was El Árbol Negro.

The fat man who'd kicked her out of the storage room was standing beside the amethyst structure. He'd changed clothing, into what she had started to recognize as the national menswear of Uruguay: a navy-blue sweater over a collared shirt. A blingy ring glittered on his pinky: the flashiest thing she'd seen so far.

Though he was talking in extremely rapid auctioneer Spanish, Ainsley could understand enough to know that he was hyping the object.

Suddenly he said, "*Cincuen, cincuen mil.*" At least thirty hands shot up. He pointed at a small woman wringing her hands. "*Primera.*"

Diego, who'd been standing quietly on the side of the room, slid over to the woman and handed her a small placard. She'd won the first round.

The fat man continued describing the virtues of the treasure. The people were listening patiently. Ainsley sensed that a lot of them knew of El Árbol Negro and didn't need the extraneous detail. Maybe they'd heard about it from their parents or grandparents. It didn't matter.

She knew that the average person in Uruguay made about ten thousand U.S. dollars per year. Ainsley would wait until most people had priced themselves out.

"*Sesen, sesen mil,*" he said, and the same thirty hands shot up. "*Primero.*" This time he was pointing at an elderly man in a gray coat who accepted Diego's placard with a cynical shrug.

Another minute of hype, then: "*Ochen, ochen mil.*" Not as many hands this time. The placard was passed again. Ainsley sat on her heels, satisfied that she was the whale in the room. Lurking and waiting to sweep the entire school of minnows into her jaws.

After all, she had the unlimited funds of Associated Industries behind her. Everything would work out fine if she were the only whale.

But she wasn't.

CHAPTER FOURTEEN

On the other side of the circle stood a dark man, dressed in a crisp sport coat, no necktie, and a thick paste of scruff on his face. His lips were pursed and sensual. His dark eyes roved the group.

He wasn't bidding either. He was just watching people.

Another whale.

As the auction went on, Ainsley saw him pick out bidders, one by one, and pin them with that gaze until they stopped bidding. It was intimidation, pure and simple. His way of keeping the price down.

He definitely wasn't working for the *remate*.

Thirty minutes later, the price had skyrocketed to six hundred thousand pesos, leaving Ainsley and the four or five hands that still dared to go up. The rest of the bidders had backed away a few steps, leaving herself and a few others in the action.

That guy couldn't scare her with his mad-dog stare. It was time to jump into the fray.

The fat auctioneer said, "*Seis cien y cincuen mil*". Six hundred and fifty thousand. She raised her hand. She felt like a third grader who desperately wanted to be called on. When he saw her, his face dropped. "*Primera*," he said.

Diego was over in a flash, pressing the placard into her hand. "You are a brave *yanqui*," he said.

"For bidding at an auction? I don't think so."

"But you cannot take back the bid."

"Do I look like I would?" she said.

"No, *senorita*, you do not," he said, backing away. "I apologize."

She felt a prickly sensation rising on the back of her neck. Then she knew why. On the other side of the circle, the dark man's eyes had found her. They were boring into her own, to the very back of her skull, sending tingles down into her belly. She didn't know if it was frightening or arousing.

The fat auctioneer was still orating, more for theatrical effect than for anything else. With a dramatic flourish he said, "*Siete cien mil*." Seven hundred thousand pesos. Almost thirty-five thousand dollars.

The dark stranger raised his hand. "*Primero*," said the auctioneer, and Diego went hustling over to the man. His burningly intense eyes were still fixated on Ainsley. The three remaining people backed away from the front line.

It was down to them now.

Major psychic intimidation heading her way.

Ainsley had never been one to back off from a challenge. In fact, she loved confrontation, relished it. She punched a saucy hand on her hip, cocked her head, and mirrored that riveting stare right back at him. Ainsley liked the feeling this gesture gave her.

As the fat auctioneer's mouth continued yammering about the quality of the amethyst, Ainsley felt the eyes of the crowd peeling her apart. She had never felt so obviously foreign. Could they tell that she was an American, a gringo interloper from a land of ten-gallon hats, outsized energy consumption, and enormous self-regard?

If so, would they allow her to bring home their prized gemstone?

"*Siete cien y cincuen mil*," said the auctioneer. Seven hundred and fifty thousand pesos.

Ainsley's hand shot up. A look of annoyance passed across the auctioneer's face. "*Primera*," he said. The dark man's gaze flicked towards the auctioneer. She'd pissed off both of them.

Diego appeared at her side again and ceremoniously handed her the placard. "You must care about El Árbol Negro very much."

"No, I'm just bored," she said, keeping a straight face.

"If this is what you do when you are bored," replied Diego, "then I would very much like to move to America."

The auctioneer had finally dispensed with the hype and went straight to the next bid: "*Ocho cien mil*." Eight hundred thousand pesos.

All eyes turned towards her opponent. He nodded and raised his hand. The crowd breathed out. A few even clapped. Diego handed him the placard.

The stranger's eyes fixed distantly, on the far upper corner of the room, as if there was nothing left to be done here. A satisfied smile settled on his mouth.

Ainsley didn't know why he looked so relaxed. She was going to take him to the cleaners. He was going home empty handed.

She braced herself for the next bid. The fat auctioneer took a deep breath, paused dramatically, then made the announcement.

"*Final. Esto se vende al señor.*"

She did a quick translation in her head. *The End. Sold to the man.*

There were a few gasps, followed by an enormous round

of applause. The other defeated bidders were watching her curiously, cynical smiles curling the edges of their mouths. It took a few moments for the message to sink in:

You're a loser now too.

The auctioneer had cut her off. The game had been rigged.

A woman patted her shoulder, but Ainsley struck it away. She didn't want consolation. She wanted the amethyst. She watched the fat auctioneer congratulate her opponent, then kiss him on the cheek in the male South American style of greeting. They chatted like a couple of old friends.

Ainsley was disgusted. She'd just been cheated, duped.

Blatantly and royally screwed.

The gravity of what had just happened suddenly crushed her. She would have two very angry employers back in the States. She pictured the seventy-five hundred promised dollars vanishing from her online checking account. All followed by more financial desperation.

"You can't *do* this!" she shouted.

The fat auctioneer ignored her. Didn't even risk a glance.

She raised her voice. "Is it because I'm a woman? Nothing swinging between my legs? Or is it because I'm a foreigner? You can't let the *gringa* take home a piece of the *pais*? Somebody tell me the reason so I can sleep tonight. Please!"

The fat auctioneer tossed her an amused sneer, then turned his pudgy back on her.

Diego appeared at her side again. "You have a strong spirit," he said, touching her arm. "Follow me. I want to talk to you."

She followed him out of the auction room, through the towering aisles of antique chairs and old boat equipment. "That man is well known to us. He comes to the auction almost every week, and whatever he likes, he gets. His money has been very good to us."

"Then you could've told us that the game is unfair," she replied.

"Everybody knows him. He is the prince."

"Everybody except me."

"Now you know too."

Ainsley grabbed his shoulder. "Diego, I need to talk to that man."

He shook his head. "No, that is *not* possible."

She reached into her pocket and unrolled another wad of bills and pressed them into his hand. His second bribe of the day. She was becoming an important source of Diego's income.

He grinned like a little schoolboy. She waited for the inevitable change of mind.

"I enjoy your form of persuasion," he said. "Let's go outside."

They exited through the front door and walked down the industrial road in the late afternoon sun. This was one of the *cantegriles*, or small shantytowns on the edge of the city. Dogs were lapping the still black water in the drainage ditch. A faded brown bed frame lay abandoned in some high weeds— and just beyond, a shack with a corrugated metal roof and laundry hanging outside on a line.

Pathetic as it was, that shack was still someone's *home*, repository of somebody's hopes and memories.

"Okay," Diego finally said, checking over his shoulder, "that man is from a very important family in our city. His wife moved back to the interior last year and is divorcing him."

"If he stared at me like that, I'd divorce him too," said Ainsley.

"He comes every week and bids on the most expensive item. He always wins."

"I noticed."

"He has saved us many times, so we make sure he always wins."

"So he doesn't care about El Árbol Negro?"

"Who knows? He doesn't usually keep the items he buys. He sells them to Brazilians, Europeans, Asians."

"Why?"

He shrugged. "The man wants something to do."

"Knitting would be cheaper."

"Maybe you don't know rich people. They have different needs."

"Would he sell it to me?"

"It's possible."

"Can I ask him?"

"If you can find him. He pays us in cash and disappears. He doesn't want us to take his address. He sends people to pick up the items."

"What's his name?"

"José Ignacio Tabarez. He lives in Punta Carretas."

She pulled out a small notebook from her purse and wrote down the name and barrio. Diego looked at her curiously.

"Are you a detective?"

Ainsley made a fifty-fifty waver of the hand. "More or less. But you never met me. Understand?" She pressed another bill into his palm and walked away.

Towards Punta Carretas.

CHAPTER FIFTEEN

Ainsley stared at the ladybug as it inched across her tablecloth, feeling a bitter wave of resentment in her throat.

José Ignacio Tabarez.

Just thinking about the name made her furious.

It was ten o'clock that same night, and she was dining alone on the outside porch of a romantically lit restaurant named Balcón del Lobo.

Completely alone.

She was in Punta Carretas. This neighborhood was in fact one of the wealthiest of Montevideo, the streets lined with *ceibo* trees, their clusters of buds like long cobs of red thimbles. Flowering vines wrapped themselves around trellises and entrance arches.

A candle flickered on her table. The wind blowing off the estuary was fierce tonight, and she was glad to be protected by a canopy of elm trees and a clear plastic windbreak. Branches of trees clicked in the darkness overhead.

She sipped her wine, a glass of a local red varietal called tannat. It was heavy, floral, and strangely dead on her tongue, but maybe it was just her mood. Except for mescal and nail polish remover, there was basically no type of spirit that Ainsley would turn her nose up at.

This restaurant had been an amazing find. A three-minute walk out of a randomly halted taxi had produced this discovery, hidden amongst the trees and the residential homes. Yes, she was dining in someone's former *house*.

Ainsley had always been excited by thoughts of old homes.

She'd been greeted by a parrilla in the foyer, but at the table she'd ignored the savory aroma of sizzling meats in favor of a simple risotto primavera. She knew from a sous chef ex-boyfriend that risotto was the true measure of an Italian restaurant. Done properly, he said, it requires at least forty-five minutes of constant stirring, and doesn't forgive any cooks who cut corners.

That had been years ago. Now she was alone, in the southern cone of South America, with an excellent risotto half finished before her, still thinking about that guy. It made her angry that her life was so empty.

She studied her fellow diners on the balcony. A single table of fiftyish men, all wearing navy blue sport coats, all of European extraction, mouths set downward, a solemn bottle of red wine untouched between them. Sensible cuts of meat rested on simple plates.

So far, Ainsley thought, the average Uruguayan man seemed as exciting as a basket of laundry.

She had decided not to tell her employers about the loss of El Árbol Negro. What was the point? The women were dead weight at this point. She drained her glass and thunked her head drearily against the wall.

"Is everything all right?" said a woman's voice. "The risotto make you feel not so good?"

She was speaking English.

Ainsley cracked open an eyelid. It was her waitress, a

small black-haired girl with bright blue eyes. She was too tall for her weight, and the points of her hips projected against her long white shirt.

"Your English is good," Ainsley said.

"I learned from two friends. They are from Flagstaff. Near to the Grand Canyon?"

"I know it."

"What else do you need?"

Ainsley lifted her glass and tapped on it. "Two things: more wine and a man."

"I can get you the first one. The second is also easy if you have no ... *como se dice* ... requirements."

"I do," said Ainsley. "His name must be José Ignacio Tabarez."

The waitress laughed. "You will have better luck dancing on the moon."

"You know him?"

"Not like I know my cousins, no. But everybody knows the Tabarez family. They are the kings of Punta Carretas."

"Do you know where they live?"

"Of course." She pounded the table. "You know something? I will take you there when my tables are finished. Don't argue. Here!" She poured Ainsley more wine. "Tannat makes everything better. Wait for me. We have fun!"

The girl left the bottle on the table and swept away. Ainsley didn't object. Never in her life had she been at the mercy of ordinary strangers, hairdressers and waitresses. Now she was going to be escorted to Tabarez's house. She laughed to herself.

Fine. She would ride this wave wherever it was headed.

CHAPTER SIXTEEN

Over the next hour, the bottle grew emptier, and Ainsley watched the other diners slowly rise from their table, pat their bellies, and amble down the stairs through the verdant greenery to the sidewalk, back home to their houses, to their wives, to whatever lifestyles they'd chosen in this ambient city.

Then the waitress appeared at her side. She'd thrown a worn gray peacoat over her navy-blue sweater. Ainsley wondered if Uruguayans had ever met a neutral color they didn't love.

"I am ready," she said. "You are having a good time by yourself?"

"Happier than a pig in shit," slurred Ainsley.

"That is a stupid expression."

Ainsley felt drunk and miserable. "*You're* a stupid expression."

The waitress laughed, a sharp stabbing sound. "Excellent. Your name is now Shit Pig."

"No, my name is——"

"Stop, don't tell me. I like Shit Pig."

"Fine," Ainsley said. She had to laugh at the absurd humor. This girl was shaping up to be someone she could possibly be friends with.

"Would you like to know my name?"

Ainsley shook her head. "No. I am going to call you Wait Bitch."

The waitress laughed. "It's a very aggressive word, bitch. A little crazy. I like that. *De cuerdo y loco todos tenemos un poco.*"

Ainsley was too trashed to translate that. Neither, she found out shortly, did she have the ability to walk unassisted down the stairs.

When they'd reached the sidewalk, Wait Bitch leaned her against a streetlamp while she hailed a taxi.

"Balcón del Lobo is *phenomenal*," said Ainsley.

"Tell your friends," the waitress said. "I need business. Life would be better if I was very famous. Then people would bring me whatever I wanted, all day long."

As Wait Bitch went spinning around on her shoe, dreaming of that future day of perfect uselessness, Ainsley started to rethink the friendship.

They hailed a passing taxi and piled into the back. Wait Bitch girlishly linked arms with Ainsley. "So, Shit Pig."

"Yes."

"How do you know José ... Ignacio ... Tabarez?" She put some extra special sauce on each of the three words in his name.

"I don't know him. I just want to get something from him."

"What? Money? A baby? A future?" she said, arching an eyebrow. "He has many women who want to get those things."

"I want a gemstone."

"Which one?"

"He has an amethyst."

"*Amatista*? But they're nothing. My mother uses one to pound meat."

"This is a very special amethyst. That's all I want."

"So you don't like José Ignacio?"

"No. His eyes are too strong."

Wait Bitch smiled. "You are interesting."

Ainsley looked out the window. They were passing through what looked exactly like an inner-ring suburb of Chicago, row after row of single-family homes, the low curbs lined with tall poplars. This was the wealthy part of Uruguay.

"*Acá*," said Wait Bitch to the driver. Ainsley paid the driver and a moment later they were standing on the sidewalk.

"This is his home," said her guide.

Before them squatted the grandest house in the neighborhood, a beautiful three-story mansion, heavy, dark, and bejeweled with many European accents. Arches, pediments, balustrades, friezes of horse heads, some painted pink, some gray, and everything cloaked in a patina of aged brown.

The only problem: between Ainsley and the home stood a solid eight-foot-tall wall. There was a copper gate across the driveway, which looked even more solid. Even her untrained eye could see the security measures were pretty fierce.

"It's cold," said Wait Bitch, stamping her feet. "That fucking *pampero*." She cupped her hands to her mouth and suddenly shouted: "*Tabarez! Cabrón! Vamos morirnos de frío! Queremos tu amatista!*"

There was, predictably, no response. Ainsley scratched a square in the dirt with the toe of her shoe.

After five minutes, she said, "I'm not waiting anymore, Shit Pig."

"Quitter," replied Ainsley.

"It's not my obsession!"

Ainsley admitted to herself that coming here with this

waitress had been impulsive, silly, and useless. This had been a rookie move, the two of them kicking around on the corner outside of Tabarez's house like a pair of high-class hookers. But it was a tiny toehold, and she was desperate.

Just then, a gray Mercedes pulled around the corner and into the driveway. The copper gate started to roll open.

It was Tabarez. Ainsley knew it.

"That's him!" she said, ducking behind a tree.

Wait Bitch peered at the car. "I can't see anything."

"Shout at him!" said Ainsley. "In Spanish!"

But Wait Bitch grew nervous and fell silent.

"Oh, big mouth shuts up when it counts?" said Ainsley. "You're the cowardly lion?"

"Why are you always talking about animals?" answered Wait Bitch. "Pigs, lions. I think you come from a farm."

"Just shout at him!"

"You shout! He is your obsession!"

Ainsley stepped out from behind the tree. She started dancing wildly. "Tabarez! José Ignacio Tabarez!"

She felt like a drunken fool. But the Mercedes started forward through the gate, then stopped.

The driver's window silently rolled down. Then she felt the tingling in her innards again, and she knew that his intense stare was upon her.

"You found me," José Ignacio said, in perfect English.

"I told her," said Wait Bitch.

He peered at the waitress. "Ah," he said, "you are the little *pepperoni* from Balcón del Lobo."

"Nobody forgets me," Wait Bitch said, flinging her arms into the air. "Nobody."

"One moment, please," he said. The window rolled up, and the Mercedes pulled into the grounds. She could see the classic wooden garage opening, the orange sconces on the walls.

Mood lighting for his car. This guy had taste.

José Ignacio came back down the driveway on foot. He had changed clothing from the afternoon: he was now wearing the customary dark-blue sweater beneath a serious suit. And he was checking a phone.

"Please, come in," he said. Then he nodded at Wait Bitch. "Even you."

"Maybe I don't want to," the waitress replied.

"It's your choice. Your friend wants to talk to me."

"She's not my friend," said Ainsley. "But I'd feel more comfortable with her here."

Ainsley grabbed Wait Bitch's arm and yanked her onto the grounds of the Tabarez estate.

CHAPTER SEVENTEEN

José Ignacio Tabarez's front yard was neatly manicured, with bougainvillea cascading down the walls and tidy hedges lining the walks.

As their host walked ahead, Ainsley studied his gait. It was precise, delicate, and purposeful, like the short-legged stride of a world-class forward on alert for a cross. Tabarez didn't seem like the kind of guy who was easily derailed.

At the front door he turned to them. "Ladies, after we enter, please remove your shoes. I lived for a time in Japan and discovered the benefits of this practice."

They entered the foyer and Ainsley gasped. It was lined entirely in wood, old mahogany, first-growth stuff. The atrium extended three stories straight up, around two more levels ringed by balustrades, towards a colorful Tiffany-style glass skylight. Eighty years ago, this had been the most popular style of homebuilding in Uruguay.

Inebriated, craning her head upwards, Ainsley balanced on one leg, trying to tug off her heel. Fortunately, Tabarez stepped into a side closet to hang up his coat when the crash happened.

"*Ay mi dios*," said Wait Bitch, "you drunken daughter of a whore. Get up. You are in the house of Tabarez!"

"This house is *phenomenal*," said Ainsley, stumbling back to her feet.

"Don't you know any other words than that?"

Tabarez returned wearing slippers. He casually put his arm around Ainsley, more for steadying her than for flirtation. "Today," he said, "you have been, what is the expression? A thorn in my side."

"I have even stronger words to describe you," she replied.

He dropped his arm and fixed her with his signature stare. "I paid many thousand more pesos than I expected."

"While I missed out completely."

Wait Bitch tried to intervene. "Don't listen to him, Shit Pig. This man burns pesos to stay warm."

He turned to his countrywoman. "We are having a civilized conversation," he said, eyes flashing. "Also, because I am curious, why do you call her Shit Pig?"

"Because that how she is called."

"Who says?"

"Me."

He turned back to Ainsley. "How are you really called?"

"Ainsley Walker."

"Ainsley Walker." He repeated the word as though he'd just cracked open an oyster and discovered a pearl.

Then Ainsley realized her mistake.

She'd said her real name.

But Wait Bitch hadn't noticed. "How is your wife? Everybody is talking about how she left you."

Tabarez wagged a dramatic finger at her. "You are knocking on a door, but you will not enjoy seeing what lies beyond it," he said. Ainsley thought it probably sounded a lot more dramatic in Spanish.

He turned to Ainsley. "Why do you keep company with a woman like this?"

Ainsley was caught flat-footed. Wait Bitch had brought her here, but did she owe her any allegiance? "I don't know her name," she confessed. "We just met."

Tabarez calculated for an instant—she could almost see the gears whirring in the reflection of his eyes—and then returned to his normal courtliness.

"Of course," he said. "It is easy to make friends in Uruguay. Let's all go into the living room and discuss this matter at hand."

He escorted them up a curved stairway that had been fashioned out of a rich, reddish wood. Ainsley dragged her fingertips along the slick wainscoting. This family really knew their stuff.

At the top of the stairs they entered the *sala*, a grand living room. "Please, wait here," he said.

Ainsley knew immediately that Tabarez was a serious scholar of Uruguayan art and culture. Hanging on the walls were oil canvases of galloping gauchos in red shirts. On pedestals, sculptures of tango dancers. Stacked against the wall, several more portraits of early *libertadores*. The history of this small country was represented here.

"Don't touch anything," said Wait Bitch. "Tabarez might charge you."

"He's being very nice to us," said Ainsley.

"Don't trust him."

"Maybe I shouldn't trust you."

Tabarez returned. He was followed by a butler carrying a tray with three yellowish cocktails, each garnished with a bright red cherry.

"Please," he said, "it's a whiskey cocktail. My favorite." He took one and sipped it.

"Thank you," said Ainsley, "but I've had enough already tonight."

"I haven't," said Wait Bitch, grabbing both remaining cocktails and stalked away. Ainsley felt relieved. Her attitude was threatening to ruin this opportunity.

"You have a fantastic collection of art," said Ainsley.

Tabarez didn't respond. Instead, he walked over to a side table, on which lay an oddly twisted piece of metal. "This is my favorite," he said. "Do you recognize it?"

"Nope," said Ainsley.

"It's from the Graf Spree."

Ainsley recognized the name: the famous German battleship that was purposely scuttled outside of the Montevideo harbor to avoid capture by the English navy.

He continued. "This is from the captain's bridge. He gave it to my father before committing suicide in Argentina."

"You must be proud to own it."

"I am." He studied her again. "You are here because I have something you want."

"Yes."

"I will not ask why you want this thing. But I will ask what you are willing to offer." She felt the tractor-beam eyes pinning her.

She felt emboldened by the warm feel of tannat, the familiar sounds of English dipthongs, and the bitter taste of desperation.

"I'm willing to match your price plus one thousand dollars. For your trouble."

Driving up the price at an auction couldn't really be defined as *trouble*, but kissing up a little would probably help her. Besides, it was an even deal for him.

Ainsley met his eyes and tried to elegantly lower herself onto his tuffeted brocade couch. However, the edge of her butt clipped the corner of the cushion. In an instant, she was sprawled facefirst on the baize carpet.

She'd fallen. Again.

"Let me help," said José Ignacio. She felt his hand under the small of her back.

Then she was upright again, Tabarez next to her. His arm had been laid across the top of the seat. His black eyes were staring directly into hers.

"This couch is very dangerous," he said. "Many have not escaped it alive."

His dry humor didn't impress her. She was determined to recapture her dignity. "What about my offer?" she said.

"El Árbol Negro means very little to me," he said, "so I will probably accept your offer."

"Maybe this will help you decide." She pulled one of the cash bricks from her purse and set it down on the coffee table. "Two hundred thousand pesos. I'll give you the rest tomorrow when you give me the amethyst."

His eyes glanced at the brick, then returned to her. Suddenly it dawned upon her what an idiot she must look like, trying to tempt a rich man with money.

"When will you decide?" she said.

"Soon."

His fingers moved towards her hair and began playing with her tresses, winding them around his fingers. The soft tugging on her scalp caused her to bite her lip with pleasure. If she'd been more sober, she would've found many reasons to resist him.

But being decidedly unsober, she was finding many reasons to agree with his unspoken suggestion. José Ignacio was wealthy, handsome, charming, almost single, definitely intense, and *not* the Legal Weasel. She began to feel resentful towards Gugina and Martina. Their desperate need for this damn amethyst was injecting a distasteful dimension into

Ainsley's evening that didn't belong there. She didn't want to feel like a whore.

In short, Tabarez was toying with her, and she knew it—but she wasn't saying no.

She didn't resist when he pulled her face closer to his. She didn't resist when their lips touched, zipping excitement down the front of her body. And when he took her by the hand towards the bedroom, she didn't resist that either.

CHAPTER EIGHTEEN

Ainsley woke up to the lazy sound of rain drumming against the window.

She lay naked and swaddled in sheets, which by their feel against her skin were very high thread count. It was quite a change from her hotel's rough fabrics and weird nighttime rattles and bangs.

She was in what appeared to be a guest bedroom, which looked as pristine and as tasteful as any back home. A white Queen Anne chair in the corner, a dressing mirror opposite.

Ainsley couldn't remember much of what happened after Tabarez'd taken her up to this bedroom. She did recall some long passionate kisses, some groping, and her shirt falling off, but everything after that was a blur. She wasn't even sure if they'd actually shagged or not.

One thing was certain, though: if the deed had been done, she hadn't been alert enough to demand that he use protection. She consoled herself with the fact that Tabarez probably would have. He was that kind of guy.

She lifted herself up on one arm and felt a new presence, a little goblin, begin to hammer inside the front of her skull with a jackhammer. She'd met this little goblin before, played with him often. He was known as the Morning After, and he was the wicked child of Wine and Dehydration.

Ainsley rolled out of bed, fell onto the floor. Her legs felt like absolute rubbish.

She hoisted herself to her hands and knees and crawled naked across the carpet, gathering her scattered clothing with shaking hands. Her ass faced the door. It occurred to her that she'd be giving a real eyeful to anyone with the unfortunate timing of entering the room at that moment.

She dressed slowly because any other speed wasn't an option. Her fingers wouldn't work on her blouse. She barely had the strength to squeeze herself back into her jeans. When she breathed out of her mouth, her tongue felt like a dried piece of paste. One glance in the mirror reminded her that she'd slept in her makeup, and she didn't dare look in the mirror again.

Finally she finished dressing and stumbled down the stairs to the second floor. Her fingers gripped the handrail on the stairs as the goblin sawed and hammered inside her skull.

She approached the rear of the couch. Tabarez was sitting on it, his thick hair washed, combed, and trimmed immaculately. He was dressed in a white robe and brown leather slippers, and his fingers were playing a small guitar.

She stood behind him for a moment, listening to his unusual rhythms. He had some talent in this area.

Finally he turned his head and noticed her. "Ainsley Walker," he said, putting the instrument down and getting to his feet. She loved the fact that he'd remembered her name. "You are magnificent."

"I don't feel like it."

Here in the bright light of day and sobriety, she felt uncomfortable. Ainsley didn't regret the evening, no matter what had happened, but she was hoping he wouldn't force her to relive it either. It hadn't been her proudest moment, wangling an invite into a stranger's house, angling for jewelry and possibly giving up sex in return. She felt so tawdry.

Tabarez diplomatically changed the subject.

"Your friend left without saying goodbye last night," he said. "I didn't know her name."

"Neither did I."

"She didn't like me very much."

"Yeah, it's a mystery to me."

He thought back. "I think I remember turning her down once. At that restaurant. I was married. Also, I don't like when it's too easy."

He grinned. Ainsley felt the hot shame of embarrassment.

"But you are not so easy. You are a negotiator."

She didn't know how to take that. It was either a compliment or a sideways insult. Then Ainsley reminded herself that she didn't have to figure out how to take it, because Tabarez wasn't her boyfriend. She didn't need to care about the things he said.

But it turns out that she cared very much about the next thing he decided to say.

"El Árbol Negro is going to arrive this morning," he said.

Ainsley held her breath and waited.

"It's yours."

Yes. Absolutely bloody hell yes. Ainsley felt a rush of elation, wanted to launch herself at Tabarez, fling herself onto his body and pepper him with kisses, carry him straight back to the bedroom.

But she knew better than that. She wouldn't allow herself to give into her volcanic emotions. She had to stay professional, especially after last night, for her own dignity.

"For the price we talked about?"

"Yes." He pointed at the brick of Uruguayan pesos that she'd offered him. It was still sitting on the coffee table.

Ainsley hadn't even noticed. What a horrifically unobservant traveller she was turning out to be.

"You are wonderful," she said. "Really."

"It's nothing to me," he replied, "but it is everything to you." Diego had been right. This man wasn't passionate about art. He was passionate about the chase.

"I need to bring you the other half of the money."

"Yes."

"Can I bring it this afternoon?" The other brick was resting at the bottom of her purse, of course, but Ainsley wanted an excuse to go back to her hotel to recuperate. And figure out how to transport the tree to the gemologist.

"Of course." His eyes brightened. "I know. We will have lunch in the dining room. During this time, I will tell you the history of El Árbol Negro."

"I already know it."

"No you don't," he said. "Nobody knows. It is one of the best-kept secrets of Uruguay. Trust me. You will want to hear it."

He motioned to his butler, who had been standing in the corner, like a shadow. Ainsley hadn't seen him either. Good servants actually made rooms quieter. It was a unique skill, one also found in caddies and diplomatic attachés and all types of other people totally unlike herself.

"Heinrik will see you to the door. What time will you return?"

"One thirty?"

"And so it will be."

José Ignacio took her hand and shook it formally. Ainsley felt slightly disappointed that he'd reverted to this distant courtly gentleman again.

She followed Heinrik down the stairs to the front door. In Spanish, he said, "Do you like *ñoquis*? Today is the twenty-ninth."

For a moment she thought that she didn't know that word. Then she remembered. It was the South American version of *gnocchi*. And she remembered Marco telling her that, because of the high starch content, it was traditional for Uruguayans to eat them on the poorest day of the month: before you got paid on the first.

She nodded yes. "Especially spinach."

"Very good."

"Your name again?"

Ainsley caught herself. "Elizabeth Vargas."

Heinrik looked at her oddly. "Elizabeth Vargas?"

"Yes."

She kept her poker face. He said nothing more as they walked to the sidewalk, where a car was already waiting on the street. Heinrik opened the door for her. "The driver is called Oswaldo. He is yours for the day. It is a courtesy of Señor Tabarez."

Ainsley was shocked. The red-carpet treatment was not something she'd ever been given.

As the car moved down the street, she twisted around in her seat. Heinrik was still watching her. And he didn't look happy.

CHAPTER NINETEEN

Four hours later, the sounds of Dexy's Midnight Runners pulled Ainsley back to consciousness.

She was asleep in her hotel room. Before passing out, she'd found an old clock radio at the bottom of her closet, and set the alarm for eleven thirty am. Now she was listening to the singer yodel on about Eileen, who meant everything.

The people of Montevideo loved eighties pop.

Her phone rang. It was the first time that it had rung here. She hoped that the roaming charges wouldn't be too vicious.

She checked the display. It was Bernabé Gradín, the jeweler whom Gugina had arranged to verify El Árbol Negro. Ainsley had already loaded the number into her phone before she'd left.

"Hello?" she said in Spanish.

"Is this Aeen-sleey?" said a male voice. He sounded old but excited.

"Yes. Are you Bernabé?"

He was so excited that he forgot to answer. "Do you have it? El Árbol Negro?"

"Yes, this afternoon," she said.

"Bring it over, bring it over. You have the address."

"Is four o'clock okay?"

"Do you mean four o'clock in English hours or Uruguayan?"

"I don't understand."

Bernabé was seized by a horrific coughing fit. It was a smoker's hack, wheezy and gloppy. At last he recovered. "Will you arrive at four o'clock exactly? Or four o'clock like a Uruguayan?"

She started to laugh. "More like a Uruguayan."

She copied down directions into her notebook and thanked him before hanging up. She figured she would use Oswaldo for the delivery. She'd checked the trunk of his car, and the amethyst tree would probably fit.

For the next half an hour she occupied herself with another horrific cold shower, followed by the careful application of new makeup. Yesterday had been a rough day, and it pained her to stare into the mirror. She looked like six kilometers of bad *ruta*.

Then she had to pick out a new outfit for the day. She was confident that, no matter what, she would look better than these Uruguayan women. They dressed so *dowdy*. Ainsley wouldn't stoop to their level.

Besides, she was going to meet José Ignacio Tabarez for a personal lunch in his grand dining room. She needed to bring her A game.

She ransacked her suitcase until she found her best pair of jeans, then chose a cream top with gold ruching down the front. She'd gotten compliments on her shoulders every time she'd worn it. For footwear she chose a pair of expensive heels, which had been an impulse buy in her earlier, wilder, carefree days. Over the top was the same winter coat as yesterday: she had only brought one. The purse went almost without saying. She wanted it by her side when she took possession of El Árbol Negro.

After dressing, she locked the door of her room and made her way down into the lobby. The same idiot front desk clerk from yesterday was there. This time, though, he shot up from his chair and offered her a hair dryer.

"Señorita," he said.

"Too late," Ainsley said, "I already have a hair stylist waiting for me." She was glad to see that he flinched when she tossed him the room key.

Outside, she stopped on the sidewalk and spun around. It was noon. The weather was even colder than yesterday, but thankfully the wind had died down. During gaps in the traffic, everything felt quieter, more still. Even the sky seemed a crisper, brighter blue.

The goblin inside her cranium had finished his hammering, and Ainsley suddenly felt her accomplishment more clearly. She'd done it. She'd used her cunning, her sense of adventure, and, okay, her body to win El Árbol Negro.

Ainsley lifted her chin up, looked at the passing people in the eyes. Every step seemed infused with meaning.

She hiked the few blocks to Sofia's hair salon. Stepping inside, she saw there was only one other patron, a toothless elderly woman pointing to her head and talking in indecipherably gummy Spanish.

Sofia was standing behind her with her hands on her hips, pretending to listen intently. Ainsley guessed that this *vieja* had been one of her grandmother's clients.

The stylist saw her and brightened up. "You wake up so late," she said in Spanish. "I thought you weren't coming."

"It was a crazy night."

"Here," she said. She directed Ainsley to the chair by the window, then turned a bright light onto her. "First, I must advertise you. My only fee. Otherwise this salon will never find a client under the age of seventy."

Ainsley glanced at the *vieja*. "Careful, she could hear you."

"She can't hear anybody," said Sofia. "This country is full of old people. All the young ones..." She made a sound like *pffft*, and flew her hand away like a bird. "Now. Tell me what happened."

"I lost El Árbol Negro," Ainsley said. "And then I found it."

"How?"

Sofia turned on the hairdryer, and Ainsley raised her voice to tell the story. By the time the salon girl had finished, her hair was fluffy and dry, and they were sipping coffee on the couch. It felt good to Ainsley to get everything off her chest.

"So now you are going to eat *ñoquis* with José Ignacio Tabarez?"

"Yes."

"And you slept with him last night."

"I don't know. Maybe."

"And this afternoon he's going to sell you El Árbol Negro."

"Yes."

"All in one day."

Ainsley nodded. Sofia sat back, studying her visitor. Then she drummed her fingertips against her thighs. "How do I get to do your work?"

From the corner, the *vieja* murmured something. Sofia waved the woman off. "Let her rot. She has nothing to do anyways." She returned to Ainsley's eyes. "I need to travel like you. I need to see this world."

"You can."

"No, this salon has my hands tied. I can't do anything, go anywhere."

"That's an accomplishment. You have your own business. You're going somewhere with your life."

"So?"

"Back home," Ainsley said, "I have nothing. I'm exactly where I was ten years ago."

"But you get to travel."

"It hasn't been easy so far."

She could see the girl chewing over her dilemma. Ainsley thought about their inverted lives. This hairdresser, who'd grown up on the other half of the world, suffered the opposite problem. Still, they were two sides of the same coin.

Ainsley dialed Oswaldo. He answered on the first ring and agreed to pick her up at the salon in five minutes.

Sofia watched Ainsley closely throughout the phone call, with that unnerving stare that is customary in Uruguay. "You will tell me if you need any help in your mission," she said.

"Thank you, I will."

"I really mean it." Her eyes were burning as red as coal-fired stoves.

"Yes, I know you mean it," Ainsley said.

Her car rolled up to the hair salon, and Oswaldo popped out of the driver's seat. He opened the back door and stood there, waiting.

Sofia's mouth had dropped open.

"Tomorrow?" said Ainsley.

"I'll be here," said the stylist.

As she left the shop, she didn't need to look back to know that Sofia was still watching her.

CHAPTER TWENTY

Ainsley pulled the backseat door closed. Her driver's eyes looked at her in the rearview mirror.

"Where can I take you?" Oswaldo asked in Spanish.

"Back to Tabarez," she said.

He nodded, and they pulled away from the curb. Ainsley studied him in the mirror. His jaw was set firmly. She decided to see what she could learn from him.

"Do you like working for Tabarez?" she said.

"Yes," he said. Nothing else.

Of course he wouldn't comment on his employer. She decided to stick to facts.

"Oswaldo, after lunch I will need you to help me take a very large package to this address." She handed him the paper with Bernabé's address. "Can you find this place?"

He read the address and nodded. Not a word. Ainsley was beginning to wonder if he was a bit simple.

The car was slicing down La Rambla, and Ainsley contented herself with staring out the window, at the blurring breakwall and at the choppy brown water of the delta. The sky was bright blue and the clouds puffy and white and a chill wind was blowing again.

It was mesmerizing. She wrapped her coat around herself more tightly and snuggled in.

Then she woke up to Oswaldo touching her knee. The vehicle had stopped. She was outside Tabarez's house.

Ainsley emerged from the vehicle and buttoned the top collar of her coat. "It's so cold here," she said.

Oswaldo didn't respond. Conversationally, there was no difference between her driver and a piece of drywall. She decided to just issue him orders instead. It would save both of them a lot of trouble.

"Stay here until I return."

He lit a cigarette and looked straight ahead.

Slinging her purse over her shoulder, Ainsley walked alone towards the house. Her stomach was twisting itself into anxious knots. Partly because of El Árbol Negro, partly because she was so hungry.

And nervous. She was about to enjoy homemade *ñoquis* in a private dining room with an extremely wealthy and attractive man who may or may not have refused to sleep with her, even after she'd thrown herself at him. Why did she have to black out on *that* night of *all* nights? And now he was going to sell her a famous amethyst after telling her its secret history.

This felt too good to be true.

The copper gate was rolled wide open. Ainsley cocked her head. That was strange, given the value of the contents inside the mansion.

She stepped through the open gate onto the driveway, then moved into the manicured yard. It made her heart sing again. She touched the bougainvillea, listened to the branches clacking in the breeze from the estuary.

Then she rang the front doorbell and waited. The slab of wood before her was exquisite. Spirals and whorls had been dug into its surface, like the enormous thumbprint of a criminal.

There was no response. That was weird. Heinrik was the epitome of the efficient manservant. He should've been there in a flash.

She rang the doorbell again, then turned and surveyed the landscaping. Water was trickling from some unseen fountain. She couldn't find it. An invisible bird sang crookedly from the branches of a tall ash. She couldn't find that either. A sinking feeling filled her stomach.

Had she been lied to? Had Tabarez cast her aside that quickly? Had he decided to keep El Árbol Negro? She'd heard the old cliché of how Latin people lived for the moment, but this expulsion was quicker than she'd expected. She felt anger sprouting from her back like a bouquet of hot orange flames.

Upset, she turned back to the door. If he wouldn't answer the door, she would invite herself inside. She gripped the doorknob and turned it. The slab of wood swung open easily, as though it weighed ten pounds instead of twenty times that much. Of course Tabarez had made sure that the hinges were well-oiled.

She entered the foyer and noticed a large object, wrapped in black plastic, resting immediately next to the door.

El Árbol Negro.

With her fingertips she traced its lovely branches beneath the plastic. So beautiful. She noticed a dolly sitting next to it. How thoughtful.

Remembering her host's orders, she kicked off her shoes, then crept around the edges of the carpet. The house was completely silent.

"José Ignacio?" she shouted. "Heinrik?"

Still no response. She crept up the stairs to the second floor sitting room where she had last seen him, in his white robe, strumming his instrument.

As she rose to the landing, she caught her breath.

José Ignacio was still sitting on the sofa in the sumptuous second floor *sala*. The guitar was laying next to him. His head was tilted back, and his eyes were shut. A thin smile decorated his mouth.

Another thin smile, this one quite a bit redder, and eight inches across, decorated his throat.

José Ignacio Tabarez was not going to be dining with her this afternoon.

He was dead.

CHAPTER TWENTY-ONE

At the edge of the staircase, Ainsley Walker screamed. It was a single choked cry. She teetered backwards.

In a flash, she was tumbling backward. This was an epic fall. All her other crashes thus far had been minor league. She bounced for what felt like hours, arms flailing, knees clattering, her vertebrae bruising.

She came to rest facefirst on the bottom step, her toes pointing back up the stairs.

How humiliating.

She carefully pulled herself up to a sitting position. Her lip was split—she could tell from the tangy taste of iron on her tongue—and her shirt was torn in the shoulder. Otherwise, she seemed to have survived intact.

One more tumble like that, she vowed, and she would get on a plane and leave South America. If she couldn't walk on a continent, she shouldn't be there.

Then her eyes were drawn backwards, over her shoulder, back to the top of the stairs. None of this felt like it was happening. José Ignacio was supposed to have lunch with her. He was supposed to tell her the history of El Árbol Negro.

Now he was dead.

Who could've wanted him killed? His ex-wife? That seemed most likely. Divorces could go bad.

Ainsley couldn't resist another look. She crawled up the carpeted stairs, her knees smarting with every contact on the rug. At the top, she peeked over the last step, her eyes, nose, and forehead visible.

Jose Ignacio's robe was soaked with blood all the way down the front of his chest. On the coffee table sat a glass of what had been ice water. A wet circle of melted condensation around the base indicated that it'd been poured quite some time ago. Next to the drink sat the cash-brick of pesos.

Her money.

Now Ainsley found herself in a moral quandary.

She had three options. One, she could run quickly from the house, never look back. Two, she could run quickly from the house, never look back, with El Árbol Negro.

Or, three, she could run with El Árbol Negro *and* the brick of Uruguayan pesos.

Would it be thievery of money? Technically, no. Those were her pesos. She'd merely forgotten them at his house. Plus, there was no signed contract. And a big stack of money would look very suspicious to whatever authorities eventually found him. A stack of money that was possibly traceable.

Would it be thievery of the amethyst tree? Absolutely. And the mercenary in her didn't feel one bit bad about that. Obtaining that treasure was her entire purpose here.

She felt the decision in her gut.

Do it.

She crept forward stealthily into the room, as though José Ignacio would waken if she made any noise. The weird stench of death was thick and unmistakable. It smelled unnatural— even though dying was the most natural thing in the world to do.

Ainsley lifted her brick of pesos from the table, careful not to touch anything else, and dropped it into her purse. She thought for a moment how convenient it was that she had taken off her shoes at the front door: no heel marks. Then she thought about the sheets upstairs and hoped that Heinrik had washed them in the morning. Being framed for a murder was not in the cards for this journey.

She was only a few feet from the body, the closest she'd ever been to a murder victim. She paused to gape. He already seemed waxen and stiff. For a moment, she felt a pang of sorrow. He'd seemed to be a dignified and refined man—despite having been left with no dignity or refinement whatsoever, in the end.

From the open front door downstairs came the distant roar of a truck passing by on the street. Ainsley jerked back to reality. The outside world indeed existed, was going about its business, and soon, in days, hours, even minutes, one tendril of that business would curl into this house and find the corpse of José Ignacio Tabarez.

Ainsley would not be there when it happened.

She raced down the stairs, slipped her shoes back on, and left the house. On the street, she crouched on the sidewalk, dry heaving.

Down the sidewalk, she spotted Oswaldo leaning against his car, smoking. She composed herself, straightened her shirt, and approached him.

"Oswaldo."

He tossed the cigarette onto the ground and buttoned his coat. That was his way of acknowledging conversation.

"I need you to help me carry the treasure to your car."

It was taking a risk, but what choice did she have? The fewer people who knew she'd been here the better, and Oswaldo was obviously known to José Ignacio.

"You don't eat lunch?" he said.

"Nobody's home. I went inside but didn't want to look around too much."

"Tabarez," he said, shaking his head.

Ainsley had never been so relieved to hear that somebody was known for empty promises. And for Oswaldo to make such a disparaging comment about his employer was good news: he could be a potential ally in the shitstorm that was sure to follow.

The driver followed her back into the Tabarez estate. They walked to the front door, which Ainsley had left open, and entered the foyer.

She pointed at El Árbol Negro, which sat demurely under its anonymous plastic wrap. "This. It's heavy."

Oswaldo squinted at it. Then he looked up towards the second floor with searching eyes. Ainsley felt her inner organs tighten and she prayed that he wouldn't decide to look around for permission.

Finally he squatted down and grunted as he shifted the base onto the dolly. Then he wheeled it outside, down the steps, and towards his car. Ainsley followed, her gait quickening, checking over her shoulder, feeling very much like a burglar.

The driver popped open the trunk of his car and gestured for Ainsley to help. Together they lifted the awkward package into the small space. It fit perfectly.

"Good?"

"Yes," she answered. "Now to the address."

He started to return the dolly to the house, but she grabbed his hand. "Let's take the dolly with us. In the back seat. We might need it."

She knew she probably sounded a little too insistent, but Oswaldo just shrugged and loaded the dolly into the back. Ainsley took a seat in the front.

Oswaldo started the engine and wheeled the car back

down the hill towards La Rambla. Ainsley watched his hands spinning the steering wheel and his other hand holding a new cigarette. The smoke wafted up to the crack of the window that he'd thoughtfully left open.

She gripped the handrest until her fingers turned white. She didn't let up until Punta Carretas had disappeared from her rearview mirror.

CHAPTER TWENTY-TWO

There was nobody out on the commercial block of Montevideo where Bernabé's laboratory was located.

This was fortunate for Ainsley for two reasons. One, she was transporting a giant stolen amethyst statue.

Second, she was feeling like a basket case.

Alcohol, possible sex, large sums of cash, murder, and gemstone theft. The events of the last twenty-four hours had scrambled her brain so much that the possibility of her forming coherent sentences was about as remote as her brokering peace in the Middle East.

At least she knew that she could trust Bernabé.

Martina had told her a bit about him one night. Back in the fifties, Bernabé Gradin had been one of the most famous jewelers in Uruguay, but he'd fallen on hard times when the country did. He'd managed to hang on, diversifying his business, getting away from retail and towards laboratory and chemical work.

Now he was in his eighties, working only part-time, which Ainsley calculated was about quarter time, since Uruguayans hardly work anyways. But he was apparently still a force to be reckoned with. Martina had sworn that his eye was the best in the business.

That smelled like hero worship to Ainsley. Martina would've been a young teenager when he was a successful younger man. She wondered if there had been more to their story.

Oswaldo pulled to a stop beneath a maple tree. Ainsley retrieved the dolly from the back seat and helped him lift the treasure out of the trunk. It had survived the ride intact. They placed it gingerly on the dolly and Oswaldo carted it towards a glass door marked *Gradin Gemología*.

She stopped the driver as he reached for the door. "That's enough. No more help."

He paused. "You don't want help to bring it inside?"

"No, the owner requested no visitors. But thank you very much."

"You don't need another ride?" he said.

She shook her head. "But you've been excellent."

She pressed three thousand pesos into his palm. It wasn't quite a bribe, but she hoped that he would remember the kindness later when, she assumed, the police would be asking questions of him.

Ainsley planned, of course, to be long gone by then. Nobody in Uruguay knew her real name, and she'd paid in cash everywhere else she'd gone. If the police had any questions, they could call her back in North America, seven thousand miles away. She wondered how efficient the police would be anyways. If they were anything like the wait staff in the restaurants, the murderer would probably live a long and tranquil life.

Oswaldo looked at the pesos. His eyes widened as he counted them. Ainsley caught his eyes and lifted a single finger to her lips. *Shhh.*

"For me?" he said.

"For you."

He nodded dumbly and returned to the car without a word. Not surprising. Once the news broke, she hoped that Oswaldo would have the good sense to avoid admitting any knowledge of the day's events. He probably would.

But she had her doubts about Wait Bitch. There was nothing she could do about that, though.

She pushed these thoughts from her mind. This gemology lab was a safe haven. She propped open the door and wheeled El Árbol Negro inside.

CHAPTER TWENTY-THREE

The air in the gemologist's laboratory was musty and warm.

Old microscopes sat on a countertop that ringed the room. Thousands of small plastic bins were jammed into cupboards, and various items of the gemology profession were scattered on high desks, loupes, calipers.

A heavy old man in a rumpled gray sport coat was heaving his bulk around the counter towards her.

"My baby, my baby, there you are," he said in Spanish.

"It's nice to meet you too," she said.

But he passed her and crouched next to the wrapped treasure. He threw his arms around it. "Light of my life, you've returned to me."

Then he seemingly noticed Ainsley for the first time. He pressed his pudgy hand on the countertop and hoisted his bulk back onto his feet. She couldn't help smiling. He had a young spirit. He would always seem young.

His thick glasses magnified his eyes, and his mouth was expressive and friendly.

"I was speaking of El Árbol Negro," he said, "though I

would like it if you returned to me too," he said. He took her hand and kissed it.

"You are Bernabé Gradin," she said.

"And you are Ainsley Walker," he replied. He held onto her hand. "For eighty-one years people have been showing beautiful women to me. You are the first I have truly seen."

Ainsley blushed. She'd always presented well, knew most of the tricks, but a great beauty? No, not really. Bernabé was a flatterer, had probably always been. Though the year had changed, she was willing to bet that his line had stayed the same.

"Thank you," she replied.

"Now," he said, "let's unwrap our celebrity." Ainsley started to reach for the treasure, but he placed a warm hand on her arm. "No, please, allow us." He stuck two fingers into his mouth and executed a surprisingly strong dog whistle. "*Héctor, mira! El Árbol Negro!*"

From the rear of the laboratory came his assistant, a middle-aged man in a white smock. Héctor. Ainsley felt instantly sorry for him. He owned the saddest face she'd ever seen outside the psych ward. She was betting that he'd either suffered a stroke or was clinically depressed.

Now he swung his hangdog head towards the amethyst tree, regarding it with the same expression that a busboy has upon seeing an empty table full of dirty plates. More crap that needs to get done.

Together he and Bernabé wheeled the package onto a makeshift platform in the middle of the laboratory. It was a pair of pallets that had been hammered together under a piece of flimsy plywood. The planks bowed as the two men carefully laid the weight of El Árbol Negro upon it.

Using a pair of scissors, Héctor carefully began to slice open the plastic wrap, while Bernabé issued directions.

Ainsley smiled at their obvious chemistry, the type that came with years of close cooperation.

Finally the plastic came unpeeled, and fell to the floor, and the three of them were gazing upon the lost treasure of the Uruguayan homeland. "The light," Bernabé said impatiently. Héctor flicked on a circle of overhead lights that lit up the pallets like a stage.

Ainsley sucked in her breath. Even more than the first time she'd seen it, a day ago in the *remate*, the brilliance of El Árbol Negro showed. The color truly was beyond a dark indigo, the clusters somehow absorbing the light, containing it, holding it down.

"The door," said Bernabé. Héctor obediently locked it and pulled down the shade. Ainsley couldn't help but think that he went through life like a sad metronome.

Bernabé circled the pallet, furrowing his brow. He tucked one hand under his chin. His large magnified eyes darted left and right behind his thick lenses. He was locked in intense concentration. She sensed that he was bringing all his knowledge, experience, and power to bear upon this treasure.

He suddenly swore loudly and spat on the floor. He turned his back on the amethyst and walked to the corner of his laboratory. Blinded by the lights of the stage, Ainsley could only see the two glary circles of his eyeglasses shining in the darkness.

Then Bernabé stormed back into the spotlight with tightened lips and clenched fists, like a fighter leaping off his stool and charging towards the middle of the ring. He hummed around the amethyst like a bee looking for nectar. He finally chose a branch and used a loupe to examine its various points.

"Here it is," he said. "I knew it." To Héctor: "What did I tell you?"

The glum assistant scratched his cheek but said nothing. Ainsley was curious. "What did you find?"

The old jeweler turned to Ainsley. "This is very good work," he said. "The Russians are very skilled."

"This isn't Russian," Ainsley said. "It's from here. Uruguay."

"No, it isn't."

Ainsley felt panic in her stomach. Suddenly she knew what was coming next.

"Let me show you," he said. He beckoned her closer. She gingerly stepped on the pallet and crouched next to him. He expertly positioned the loupe over a single facet of and held it still. "Look here," he said, "very closely."

She peered into the lens. She saw an expanse of smooth, elegant, dark purple. Except in the far corner. There was a weird blob.

"I see ... something."

"What is it?" he said. "Tell me."

She didn't have the Spanish to describe it. "It's like ... a tiny piece of bread, I guess."

"Exactly," he said. "You have said it perfectly. It's called a bread crumb inclusion."

"So what does that mean?"

"It's a result of the thermal process."

"What does that mean?"

"This is synthetic," he said. "Natural amethysts don't have that."

He let that sink in for a moment. "But it is still excellent work. I've never seen a lab gem this intricate, or with such brilliance." Bernabé saw that she was crushed. "Of course, there is a small chance that I am wrong. I need to verify with that twinning test."

He glanced at the tree again and seemed to forget what he'd just said. "Maybe this could be the Japanese. They are almost as skilled. Thirty years ago, I went to Tokyo when the synthetics first arrived on the market. We knew nothing about them. We were like lambs walking into the lion's den—"

Ainsley didn't want to hear any more. The disappointment had flooded her entire body. She felt tears brimming in her eyes.

She ran to the front door, scrambling to unlock it, and fled outside.

CHAPTER TWENTY-FOUR

Ainsley ran down the sidewalk, towards absolutely nothing, punching the air with her fists. Pedestrians gave her a wide berth. She knew she looked like a flaming madwoman. She didn't care. All of the ugly behavior she'd encountered or even engaged in thus far—possible unprotected sex, definite murder, under-the-table payment, and outright theft.

All for a *fake*? A *synthetic* amethyst, grown in some *laboratory* in goddamn Siberia? She had more questions than answers. Who would've ordered such a fake to be made? Why? And how did it get into the *remate*? Why didn't the auction house verify its authenticity? Or had they been fooled too?

Then she felt herself falling. Again.

In the flick of a rat's tail, she'd tumbled halfway into a yawning canyon in the sidewalk. Again? This one had probably left by some underpaid construction crew who'd walked off the job when the funds ran out.

She hauled herself out and turned her head. One small orange pylon marked a corner of the pit. Nice to know.

Ainsley touched her fingers to her face and pulled them

away. Blood was on her fingertips. She looked down at her clothes. Her pants had ripped at the left knee. Even worse, her coat was ruined. The front and sleeves looked like a Pollock canvas, decorated with splatters of dirt, blood, and unidentifiable black smears.

Then she remembered her purse. She leaned over and peered into the hole. It was sitting in a pool of black seepage at the bottom of the pit.

She reached in and lifted the purse out by its strap. It was soaked with a disgusting fluid. It smelled like a sanitation pipe.

She clutched it to her chest and lay flat on her back on the sidewalk. There were no tears this time. She would've preferred them, though, to the gut-wrenching pain that shook her whole body.

Ainsley Walker had reached her absolute limit. She rolled over onto her side, her face frozen in a grimace. She watched a ladybug as it crawled across the sidewalk in front of her nose.

She suddenly knew her next move. It was simple.

She would go home.

No more searching for some mythical amethyst tree. No more wild goose chases in a country whose language she halfway understood. The two women of Associated Industries, as accommodating as they had been, could fly here and look for the treasure themselves. Or send some other desperate girl. Ainsley's thoughts raced forward. She'd have to put in notice at her apartment because her credit score couldn't take another eviction. Normally she'd ask to crash on her friends' couches, but all her girlfriends were having children, she was going to be homeless, but there was always Talal, a guy she'd briefly dated who owned a summer cabin, he had a serious girlfriend now, but maybe they would let her live there during the winter, when nobody was using it, maybe she could work behind the counter at the local deli up in the mountains, she would eat bologna at night by candlelight and wait for the cold sun to dawn over the icy windswept lake, waiting for death...

Then hands were shaking her, dropping a curtain on the imaginary melodrama of her future. She was back in the present tense.

Laying on a sidewalk in Montevideo, the capital of Uruguay.

Above her was the jowly, kindly face of Bernabé the jeweler. It was peering down at her. His hands were resting on her arm. They felt good.

"My poor little pumpkin," he said. "You smashed yourself." He was breathing heavily and perspiring. Part of Ainsley felt glad to know that he must've run after her.

"Then scoop me up and make me into a pie," she said.

He chuckled. "How many fingers do you see?" He was flashing them: two, four, three, one, two, five.

"I see an old bastard who doesn't want to help me," she said.

The old jeweler laughed again. "Héctor, let's get her up." She craned her head and saw the hangdog face on her other side.

The two men inserted their arms beneath her back, and she hooked her arms around their necks. With groans and strains, they hauled her to her feet. Their hands remained strong on her.

"You didn't see this hole?" Bernabé said.

"No, I didn't. In America we have fences around our holes."

"Fences are for rich people," he said. "We have been a poor country for many decades."

"I'm leaving this place," she said. "El Árbol Negro can find itself."

Bernabé grinned. "I have felt that way about Uruguay many times. But I never leave."

Suddenly she didn't want anybody's help. "I'm fine now. Really." She twisted free of the two friendly men—and staggered briefly. They grabbed her and steadied her again. Bernabé said something rapidly to his assistant, and Ainsley found herself being propelled forwards.

"Where are you taking me?"

"To a safe place," he said.

CHAPTER TWENTY-FIVE

As the two men propelled her down the street, one on each arm, Ainsley closed her eyes. She didn't have the energy.

"That's right," said Bernabé. "Trust us. Now, lift your feet. Up two steps. One, two, good. We are entering a special store."

Ainsley did as she was told. Her nose was enveloped by the scents of butter, lemon, sugar, coconut, and caramel. She heard the soft thud of dough landing on wooden counters. The metallic shish of cookie sheets being slid out of ovens.

"Okay," said Bernabé, "open your eyes."

She obeyed. They'd led her into a *confitería*, or dessert bakery. These were everywhere in Uruguay. Racks of cookies, cakes, twisty pastries, and hundreds of other varieties of sweets filled the shelves.

"This *confitería* belongs to my daughter," said Bernabé. "Here she is."

A matronly middle-aged woman greeted them. Her nostrils flared as she saw Bernabé with his arm around Ainsley's waist. "Isabel, this is Ainsley," he said.

"*Mucho gusto*," she said flatly.

"Equally," mumbled Ainsley.

There was an awkward pause. Bernabé said, "Isabel, this is a *client*."

His big eyes were pleading with his daughter. Ainsley guessed that the old jeweler was a man whose lifelong habits of seducing women had stretched his family's toleration to the limit.

"This one?" Isabel said. "A client?"

"Yes. Can we use the upstairs?"

She looked Ainsley up and down. Ainsley guessed what was going through the woman's mind, that this strange *yanqui* wasn't dressed like a strumpet, didn't have the dead-eyed brassiness of a whore. That she just looked pathetic, bleeding, and dirty. Bernabé would get a pass, at least this time.

Ainsley's guess was right. "Go ahead," said Isabel. She tossed him a key and gestured upwards.

The old jeweler and his assistant helped Ainsley up the narrow stairs. They slowly circled three flights up, around a beautiful iron chandelier.

An old heavy door awaited them at the top. But Ainsley was spent, done, out of fuel. On the last landing, with only seven more steps to go, she sat down unceremoniously. She couldn't summon another ounce of energy.

Bernabé collapsed next to her, coughing horrendously. "Getting older is not for cowards," he said.

"I imagine."

"It's like walking in a dark forest after night has fallen. You can sense all the predators watching you." He handed his keys to his assistant. "Héctor, the door, please."

Ainsley could hear his assistant dutifully clomp up the last set of stairs and open the door.

"There is no rush," he said. "Whenever you are ready."

By this point Ainsley was feeling a little better. She craned her head towards the final door. She could see natural light streaming in from whatever lay on the other side.

"Why are you taking me here?" she asked.

Bernabé looked at her with serious eyes. "Because you ran out before I could tell you everything about El Árbol Negro."

"There is more to know?"

He nodded. Ainsley could feel herself thinking more clearly now. She could feel her obsessive curiosity stirring again.

"Please," he said, "if you are ready."

Ainsley stood up wearily, pulled herself up the final seven steps, and moved through the open doorway.

She found herself in a disused dance hall. The long parquet floor featured a fireplace at one end, alongside an old bandstand and a dusty piano with a paint-splattered sheet thrown over it. Piles of chairs and tables had been pushed against the wall.

"We used this room for Isabel's wedding twenty years ago," said the old jeweler, "but almost nothing has happened here since."

Héctor pulled over an old table and two chairs. A moment later, Isabel appeared with some towels, soap, antiseptic, and bandages.

"Thank you, my dear," said Bernabé.

"Take as long as you need," Isabel said.

Bernabé pulled his chair alongside Ainsley. He squirted antiseptic into a cloth.

"Don't resist," he said. "It is useless in the face of my immense charm."

"If you were younger, you might have a chance," she answered.

He laughed and began to swab the abrasions on her face.

Ainsley winced with the sting of the antiseptic. But he chatted in that amiable way that people have as they set about work.

"Do you know that I received a phone call just before you arrived today?" he said.

"From who?"

"Just a friend. He said that a man named Tabarez has been murdered." His magnified eyes flicked into hers, then back to her cheek. "Inside his home in Punta Carretas."

That had been quick. She hadn't left José Ignacio's home but two hours earlier. She could feel the red rising in her cheeks.

"Should I know who Tabarez is?" she lied.

Bernabé continued. "I also heard from my friend that he purchased El Árbol Negro from a *remate* yesterday."

Ainsley felt emotions rising again. She was *not* having this conversation. Nothing good could come of it. She wondered if she could even trust him. Maybe Bernabé had lured her into this room to hold her for the police.

She shot up from her chair, knocking over the antiseptic on the table, and headed for the door. The old jeweler motioned to Héctor, who stood in front of the exit.

"I'm not blaming you," Bernabé said, following her. "You are sweet like milk. Gugina tells me this too. It is clear to us you are not a murderer."

Ainsley was spinning in the middle of the dance floor. Everything was in pain: her face, her leg, her stomach, her heart.

He continued, his palms up. "I just want to help you find the real Árbol Negro."

"Why?" she shouted. "Why do you want to help an *extranjera* so much?"

"Because I promised to Gugina."

"Why is Gugina so important to you?"

Bernabé became very solemn. He fixed her with an intense stare, much like the one Tabarez had done across the floor of the *remate*.

"Gugina is my wife."

CHAPTER TWENTY-SIX

This revelation stopped Ainsley in her tracks. It added a whole new dimension to the mission. She suddenly felt like she was standing on an iceberg, on top of frozen history, events out of sight, forgotten miles beneath the surface.

"Wow," she said, honestly surprised.

Bernabé tilted his head. "What is this 'wow'? I hear Americans say it all the time." He repeated it, elongating the vowel. "*Wo-aa-ow*."

"So what happened?"

"Many years ago we had a problem, and I have been paying her back ever since."

"Can I ask what was the problem?"

The old jeweler waved it off. "No, this story could take a week to tell, and I have said too much already. Now sit down."

Ainsley reluctantly obeyed. The old man groaned as he bent down for the antiseptic. Then he resumed dabbing her face, as though he were a painter.

"I'm not asking how you obtained El Árbol Negro," he said quietly.

"I want to tell you anyways," she said.

"I'm listening," he replied.

"I had an agreement to buy it from Tabarez. When I went to pick it up this morning, I found his body. I ran out immediately. I didn't call the police."

"That was very wise," said Bernabé. "Apparently a cleaning lady found him after you. Now she will be grilled like provolone." He laughed. "Don't worry. Everybody will suspect his ex-wife first. They're in the middle of a very angry divorce. Does that make you feel better?"

Ainsley felt her heartbeat slow. She exhaled mightily and relaxed in her chair. "Yes. The last thing I have in my heart is to kill another human being."

"We feel the same way." He took her hand. "Don't think Uruguayans live like this every day. In Rio de Janeiro, yes, those thieves are crazy. Not here."

"I know."

He swabbed her cheek again, then sat back. "Okay," he said. "Your face is beautiful again. Now for the knee." He switched his attention to her pants leg and began cleaning the scrape.

"So," he said, "do you think it's possible for us to hold a conversation about the amethyst now?"

"Probably," she said.

"And you won't run out again?"

She tried not to smile. "I can't promise that."

"I have studied synthetic amethyst for thirty years," Bernabé said. "I was one of the first to identify the hydrothermal technique in Asia. I can tell you one thing for certain. The forgers have stayed ahead of us. They have contaminated the entire supply with synthetic."

"Really."

He nodded. "It's very hard to separate. See, rubies, emeralds, sapphires ... those are different. They often have tiny flaws, so when I see a clean specimen, I suspect it's been created in a laboratory. But amethyst is a quartz crystal. It's naturally clean. So the real and the synthetic look the same. And so then to verify, I have to compare the structures, which requires an expensive test. And that test usually costs more than the stone itself. So people don't like to test their amethysts. As a result, nobody trusts the quality of anything." He excitedly poked a finger at Ainsley's sternum. "And that is why the global price of amethyst is so low."

"It sounds like amethyst needs a good public relations firm," she said.

"Yes. And it's why I was so suspicious of your tree. Héctor will perform the test tonight, but I'm certain it's synthetic."

"So that little bread crumb—"

"That was a mistake. They missed it on the inspection, or else they would've removed it."

"But who could've constructed this?"

Bernabé shrugged.

"And why?"

He shrugged again. "Who and why? I don't know. The question now is different." He leaned forward. "Who has the *real* Árbol Negro?"

That was a good question, but Ainsley announced her decision. "Someone else will need to find the answer to that question. I'm finished here."

Now it was Bernabé's turn to look confused.

"This is just a temporary job for me," she said. "Coming to Uruguay, being confused by your weird Spanish dialect, getting cheated, finding a murdered corpse, getting cheated again, falling into pits—no more. The job is too hard."

He took off his glasses and massaged his forehead. He looked suddenly old. "Gugina really needs you," he said.

"I don't need her," said Ainsley.

"But where else can you find such an assignment?" he said. "You get travel, adventure, to chase after gems. It's a dream."

Ainsley admitted that he had a point. It had occurred to her that she would be turning her back on something that *was* difficult and dangerous, true, but also phenomenally rewarding.

"Come outside," he said, rising. "I want to show you something." He offered his elbow, in the old-fashioned way.

He must've seen the hesitation in her eyes. "You can trust me," he ordered her.

Exhausted, Ainsley accepted the offer.

CHAPTER TWENTY-SEVEN

Ainsley followed Bernabé across the dance floor, her shoes clicking on the parquet tiles, and through a set of heavy wooden doors on the other side.

They emerged onto a long, narrow, tiled balcony. It was late afternoon and a stiff breeze was numbing her cheeks. A row of tables and chairs were arranged along a lovely wrought-iron railing. On the other side of the railing lay a gorgeous view: the entire sea-facing side of the Montevideo peninsula.

She gazed over the gray and brown rooftops of the city. The spooky stateliness of the dilapidated mansions and cafes of Ciudad Vieja. The flashy steel of the freighters in the port winking in the distance. The towering condominiums in Punta Carretas. And where the rooftops ended, the brown choppy waters of the enormous estuary.

"This city is a hidden treasure," he said. "Forgotten by the world."

"Absolutely," she agreed.

Héctor brought them two espressos from the *panadería* downstairs. Ainsley added sugar and sipped from the small cup, letting the bitter taste fill her mouth. It was bracing, tough ... but not disagreeable.

"However," he said, "there is more to Uruguay than this city."

He offered his arm to Ainsley again. She accepted, and he escorted her towards the other end of the balcony, where they turned the corner. Before them lay a very different view, one that pointed away from the sea.

Inland.

"That is the Interior," he said.

Ainsley squinted her eyes. Another sprawl of gray buildings, followed by an outer ring of scattered gray dots, and then nothing but green to the horizon. Beyond that was the cold blue sky.

"What's there?" she said.

"Mostly cows. But go beyond them, to the very northern part of the country, and you will find the department of Artigas."

"So?"

He looked at her carefully. "That is where you can find the real Árbol Negro."

"Don't joke," she said.

He lifted his palms again. "No joking," he said. "I speak the truth."

"How do you know this?"

He smiled. "What did Gugina and Martina tell you about the history?"

She recited the information wearily. That El Árbol Negro had been mined in the 1800s by Tarasconi. That it was the darkest of the dark amethyst. That it had been stolen from the Ferreyra family in the 1960s and been lost ever since.

"That's all true, but Gugina has been gone too long. She doesn't know the whole story." A look of pride hung smugly upon the jeweler's face.

"Then tell me."

"It was never stolen," he said.

"Really."

He nodded. "The Ferreyra family is lying."

"So they've been holding El Árbol Negro all this time?"

"That, I don't know. This is where my knowledge stops and I must rely on rumors. But I have heard, more than once, that it has been hidden in Artigas. The place where it was mined."

"What's your opinion?"

He leaned against the railing and stared at the horizon for a long time. "Did you ever read *The Pearl*? By your American author? Steinbeck?"

Ainsley had, in the eighth grade. "I don't remember much," she said. "Tell me."

"Kino, a fisherman found the most valuable pearl in the world. It destroyed him, and so he threw it back into the ocean."

Ainsley remembered now. She hadn't thought about that story in years. There was no need, since she hadn't enjoyed any great blessings. Wasn't it obvious now, as an adult, that there was no such thing? That every great blessing was a double-edged sword?

The jeweler continued: "So my theory. I think the Ferreyras felt the same way. Holding El Árbol Negro caused them too much stress. To make it worse, the sad times began. Ferreyra was probably worried that the amethyst would be seized by the junta. So the family probably concocted a story about a theft. Then they probably sold it to a private investor with the guarantee that it would be kept a secret."

"It sounds possible," she said.

"I have heard this same theory many times over the years, always with the same name attached."

Ainsley leaned forward. "What is it?"

He regarded her with cunning eyes. "Why do you want to know? You just quit the job."

She fidgeted in her seat, fighting with her inner self. "I don't know. Maybe I'm still interested."

"Pffft," said Bernabé, waving a dismissive hand. "You are acting like a woman who cannot make up her mind."

She felt upset at his casual insult, mostly because he'd touched on a hard kernel of truth. In a single sentence, this man had just described the whole of Ainsley's adult life. She had sifted through friends, boyfriends, jobs, apartments, and worldviews the same way a gold miner sifted through gravel. And now she was realizing that the holes in her sieve had been too big, that everything had slipped through, and that now she was holding nothing but an empty pan.

She felt an immense surge of frustration course through her body. She wouldn't allow another piece of life to pass her by.

She set down her miniature espresso cup with a bit more force than necessary. It sloshed onto the table. "You're right."

Bernabé waited, saying nothing.

"I want to find this amethyst," Ainsley said. "I have girl-friends who are celebrating wedding anniversaries, having babies, getting promoted. None of that is happening for me. This is the one thing I can do. It's the only thing going for me right now."

He looked at her quietly. "How do I know you are serious?"

"I am."

"Then prove it to me."

Ainsley knew exactly how. She fished around inside her purse for the small packet from Gugina and Martina. She removed a slim leaflet with *Aerolíneas Argentinas* printed on it.

"My plane ticket. I'm supposed to return to the U.S. in three days."

"If you go to Artigas, you won't be able to."

"Exactly."

Holding Bernabé's eyes, she ripped the ticket in half and tossed the pieces over the railing. The old jeweler watched them scatter to the street below.

"You are like an actor. You have the drama in you."

Then Bernabé began strolling very slowly along the balcony. He crooked a finger, beckoning Ainsley to follow.

As they walked, he said, "Here is what I know. The man's name is Guarasquil."

"Guarasquil?"

"Yes."

"That's all you know?"

"I have never met him. There is a rumor that he is wealthy. There is a rumor that he is poor. There is a rumor that he lives in a mansion. There is a rumor that he lives in a cave. There is a rumor that he is white, that he is black, that he is yellow, brown, green. There is even a rumor that he is *charrúa*."

"So he's a myth."

"No, he exists. I remember, decades ago, hearing about this same man in a different way. They said he lived on a ranch in the interior and raised peacocks."

"Then I will find him."

"Tonight," he said, "we will talk more over dinner. My daughter will get your coat cleaned."

Ainsley bowed her head. This funny, slightly lecherous, intelligent old jeweler was controlling her. She may as well enjoy it.

After all, she was going to be in Uruguay for longer than she'd expected.

CHAPTER TWENTY-EIGHT

There was a predictably sleepless night back in the Hotel Real. Ainsley's mind was racing with ideas, worries, and confusion.

Bernabé had taken her to a local *parrilla* at ten in the evening, where she'd looked at the hunks of meat cooling on her plate and wished that her stomach would stop flipping with anxiety. He'd told her everything he knew about the Artigas area, some of it relevant, most of it not. She'd tried to remember everything, even taking notes. They'd stayed at the restaurant until one o'clock in the morning.

Now, as she lay in bed watching the hour hand sweep past, something was bugging her about Tabarez's murder.

It was too coincidental that he was killed the day after the purchase of El Árbol Negro. The two events had to be related. And if so, why would someone murder him for a fake gemstone? It's possible that neither he nor the murderers had known it was synthetic. In which case, had the *remate* known? Or had they also been snookered? She was starting to feel paranoid, that there were some unknown powers manipulating the strings. Gugina and Bernabé suddenly didn't seem like the biggest fish in the sea anymore.

At six a.m. she went through the freezing shower routine for the third time. Afterwards, though, she chose a less glitzy outfit: safari pants, long t-shirt, vest, knit scarf, jean jacket. She sized herself up in the mirror. She looked like a bohemian explorer.

Perfect. She was leaving for Artigas.

She had no definite plans beyond heading to the bus station and catching the first bus out of town. When she arrived up north, she would improvise. Chat with people. Sashay down the street until some off-duty miner asked her into a bar for a drink. Her imagination took off.

Oh hell. That was a complete sham.

Artigas lay on the border with Brazil. Though she was wrapped in a cloud of ignorance about that specific town, she knew about border towns in general. They were the same everywhere: dangerous, filthy, and filled with unsavory characters.

She thought back to an ill-advised trip to Tijuana she'd taken with a group of guy friends, to the even more ill-advised afternoon they'd spent knocking back tequila shots on Revolución Avenue. The moment they stepped out of the bar, they'd been robbed. It had taught her the value of keeping her money in a special belt under her clothing.

She piled her wet hair on top of her head, left the hotel, and walked to the salon. Sofia was alone inside, cleaning the floor. It was a sad picture. Ainsley caught a glimpse of the lonely feeling that sometimes visited this country.

"Oh my God," said Sofia, "it's you." She dropped the broom and flung open the door.

"Are you open?"

"Come inside! Quickly!"

Ainsley ran inside the salon. Sofia slammed the door shut

behind her and hung the closed sign. Then she dropped the Venetian blinds. Each made a sharp crack as it hit the windowsill.

Then Sofia turned to her. Her body was trembling and her fingers shook as they touched her stomach. In English, she said, "In my family we have ability to understand people. It's almost like psychic. So I meet you and I feel something special. It doesn't feel that you are murder somebody."

"I'm not a murderer."

"You swear."

"Absolutely."

Sofia held her breath—and her American friend's eyes. It made Ainsley feel uncomfortable. When she finally spoke, she switched back to Spanish. "I know you are saying the truth," she said. "There is no lying in you."

Ainsley dropped into a styling chair. She was starting to feel the stress of being a fugitive—even from something she hadn't done.

"I walk in for lunch and I find him," said Ainsley.

"Where?"

"On his couch. Dead. Then I fall down the stairs because I am an idiot."

"Your favorite activity. And next?"

"I leave. Run away."

"Nobody sees you."

Ainsley shook her head. "There was a driver, but I gave him money. We'll see if that lasts."

"The news media," Sofia said, "say the police are suspecting Tabarez's ex-wife. But you have a different problem."

"Yeah."

"That waitress."

"God, I *know*." Ainsley had been worrying about her.

"She took you to his house. Did she know your name?"

"No. She called me Shit Pig."

That broke the tension. Sofia giggled. Ainsley pitched over sideways over the edge of the chair. Her long wet tresses swung and whapped against the side of the chair.

"There is a good story there," said Sofia, "but what happens if she describes you to the police?"

Ainsley didn't answer. That very question had been vexing her for the last twenty-four hours. She didn't have a reason to distrust Wait Bitch—but she didn't have a reason to trust her either.

"And the *remate*," said Sofia. "How many people were at the auction?"

"A hundred."

"They all saw you bidding against Tabarez. They all saw you lose."

It was true. Someone from the *remate* might recognize José Ignacio Tabarez on the television, and might even remember the *extranjera* who lost out to him.

"This doesn't look good for you," said Sofia. "Not bad, but not good either."

"I've paid in cash everywhere. Nobody knows my name."

"But Wait Bitch can describe you. The people at the *remate* can describe you."

The room fell quiet while they both thought. From the supply closet came the peaceful slurp of a percolating coffeemaker. Ainsley chewed on her lip.

"There is one thing you can do," Sofia finally said.

"What?"

"Change your description."

Sofia pointed at Ainsley's head with a pair of scissors.

Ainsley suddenly understood. She flung her arms out wide. "Oh my God, *yes*."

"You like the idea?"

"Without a doubt."

"You want to do it? Right now?"

"Absolutely. And hurry up before I change my mind."

Sofia sized up her face in the mirror. "Your face is shaped like an egg. I want to frame it. Chin length." The scissors snipped impatiently in her hands. "Give me the signal, little sweetheart."

Ainsley nodded and closed her eyes. She felt Sofia's hand steadying the crown of her head, the cold edge of the metal scissors nipping against her neck.

A minute later, Sofia said, "Done."

Ainsley opened her eyes. Her hair was gone. Her neck felt exposed and freezing. She looked down. Her tresses were laying like dead wet snakes on the floor.

Ainsley felt an overwhelming rush of excitement. For fifteen years she hadn't dared to even give herself bangs. And now, in less than two minutes, she'd hacked it off. Would there be regret today, tomorrow, next week? Possibly. But she would be too busy to think about it.

Then they settled on a new hair color: a deep maroon that was currently popular. They spent the next hour dyeing and drying. Several towels were killed in the process.

When they were finished, Ainsley looked in the mirror. She saw a leveled maroon bob hanging from an unfamiliar face.

"I look older," she said.

"Don't talk in this way," said Sofia. "Always you are gorgeous."

"It doesn't matter. Where I'm going, nobody will care."

"Where are you going?"

Ainsley looked up. "Artigas."

The salon girl dropped the brush she'd been holding. "Why do you want to go up there? There is nothing but cows and dirty miners."

"To look for El Árbol Negro. The real one."

Sofia laughed. It was funny to watch. The laughs built in size, volume, and intensity. Soon she was stretched out on her sofa, kicking her feet. It even brought a smile to Ainsley's face.

"I'm serious," said Ainsley.

"Do you know that we make jokes about the people who do this? There are some Uruguayans who have searched for decades."

"But I have good knowledge. A very dependable source told me the name of a man."

Sofia looked at her with great pity. "Maybe, but you don't have good Spanish. I am sorry but it is the truth."

Ainsley shrugged. "This is my job, and it's taking me to Artigas."

"So close to Brazil. It's not safe."

"It's my mission."

Suddenly Sofia tossed her scissors onto the countertop. She whirled Ainsley's chair around, placed her hands on each armrest, and looked at the American guest straight into the eyes.

"You will need help on your mission."

"Maybe."

"I will go with you."

Ainsley was taken aback. It wasn't phrased as a question, or a possibility, or a joke. It was a statement of fact. She stuttered a response until Sofia pressed a finger to her lips.

"You need someone with good Spanish when you travel into the Interior. Someone who knows the customs."

"You know the Interior?"

"I spent all my summers there, helping my grandfather on his *estancia*. The people are very different."

"What about this salon?"

"The other girls can run it for a few days."

"Are you sure?"

"Of course. I don't waste my words." She crouched next to the chair and took Ainsley's hand. "I told you, I sense that you have a special quality."

Flattery would get her everywhere. Ainsley thought about it.

"I trust you," said Sofia. "Do you trust me?"

And there it was: trust. The very heart of the matter, dragged right out into the open, like her most embarrassing outfit pulled out of her closet and laid on the front lawn for everyone to see.

"Yes," said Ainsley. "I trust you. But I can't guarantee success. Or comfort."

"It's not important. I can sleep anywhere. I'm a *gaucha*." Sofia mounted a salon chair and rode it like a horse, pretending to lasso a calf.

"And a bit crazy," added Ainsley.

"Maybe," she said, hopping down.

"Do you know anybody in Artigas?"

"Not even one. Every face is unfamiliar to me."

"I'm going right now."

"Now?"

"This afternoon. In two hours."

Sofia flipped the sign from *Open* to *Closed*. "Then I will meet you at the bus station."

The two women met in an enormous hug. She felt Sofia's small but sturdy bone structure beneath the embrace. Then Ainsley stepped back. "Don't forget: I'm on a mission. This means a lot to me."

"And me too. Who is this man who has El Árbol Negro?"

Ainsley thought for a moment. "I'll tell you the name when we get there."

CHAPTER TWENTY-NINE

Ainsley arrived at the Tres Cruces bus terminal a few hours later. Under her arm was her white bag, which had been newly restored. The cleaning had cost her almost two thousand pesos, but it was worth it. She'd spent forty-five long minutes at a cleaners recommended by Bernabé, watching the owner use a soft bristle brush and a bar of glycerin soap to remove each stain individually. He'd sold her a bottle of leather conditioner and instructed her to apply it only after it had dried.

Inside the bag were all her usual items, plus a change of underwear and socks. She'd decided that travelling light was the best choice. All her other belongings she'd elected to keep in her room at the Hotel Real until she returned.

And the cash-bricks were inside one of the zippered pockets, wrapped inside a t-shirt.

Ainsley smiled when Sofia appeared at the far end of the concourse. The girl was followed by a porter who was dragging what looked to be a steamer trunk on a handcart. It weighed at least sixty pounds.

"I couldn't decide what to bring," she said.

"So you just brought it all."

"No, not everything. I left my second-favorite black skirt at home."

Ainsley rubbed her temples in frustration. Sofia understood the message. "Listen," she said, "I have a secret to tell you. I have never travelled anywhere before. I have never been outside of my country. I am like a caged bird!"

"Neither have I," said Ainsley. "But I know the first rule of travel."

"What?"

"Lay out all the clothing you think you will need. Then lay out all the money you think you will need."

"So?"

"Leave half the clothing at home and double the money."

Sofia looked distraught. "But it's too late for me to repack."

"Don't worry. We'll figure it out. Let's just go."

They boarded the noon bus and chose the only pair of seats remaining: in the back, next to the restroom. The bus was scheduled to make several stops along the way and would arrive in Artigas at ten o'clock that night.

Sofia suddenly tugged Ainsley's sleeve. "I have an important question," she said. "Do you have any makeup?"

"Yes. Why?"

"Because I need to look good when we arrive." She sucked some lipstick off her teeth. "It's the first rule of Uruguay. People talk a lot. Especially in small towns in the Interior."

The driver gunned the enormous engine to life, and a moment later the bus pulled out of its berth and began snaking through the streets of Montevideo. Ainsley's stomach immediately felt queasy. She'd never been able to tolerate buses, trains, long car rides.

But Sofia was happily yapping next to her. She was describing a national holiday every February called Lemanja, named after a West African sea goddess. People from the interior, she said, visited the beach dressed in white, where they launched small boats full of blue offerings to the goddess.

Ainsley had to pinch herself. This was South America? A pagan offering to an African sea goddess? She'd always associated the continent with five hundred years of strict Catholicism—the *pietà*, the *semana santa*, skinny Jesuit seminarians in brown frocks.

The bus sped up as the streets turned to two-lane blacktop, and the houses gave way to open grass, and Ainsley occupied herself with gazing at the gray-skied landscape. The rolling hills, the *cuchillas*, were dotted with hundreds of grazing cows—occasionally one looked up from its endless meal to stare dumbly at the road. Ainsley smiled at how their eyes were spaced so far apart. It was ironic that fashion models were hired for the same characteristic.

"Let's play a game," said Sofia.

"We can't," said Ainsley. "I forgot to bring cards."

"No cards for this game," said Sofia. "It's called Lie Detector. You ask me three questions about my life, and I answer. Two of them will be lies. One will be the truth. You have to guess which is which."

Two lies, one truth. This sounded like a good way to pass a bus ride. Ainsley was ready.

"You go first," said Sofia. "Ask me anything."

"Do you have a boyfriend?" Ainsley said.

"Of course," replied Sofia. "He is a respected man who works in the legal center downtown. His family is very close to mine."

"That's a lie," said Ainsley.

Sofia laughed. "How did you know?"

"He wouldn't have let you come on this trip."

"Maybe I didn't ask him?"

"Then it doesn't matter because it won't last anyways."

Sofia became quiet. "I don't have a special man," she said. "I have never found one who was worth my attention."

Ainsley knew how that felt, but she didn't feel like sharing her own script yet. "Second question: Have you ever stolen anything?"

"Of course."

"What was it?"

"A piece of *chicle* from the store. I was seven."

"That's a lie. You're a terrible liar."

Sofia laughed. "Yes. Oh my God *yes*. Everybody can see this. I have no control over my face."

"Third question," Ainsley said. "And now I know you have to tell me the truth. How far would you go to protect your friends?"

"As far as necessary."

"Any distance?"

"Yes."

"Even if it meant sacrificing your freedom in some way?"

"Of course. Wouldn't you?"

Ainsley chewed on that one for a while. She wasn't sure. But Sofia was certainly loyal to her, no doubt about that. "I suppose that it's my turn now?" she said.

"No," said Sofia, "I have no more interest. This game is too hard." She began filing her nails instead.

"Maybe you just wanted to talk about yourself."

"Always," Sofia said, nodding. "Every day I enchant myself like an idiot. It is my great weakness."

They fell silent for a while, and Ainsley contented herself with watching the landscape again. Groves of shimmering gray-green olive trees rolled past. They had probably been planted by the early Italian and Spanish immigrants, yearning for a taste of home.

"Guarasquil," she suddenly said.

Sofia looked at her oddly. "Guarasquil?"

"That's the man. He is the one who holds El Árbol Negro, according to my source."

Sofia stared at the back of the seat before her. "Never before in my life have I heard of this person." Then she looked at Ainsley. "Thank you for trusting me."

Ainsley nodded. "You have to keep it a secret."

"I will never speak the name again."

The rocking of the bus, the exhaustion, the sleepless night—all of it conspired to close Ainsley's eyes.

"You can put your head on my shoulder," said Sofia.

"No, thank you," said Ainsley. "I'm just fine here."

She nodded off a few minutes later, her head on Sofia's shoulder.

ARTIGAS

CHAPTER THIRTY

Several hours later, they stumbled off the bus, Ainsley feeling groggy from the too-long nap.

The women found themselves standing in an empty outdoor bus port, beneath an aluminum trellis that was rusted brown from years of harsh weather. The four other bus docks were empty. Ten in the evening, and the dark air felt richer and colder here, hundreds of miles away from the ocean's biting winds. And everything was much quieter.

They walked towards a taxicab waiting beneath the single streetlight, the rolling sound of Sofia's suitcase echoing across the lot. The driver greeted them with a mumbled *mucho gusto*. He grunted as he heaved the suitcase into the trunk.

Ainsley held her shoulder bag on her lap as they entered the backseat. Here is where things could get really sketchy.

"Where can I take you?" said the driver, when he'd slid into the front seat.

"We need a room for the night," said Sofia.

He looked up into the rearview mirror. "You have no hotel?"

"It was a spontaneous trip."

"I can't recommend anything," he said. "I just arrived from Asunción."

Sofia turned to Ainsley and said in English, "Do you want to find a different taxi?"

Ainsley peered around. The area was dead: no vehicles in sight, nothing but a few closed-up buildings across the street.

"No," she said. "Let's just drive and hope for the best."

They tooled down the quiet streets of Artigas. Simple concrete homes and storefronts lined the broad street. A constellation of white pinpoints punctured the nighttime sky.

"This place is popular," said the driver suddenly. "I have taken many people here."

His finger was extended towards a slouchy joint decorated with a red neon sign that said, simply, El Hotel Bueno. A group of five men were standing outside smoking cigarettes. A pair of women leaned against the entrance watching the cab closely.

"Is there someplace else we can go?" said Ainsley.

"I don't know any. We can keep driving but..." He tapped on his meter and shrugged. Ainsley thought it was nice that he was so concerned about the cost, since by her calculation the fare had only topped two dollars.

Sofia looked her. "How bad can it be? Some asshole calls us *puta* and we slap him?"

"I hope the lock on the door is strong."

They paid the driver and hauled Sofia's luggage across the street towards the hotel. The men smoking cigarettes watched them closely. They were members of the rural class: shorter, stubbier, stained with the signs of manual labor. Definitely not the type of man that she had seen back in Montevideo.

The women, on the other hand, confronted them immediately.

"What is wrong with you?" one said as they approached.

"This is a respectable place! Do you want to destroy our reputation?" The other woman cackled. They were bulky and square, built like a pair of coffee tables.

"We just want to stay in a room for the night," Sofia said. "You have one?"

"One room? For both of you?"

"Yes, one room," said Sofia. "Is there one vacant?"

"We don't know. We are just staying here too." The other woman cackled again. Ainsley got the sense that some joke was being played on them.

Fortunately Sofia must've felt the same way, because she lifted her head high and cruised past the gatekeepers. The first woman kicked Sofia's enormous suitcase. The other cackled yet again.

The lobby was a shabby space: concrete block walls, a black couch with stuffing spilling out of its split cushions. An old beaded floor lamp in one corner provided crappy yellow half-light to a small circle of carpet.

The front desk was a high wooden countertop. Behind stood a heavy woman with a wild mass of frizzed black hair and intense eyes. She wore a spandex green top that was way too tight for her weight. Just because you *can* wear it, Ainsley thought, doesn't mean you *should* wear it.

The hotel clerk fixed her elbows on the counter and rested her chin on one palm. "*Bom dia*," she said.

Ainsley was taken aback. That was Portuguese. Of course, they *were* on the border of Brazil—and in border towns everything spills over.

She let Sofia do the negotiating. As Ainsley listened, she didn't recognize some of the unfamiliar glottal sounds coming from her friend's throat.

Sofia turned to her. "They have a room. It's two hundred."

That translated to less than ten bucks. Ainsley happily

peeled off a couple of bills and slid them across the counter-top. The hotelier watched her with great interest.

They were directed towards a back hallway, illuminated by overhead florescent lights. The air smelled moist and dirty.

"I thought you said you hadn't lived outside of Uruguay," said Ainsley.

"I haven't," said Sofia.

"But you were speaking Portuguese."

"That was Portuñol. I learned it by listening to the gauchos every summer."

Ainsley remembered that word. Her tutor Marco had mentioned it. He'd said that Portuñol was a hybrid dialect of Portuguese and Spanish, spoken by only a hundred thousand or so people along the border of Uruguay and Brazil.

"Teach me."

"No way. All I can do is curse cattle and talk about women."

"What more do you really need?" deadpanned Ainsley.

"In this hotel, nothing more. *Mira*."

She nodded towards a dirty man staggering drunkenly out of an open door. A chubby woman wearing a cutoff t-shirt and lacy underwear closed the door behind him. A wad of pesos showed from her hand.

"Oh my God, we're in a whorehouse," said Ainsley.

"Not really," said Sofia. "I mean, there seems to be some of this type of activity, but—"

"Did the clerk wanted to know if I would be comfortable in this environment?"

"Yes."

"And you said—"

"Of course. These *putas* are nothing to us."

Sofia announced this as though it were the most natural fact in the world. Ainsley had to admit she was right. These practitioners of the world's oldest profession weren't going to harm her. She wasn't competition. In fact, after the events of the last few days, they'd go down like a spoonful of ice cream. Even better, this could be just what she needed. Buy enough drinks, and some lowlife would start yammering about Guarasquil.

"She said that this hotel is mostly boarders right now," said Sofia. "She said that she kicked out all of the whores last month during the storms."

"Was it bad?"

Sofia nodded. "It was raining penguins."

Ainsley smiled at the expression, but her smile was wiped off her face as they entered their room.

It was as bad as she'd feared.

A pair of twin beds with thin mattresses had been shoved up against the dirty walls. Between them, a single nightstand rested on wobbly legs, its red surface crusted with God-knows-what variety of gunk. At the foot of each bed stood a rusted metal folding chair. The edges of the yellowed linoleum were ragged and curled up at the edge of the walls, owing to the moisture.

Ainsley stood in the middle of the room, gripping her bag closer to her body. "What do you think?"

Sofia dropped her suitcase onto the bed. "We won't be here much anyways."

Then Ainsley looked around. "Where is the bathroom?"

"In the hallway."

The importance of this comment took a few seconds to sink into Ainsley's head.

She would be sharing a bathroom with a bunch of back-woods South American whores.

Sofia seemed to read her thoughts. "It's not a whorehouse. It's a—"

Ainsley held her finger up. She pointed to the wall and motioned for Sofia to listen. There was a quiet squeaking from the room next door. Then grunts, groans. The squeaks, grunts, and groans grew faster.

These were the unmistakable sounds of sexual congress.

"It's a whorehouse," said Ainsley.

"No, it's not."

"It's a whorehouse."

"Don't judge them! You don't know them. Maybe these two are in love."

Ainsley kept her bag tightly against her side. "I'll meet you outside."

CHAPTER THIRTY-ONE

Ainsley led the way back out to the sidewalk. The female gatekeepers slid their eyes the other way. Ainsley knew the rules of cattiness. She could expect zero help from them.

The gang of men had dispersed, except for one lonely soul. He had stooped shoulders, was dressed in a freshly ironed t-shirt, his thick hair oiled back. He was smoking quietly. A local laborer on his big night out. Ainsley wondered if he'd gotten too scared to go into the hotel. Maybe sex-for-money wasn't his thing. Maybe he needed something else.

"Hey there, handsome," said Ainsley. She tipped her face up and smiled.

He looked away shyly.

Sofia placed a warning hand on Ainsley's arm and spoke in English. "Don't talk like that. In Montevideo, yes. Here, only the whores are so aggressive."

Sofia tried a different tack. "*Señor*, I am so scared here. Do you know this place well?"

He brightened up. "Of course, it is my home. What do you need?"

"My friend and I need to go out. Some place where the men will take good care of us."

He lifted his head. "I know exactly the place. El Frasco de Riquezas." He gave them directions to a street about four blocks away that Ainsley copied down in her notebook. "Find Cesáreo and tell him that you know me. He will take care of you."

"How are you called?" said Sofia.

He drew himself up proudly and said, "*La Vara*."

Ainsley did a quick translation: The Twig. Undoubtedly derived from his slight build.

As they strolled down the dark streets, Ainsley thought about the difference between the two approaches. She'd chosen the direct method, the usual American liberated woman thing, executed with the subtlety of a sledgehammer. But Sofia had more accurately read the man, his posture, his clothing, and played a different game, one more fitting.

Ainsley felt ashamed at her hamhandedness. She vowed to act differently.

"Do you think he was telling us the truth?" said Ainsley.

"Oh yes. I made him feel like a man."

They passed a well-lit playground. Children were swarming all over its simple equipment, even though it was already ten o'clock at night, as the parents chatted between sips of mate from a gourd.

"What are those toys?" she asked.

Ainsley pointed to a girl clutching a piece of white rectangular plastic with lime-green trim and two green antenna. She'd seen many children in Montevideo carrying the same item. It looked like a Fisher Price product.

Sofia shook her head. "That's not a toy. That's a notebook computer."

"Really?"

"They come from a new government program. Every child gets a notebook computer. Every one."

"Even here in Artigas?"

"*Especially* here in Artigas. These children never had a chance for real education, until now."

Ainsley watched the children and reflected. She remembered that, back in the United States, in the nineteen-eighties, the Reagan administration had classified ketchup as a vegetable to save money on school-lunch programs for the children of its poorest citizens. Here, in Uruguay, the government was giving cutting-edge technology to the children of *its* poorest citizens. Which was the more compassionate nation?

She kept wondering about that while she followed Sofia, who possessed the bizarre sense of seeming to know exactly where to go.

In fact, they smelled El Frasco de Riquezas before they saw it. Ainsley's worst fears were confirmed.

The so-called basket of riches was such a dung heap that she couldn't even properly classify what, as a structure, it had once aspired to be. Broken shutters, peeled paint, and collapsed porch. The plastic buckets hammered to the rain gutters were the finishing touch.

She was sure of one thing: Nobody had ever entered this vermin-infested concrete shack with more than a hundred pesos. She also guessed that nobody had ever left with more than a lyric on the lips, a stumble in the step, or a black eye.

"This is the real interior," Sofia said.

"Oh, they're going to love me here. The tall American girl slumming it."

Sofia cast her a cynical look. "They won't know what to say to you, *extranjera*. *I'm* going to be the popular one here."

"Fine. I'll play defense."

"Yes, thank you. And now repeat, one more time, the name. Was it Guarasquil?"

Ainsley nodded dumbly. She had plunged so far into the adventure that she'd almost forgotten why they'd come here.

As they stepped into the glowing orange interior of the bar, the choking air smacked Ainsley in the face like an ugly boyfriend at the end of a three-day bender. The entire bar was packed with laborers, at least sixty by her count, most smoking hand-rolled cigarettes. She wiped the sweat off her brow and tried not to look scared.

The bartender was the first to notice them. Then one of the bar patrons did the same. Hands tugged at sleeves. Heads turned. The whispering began.

Then the drinks began to arrive.

"Señorita," said the bartender, handing Sofia a Quilmes, a local beer. "*Bienvenidos. Para ti.*"

There was another another tug on the sleeve. Another cap was popped. "*Señorita. Para ti.*" Another one was headed to Sofia. Then another.

"Do you want me to make them stop?" said Ainsley.

"No, let them. We have to make friends."

The women travelers proceeded through the mass of bodies, collecting drinks and compliments. Broken yellow teeth smiled over plastic cups of clear liquor. Ainsley minced with small, timid steps instead of her usual confident stride.

She thanked the men who made exaggerated attempts to clear a path. Some swatted each other to gain the women's favor. Others gave up on the entire charade and hung around the outside edge of the group, cackling at their buddies. Altogether, the group of men reminded Ainsley of a herd of goats, jostling and jockeying for the closest position to the trough.

A pair of stools materialized, and Ainsley and Sofia perched themselves daintily upon them. The goats immediately surrounded them.

"My princess," one said. He was inexplicably wearing a

New York Mets baseball cap. He took Sofia's hand and lifted it to his cracked, leering lips.

The goats let out an enormous roar. Ainsley could see Sofia doing her best possible acting job.

"Keep up the act," whispered Ainsley.

"I'm *not* acting," Sofia said, her eyes glowing. "I *love* this place."

The suitor stood, his legs splayed out comically wide. "Why are you visiting such a shithole like this?" he said.

"To drink," said Sofia. "Why do *you* come here?"

He took off his hat and rubbed his eyes. "I don't know. The liquor is always warm, and these bastards stink like a cow's asshole."

"There is another reason we came here," said Sofia. "We are here to meet Cesáreo."

"Cesáreo!" the man shouted to the ceiling, whipping his forearm back and forth. Ainsley had seen several men doing that here in Uruguay. It seemed like a regional sign of excitement.

The goats took up the name: "Cesáreo!" Soon the crowd parted, enough so that Ainsley could see a heavy man sliding off a stool to his feet.

Cesáreo.

His belly was distended and hung from his frame like the sac of a frog in mating season. His fingers gripped a bamboo rod that had been glossed and tipped with black rubber. He was using it as a makeshift cane.

He heaved his bulk over. "Why do you ask about me?" he said. "I don't know you." There was hostility in his tone. He seemed like an unhappy old man who'd closed himself off to beauty, excitement, pleasure.

"But you know *La Vara*," said Ainsley.

A few men sniggered in the back. It sounded like the Twig

was a punchline in this establishment. Ainsley wondered if they'd done the right thing by coming here.

"*La Vara?*" said the man. "Of course I know that piece of donkey shit. He owes me the sixty thousand I paid to the judge to keep him out of prison."

The goats howled with laughter, but Cesáreo wasn't having any fun. His watery eyeballs bulged, his chin-fat quivered. Ainsley realized that she had blundered into a situation that could derail her plans. Something about him felt like a pack leader, maybe his age, maybe the posture of the men around him, maybe the silence when he spoke. If she alienated this man, she'd probably alienate most of the bar. And if that happened, she could kiss goodbye her hopes of finding a lead on Guarasquil tonight.

She looked at Sofia. The hair stylist shrugged. She was going to sit this one out.

Then the light bulb blinked on over Ainsley's head. She pulled herself up straight on her stool and looked at Cesáreo. "We know that he owes you money. That's why we're here."

Cesáreo looked confused. So did Sofia.

"We're going to pay you," said Ainsley.

The goats made a long *oooooooooh*, followed by what sounded like a mild ruckus. They rattled stools on the floor, pounded on tables, slapped each other on the backs.

Sofia whispered, "Do you know what you're doing?"

"Not really," she whispered back.

"These men are old fashioned. A woman never pays off a man's debt."

She was probably right. Ainsley also guessed that *La Vara* had earned himself a reputation for stiffing people on loans. Maybe that's why he'd been hanging around outside their hotel. He hadn't had any money to romp around inside with the chubby hookers.

Cesáreo squinted at her. He was leaning on his cane towards Ainsley, leaning into her words. "*You* want to pay *me?*"

"That's why we're here," she said.

"I think you have a mouth of garbage."

Oh Christ. He didn't believe her. Ainsley plunged a hand into her pocket and pulled out a thick wad of pesos. She stood up and waved the money around in the air for the goats to see.

"Look," she said, "we're not lying. This is for real."

Ainsley knew how jaw-droppingly stupid this move appeared to be, one that normally would've resulted in swift robbery and back-alley rape. But she was guessing that nobody in this bar would cross Cesáreo. Flashing cash, as long as it was *his* future cash, was safe.

Cesáreo wasn't satisfied. "Why do you want to help that piece of dung?"

That was a good question. Ainsley opened and closed her mouth like a dying fish. Nothing was coming out. Her powers of bullshitting had deserted her.

Sofia stepped in. "*La Vara* is my cousin. My family is moving him to Montevideo so we can watch him more closely, but he told us that he has some debts here that he must pay before he leaves. So my father ordered me to come here and settle debts."

God bless her, Ainsley thought. The best part was that Cesáreo was totally buying it. "You can't send *La Vara* the money?" the man said.

"No, idiot," said Sofia, "he would do the same thing to us that he did to you." She looked around and shrugged. "What can you expect from a cow when he is standing in grass?"

That earned a big laugh. Ainsley didn't quite understand the expression, but some sayings just wouldn't translate.

Cesáreo looked willing to play, but he said, "I have another concern."

"What?"

"Her. The American." He was eyeing Ainsley.

Ainsley wasn't surprised by her nationality being guessed again. It'd happened too often. Maybe it was her speaking distance, or her manner of eye contact.

Sofia invented another explanation: "She is my cousin by marriage. Ainsley is like a sister to me." They linked arms.

This stylist was slick. Bringing her along had been a wise move.

Cesáreo seemed satisfied by that. "Do you want to pay me here? With everybody watching?"

"There is no rush," Sofia said. "We have many hours until the dawn. Let's everybody have a good time." She signaled the bartender. "A beer for everybody. On my father."

A big roar shook the rafters of the bar. The goats hugged each other and hoisted their plastic cups into the air.

Sofia caught Ainsley's eye and smiled. She'd just doubled down the riskiness, buying drinks for the entire bar with Gugina's money. But Ainsley knew what was going through her mind. They needed to make friends, friends who would talk about Guarasquil.

It was going to be a long night.

CHAPTER THIRTY-TWO

Four hours and as many beers later, Ainsley was still sober.

She'd watched more than half the goats crawl out of El Frasco de Riquezas, and wondered what type of fetid mattress they slept on when they weren't slaughtering cattle or blasting into the sides of hills.

The laborers had accepted her, mostly because she could hold her liquor and laugh at their jokes, none of which she understood entirely. After all, she'd been able to pick out some of the basic emotions: resignation, anger, disappointment. There was a lot of that here, and she understood those feelings too well.

A few of the savvier goats had watched her closely over the rims of their cups. Some leering, others suspicious. Others had forgotten about the women completely, and were deep into their *machismo*, hugging each other.

The lowlight had occurred at the moment that a plastic cup arrived in her hand. Inside was a clear liquid. Someone had explained that it was *cachaça*, a Brazilian liquor fermented from sugarcane juice. It was clear, potent, and harsh. She could enjoy it inside a caipirinha. But neat? The stuff could start a lawnmower. A single mouthful had scorched her esophagus and sent her into a deep coughing fit.

Drinking it, however, had won the goats' respect.

The highlight, she sensed, would be coming soon. She was chatting with a small group of the remaining goats. *Small* was the operative word: this group was very *indigeno*, not a single man taller than five-foot-four. Ainsley hunched over on a low stool to reduce the intimidation.

She'd kept mentioning amethyst, mines, and Tarasconi.

Finally, one of them made an offhand mention of El Árbol Negro, called it *una leyenda*, a legend. Another said that it wouldn't ever be found again. A third had disagreed. That's when Ainsley had jumped in.

"Did you hear that it was sold?"

"Where?" said one. He was the one wearing the New York Mets cap.

"At a *remate* in Montevideo."

The goats snickered. The baseball cap one said, "That was the Ferreyra fake. Everybody knows it."

The others had nodded agreement, offering their opinions of the sucker who had bought the synthetic one. Ainsley was torn up inside but kept smiling.

The Ferreyra fake. She needed to remember that name.

Finally she saw the opportunity to butt in again. "I heard that the real El Árbol Negro is in this department."

"Maybe," one said.

"What's the name of the man? Guaya-something?"

The goats became strangely silent. Nobody could meet her eyes.

"Guarasquil," muttered one.

"Is he close?"

The goat shrugged. "Maybe sixty kilometers. But nobody gets close to Guarasquil."

"Nobody but Cesáreo," another offered.

Ainsley's ears perked up. "Cesáreo knows Guarasquil?"

The goats buried their faces in their cups. She knew she was pushing too hard, but this was the opening she'd been waiting for.

"I want to go to this place," she said.

Sofia stumbled over and threw her arms around Ainsley's shoulders. "Me too! I want to go." She paused. "What are we talking about?" Then she lost her footing and fell backwards on her ass.

In a flash, Ainsley realized that her companion was *really* drunk. That was alarming. She thought that it was obvious that they would need to keep their wits about them out here in the fields.

"Guarasquil," she said. "Cesáreo knows where he is."

Sofia whirled around, stuck her fingers into her mouth, and wolf-whistled. The short, piercing screech got everybody's attention.

"Cesáreo!" she shouted.

The fat man had returned to his stool and was nursing a bottle of beer. He looked at them with an expression of supreme annoyance. "What more do you want from me?"

"We want you to drive us to meet Guarasquil," she said.

"Get your own car," came the reply.

Sofia punched one hand on her hip. "We want *you* to drive, old man."

"Not for nothing," he said.

Sofia cocked a hip. "When we arrive, we will pay you La Vara's debt."

Ainsley couldn't believe the bravery of this girl. But Cesáreo seemed to be considering it.

He brushed the back of his head. "Look, young woman, my only day off is tomorrow. After that, I don't have another day off for another week."

"Then we go in the morning," she said.

"I can't. It's Sunday."

"So?"

"I spend Sunday with my family."

"Then you need to take us there right now, before Sunday begins," she said.

"At this moment?"

Sofia drained her beer and tossed the empty onto the floor. It clattered and rolled to Cesáreo's feet. "Yes. Before the sun rises."

Ainsley grinned. This little pistol knew how to work the urgency card, an atypical maneuver in this country. Nobody needed to do anything in a hurry here.

Cesáreo hemmed and hawed. "It's risky," he said. "My car is a month from the scrap pile. And I don't know if they will remember me there."

"No excuses," Sofia insisted. She snapped her fingers. "Let's go, fatty."

Cesáreo couldn't argue, not with the prospect of his loan being repaid. He shrugged and found his coat. A couple of the remaining goats slapped him on the shoulders, congratulations, buddy, but he shooed them away. There was nothing in him but practicality.

When he left the bar, Ainsley followed him without bothering to finish her beer.

She was inching one step closer to El Árbol Negro.

CHAPTER THIRTY-THREE

Cesáreo drove an original Volkswagen Bug.

Not the new version, the nostalgia object with the pastel colors, flower holder, and ten-thousand-dollar markup.

No, Cesáreo drove an *actual* 1969 Volkswagen Bug. It had been white, once, long ago, but had since succumbed to an explosion of rust spots that blotched its paint like a case of leprosy. The hubcaps were a distant memory. The seats were basically craters of peeling duct tape.

And Ainsley was stuffed into one of the backseat craters, knees nearly up around her ears, wondering how she would ever pull herself out.

Despite the six inches of height between the two girls, Sofia had called the front seat, claiming the need to talk to Cesáreo better. His weight, meanwhile, was so great that Ainsley had shifted to the right to keep the vehicle balanced.

Furthermore, it was a convertible, and the badly ripped top had flapped so loudly in their ears during the first ten minutes that Sofia had demanded that it be taken down. She had a talent for asking things in a way that made the other person feel privileged to help her.

This was a quality that Ainsley hadn't yet developed. She'd always been more of a lone wolf. Her mother had always said that, if she wanted something done right, to do it herself.

Now Ainsley couldn't see anything except for the headlights trembling upon the two-lane road. So she tipped her head up to the open sky, took in the entire spectrum of colors, from the starry blackness in the west to the purpling glow of the sunrise in the east.

Then she inhaled deeply. The smells were familiar yet newly exotic—the cloying odor of cow manure, the sweet citrus tang of orange groves, the sharpness of sugar cane. The old farmers' saying was true: you really *could* smell good soil.

However, as the sun broke over the horizon, the quality of the loam couldn't explain the gangs of poor, dusty people, mostly women and children, scrabbling through piles of rubble on the sides of the road.

"Why are they doing that?" she asked. "What are they looking for?"

"Those piles are set out by the mines," said Cesáreo. "The people can keep whatever they find."

"What do they find?"

His eyes found her in the rearview mirror. "Why don't you get out and have a look?"

There was nothing nice in the comment, so Ainsley sat back. She had given up trying to control this journey. She couldn't predict what would happen in the next three hours, let alone the next three days. She couldn't even predict how somebody would react to an innocent question about a pile of rubble. The Uruguayan temperament was a mystery.

Now she began to understood the wisdom of Tao. It felt liberating to float down the river of life, possessing almost nothing, judging nothing, expecting even less. She barely even felt the need for sleep now.

In Taoism, however, the journey itself was the goal. But

for Ainsley, this drift had a very specific destination: El Árbol Negro.

An hour passed, and the Volkswagen rose and fell over the hilly landscape. Then the road turned to dirt, and Ainsley felt every rut, every declivity, jam into her backside and up her spine.

It didn't affect Sofia. In the front seat, she was snoring loudly. Ainsley let her sleep. The stylist needed to sober up before they arrived. Ainsley wondered for a moment how much *La Vara* owed the driver. Would it be two hundred dollars? Three hundred? Nobody had mentioned an amount yet.

Quietly, angling the bag so that Cesáreo couldn't see, she unwrapped one of the cash bricks, peeled twenty thousand pesos off the roll, and slipped it into her pocket. It was about a hundred dollars. Her heart was hammering in her chest. She didn't need him to see the real amount.

His eyes had been watching her in the rearview mirror. "How long have you been living in Montevideo?" asked Cesáreo.

"Only a few months," she lied.

"It is pleasing to you?"

"Yes," she said. "I lost my job back in America, so I came here to explore."

He nodded. "What is your relationship to this one again?"

Ainsley racked her brain, trying to remember Sofia's lie several hours earlier. "By marriage. My sister married her cousin Benecio."

It seemed like a good name to choose. And their driver didn't question it.

Then the road suddenly dropped into a series of sharp switchbacks. Cesáreo groaned as his arms cranked the wheel around every hairpin turn. Ainsley wondered why until she remembered that this car had been built before power steering was invented.

"What is this called?"

"The *cuesta*," he replied. "It is millions of years old."

For miles to the left and right stretched a steep cliff, and they were tacking down its face. Even though geology wasn't Ainsley's cup of tea, she was impressed. This formation gave some definition, some verticality, to Uruguay's otherwise flat landscape.

As they neared the bottom, she felt something else change: the foliage. The road sliced into a forest, the only one she'd seen so far, one dense with green and gray elms and *ceibo* trees. The air grew a little muggier, the smells more rank.

Cesáreo slowed the Volkswagen down and turned right onto a dirt track that was mostly hidden in the vegetation. Immediately they ran into a chain thrown across the way.

Cesáreo stopped the car. "Guarasquil lives down this road."

He put the transmission into neutral, threw the parking brake, and heaved himself out of the car. He walked to the post on either side of the dirt track and tried to unhook the chain. It didn't work. He tried again.

Ainsley touched Sofia's shoulder. "Wake up, little sleeper."

Sofia yawned and looked around. "Where is my suitcase?"

"You left it at the hotel."

"Oh," Sofia said sleepily. Then she twirled a hank of her hair. "I need my brush." She seemed to have forgotten about the purpose of the trip.

Outside the car, Cesáreo cursed the chain. He lumbered back to the Volkswagen and stuck his enormous round skull into the passenger-side window.

"Guarasquil must be worried about something," he said. "This used to be open to anybody who lifted the post out of the ground."

"So what do we do?"

His nostrils flared. "There is no 'we'. I go home. You can walk. Guarasquil lives only two kilometers down the road."

"Guarasquil?" said Sofia. "Is that where we are?"

Cesáreo shot her a dark look. "Have another beer. Maybe it will remind you."

"Cesáreo," said Ainsley, "We need you to walk with us. You have to introduce us."

He wagged a finger at her. "No, no, no, no, no. We are not friendly. Not like that."

Ainsley didn't quite understand who "we" referred to. But Sofia apparently did. She immediately launched into a heated argument with their driver. They began flinging what sounded to Ainsley like thirty syllables of Spanish per second at each other, inches from each other's face, barely pausing for breath.

Then Sofia slammed open her door into the fat man's knee. He hopped around outside the car, howling, his face wrenched.

"Get out, quickly, we are leaving," Sofia said. As the caboose in the conversation, Ainsley had no choice but to obey. She drew herself awkwardly out of the abyss of the backseat and heaved herself over the edge of the convertible.

Meanwhile, Cesáreo was limping around to the other side of the vehicle.

"Walk," Sofia said, "quickly, to the chain."

"But I have to pay him," said Ainsley.

"No, you don't. That's what we were arguing about. I got him on a technicality."

"The fact that he didn't personally take us to meet Guarasquil?"

"Yes."

"You're nasty."

"I am even worse than you can imagine. Then I told him that we didn't have any money left after paying for the beers."

They stepped over the chain. Behind them, Cesáreo was still screaming. He yanked so hard on the door handle of his car that it pulled off in his hand. Frustrated, he threw the handle at them. The metal clattered in the dirt at their feet.

"We should give him *something*," Ainsley said.

"No," she said. "You can't let these country people know that you have money. When the eyes see that big brick of pesos in your bag, the lips begin to whisper, the feet assemble, the hands come out."

Ainsley was taken aback. "You know about the pesos in my bag?"

Sofia looked at her with large, innocent doe eyes. "Of course."

"How?"

"I searched through your bag when you fell asleep on the bus." She patted Ainsley's shoulder. "Don't worry. I don't want to steal anything."

Before Ainsley could react, Sofia had taken her arm, and together they were striding girlishly together down the hidden dirt lane.

Here they were, in a hidden pocket of rural northwestern Uruguay, skipping towards a remote settlement to beg for their community's most valuable object.

This was ludicrous, Ainsley told herself. But Tao didn't know that word, because it was judgmental. Tao only knows what is.

CHAPTER THIRTY-FOUR

Gradually the shouts of the driver petered out, and the two women found themselves passing down a long promenade formed by carob trees.

Ainsley looked up at their frizzy leaves, which fanned together overhead, blocking out most of the morning sunlight. She felt a shiver go down her spine.

Their shoes beat a continuous *pat-pat-pat* against the earth as the two girls plunged further down the road.

Then the carob trees ended, and the road opened up into a large clearing. To one side, a small creek snaked through the high grasses. On the other side, the wall of the *cuesta* cast a shadow across the earth.

And in the foothills of the formation was nestled a small plot of land with a primitive wire fence hammered around it. Inside its boundaries, several slabs of stone were spaced out at regular intervals.

It was a cemetery.

"I love cemeteries," said Sofia. "So much history."

"Someone died recently," said Ainsley. "Look."

She was pointing at a low mound of fresh brown dirt that

had seen no more than a few weeks of exposure. A fresh grave marker stood over it.

"We have nothing to fear here," Sofia said. "I can feel it."

As they came around the bend, Ainsley spotted a cluster of small, concrete bungalows. They were huddled in the hollow between foothills like ugly trolls around a campfire.

"Guarasquil," said Sofia. "This must be his settlement."

"So do we just walk in?"

Sofia shook her head. "Rural Uruguayans are very territorial. We have to shout from here and hope they don't attack us."

Ainsley watched Sofia as she stuck her thumb and forefinger into her mouth again and blew another short, sharp wolf whistle. She loved doing that.

Immediately, the doors of several bungalows flew open. Several men stumbled out onto the hardpan, squinting. They were skinny, wearing jeans and t-shirts. Some casually carried hatchets, others clubs. One even had a poker.

Soon the small group of natives had gathered on the road, craning their necks at the girls.

"Oh God," said Ainsley, "we *are* going to end up in the cemetery."

"Of course not," said Sofia. "They just need to get a better look at us. Can I borrow your makeup?"

This wasn't a ludicrous request. A girl could gain serious mileage in this type of situation from her appearance. Ainsley fished around in her purse and handed her some goods.

Meanwhile the men had begun to approach. They were carrying a couple of two by fours. One carried a rifle. Ainsley tried to suss out the situation. What type of body language should she adopt? Hands planted firmly on hips? No, that was too authoritative. Shoulders slumped? That was too weak. A sexy hair toss? Definitely not.

In the end, she just stood there, as if she were waiting for a bus, her bag tucked safely under her arm.

The men stopped a safe distance away. Ainsley saw that they possessed a slightly different appearance than the usual white Uruguayan. Broad noses, long black hair, and shorter than a coffee table. And yet they wore t-shirts, jeans, and workboots like everybody else. In fact, they looked a lot like Native Americans living in Albuquerque.

"What do you want?" one said in Spanish. His dark eyes were like pieces of anthracite coal.

"To see Guarasquil," said Sofia.

"He is busy."

"Then we will wait until he is not."

The natives didn't budge. A pair of dogs tussled in the road behind them.

"You can wait up here if you want." Another native stepped forward and pointed at Ainsley's bag. "But we need to look inside."

The cash-brick was inside the purse. Ainsley had to think quickly. "Listen to me," she said. "I will take everything out of the purse and lay it on the ground. Then you will see that we are friends."

The men cleared their throats and shifted in their stances. That was as close to agreement as she was going to get.

One by one, Ainsley removed the items and laid them in the moist dirt: her wallet, her passport, her sheaf of information about El Árbol Negro (which she laid facedown), her breath mints, her multivitamin tablets, her underwear, her tampons. The men didn't smile at any of it.

At last nothing remained but the pesos inside the zippered pocket. With a flourish she grabbed the purse from the bottom, held the brick through the leather, and dangled it upside down. "See? It's empty. We are friends."

A childish trick, but the natives either believed it or didn't care. One by one, they turned around and walked back to their village, occasionally glancing back at the women.

As Ainsley returned her items into her purse, Sofia knelt down and whispered, "You are crafty."

"I know," she said.

They followed the men towards the settlement. Ainsley felt her stomach perform little excited flips. This was no fake Potemkin village. This was no Disney World. This was an authentic, secret village of the descendents of native South Americans who'd resisted the Spanish and Portuguese.

She thought back to a word she'd read during her tutorial with Marco.

Charrúas.

Could these be descendants of the *charrúas*? The natives who'd supposedly stolen horses from the Spanish, taught themselves how to ride, then defeated the European invaders the next spring using the enemies' own animals? The savages who had used *rompecabezas*, or headcrackers, to crush their opponents' skulls? The tribe that had been supposedly destroyed at the Battle of Salsipuedes? (A heroic-sounding word, but which translates to "leave if you can".)

If they were, the mighty *charrúas* had fallen.

Ainsley and Sofia arrived in the middle of the settlement. They stood alone.

The women stood in the doorways of the ramshackle little concrete block huts, regarding the visitors. The children clung behind the women's legs, or perched in the windows, sucking on dirty fingers and staring with unblinking eyes.

"What now?" Ainsley said.

"We wait," said Sofia. "Don't walk around, you'll scare them. Here, sit by me."

Ainsley sat down on an overturned paint bucket.

And waited.

CHAPTER THIRTY-FIVE

With nothing to do, Ainsley scanned the village.

The homes had heating, at least: large oil tanks were tucked into the side of each. Nearby was an open shed, more of a partly covered workspace, featuring handhewn tables and sawhorses. She recognized rakes, spades, and a few other agricultural tools hanging against one wall.

Everything was coated with the gray-brown grime that an outdoors existence brings.

Then she listened. She heard a generator humming somewhere. Nearby a piece of meat was frying, somewhere else a baby crying. People *lived* here. Apparently, they had fun too: empty igloo coolers and beer cans littered the ground.

Meanwhile, the children were still watching them.

"Sofia," she said, "what do you think these children think when they see me? Do they know I am an American?"

There was no response. Sofia was curled up inside a dusty wheelbarrow, fast asleep.

That girl could sleep anywhere. And now Ainsley felt even more alone.

An hour crawled by like a sick infant. Ainsley grew impatient. She was a city girl, with a linear sense of city life. She didn't enjoy the feeling of time spreading out like a shapeless oil slick.

Even worse, she had to use the toilet. She stood up. The faces instantly appeared at the windows and doors again.

"Where is the bathroom?" she asked.

One of the children pointed to her right, towards a concrete block outhouse. She walked over and flung open the door. A horrendous plume of stink billowed out. The unmistakable stench of overripe feces.

Ainsley slammed the door, covered her face, and stumbled several yards away before being seized by a coughing fit.

When she'd recovered, a stringy man stepped outside of his house. "Guarasquil is too busy to meet you today," he said.

Wiping her eyes, Ainsley highly doubted that. This little hamlet was stuck in neutral. She couldn't imagine somebody popping even into first gear.

"That's okay," she said. "We will still wait."

"Then you will be sleeping on the ground tonight."

She pointed at her dozing friend. "She already is."

The man cocked his head to one side. He was looking at Ainsley like she was a bizarre species of rainforest bird.

"Do you have any men to accompany you?" he said.

"No. Why? Do we look like we need men?"

His eyes opened wide, and he backed away into his home and shut the door. Ainsley chuckled to herself. She'd scared the native with her women-first attitude. At the same time, she knew that attitudes in the urbane Montevideo were very different. Uruguay, in fact, had the highest divorce rate in South America.

Another thirty minutes passed. The shadow from the *cuesta* passed across the yard. Chin in hand, Ainsley watched chickens peck at nothing on the ground. She felt like one of those chickens. Poking around for a jewel in the dirt—and finding nothing.

Then the hair on her neck stood on end. Someone was approaching behind her. She twisted around.

A muscular older man was striding towards her.

From his hand swung a dead snake, the blood dripping from the headless neck into the dirt. His face was etched with permanent creases. She immediately knew that this man was an authority figure.

Ainsley straightened up and waited for a greeting, but he strode past her without a word and tossed the snake into a bin.

In the open dirt that passed for the town square, he shouted a name. A small man meekly shuffled out of his bungalow. While the family watched, the newcomer pointed down the road and explained something very passionately, with chopping hand gestures. The small man nodded and scampered off.

The newcomer had to be Guarasquil.

It seems that he regarded her and Sofia as no threats whatsoever. They weren't even worth a second glance.

The other men had heard Guarasquil's voice and were coming out of their bungalows now. They quietly assembled before him. As he gave directions to each, the men peeled off from the group. One began chopping wood, another checked the oil tanks, a third stocked an underground larder with cans.

Ominously, a fourth began cleaning rifles.

And with every assignment, she noticed, Guarasquil pointed towards the main road. In fact, the more he did so, the more agitated he became.

When the men had all been assigned duties, he paced the ground for a moment. He spat some tobacco on the ground, tidied up the shed, glanced at the road again.

Then he finally noticed Ainsley. She was an afterthought.

He drew up and stopped about fifteen feet away. She'd noticed that speaking distance was much greater out here in the interior.

"El Árbol Negro?" he said.

"Excuse me?"

"Are you looking for El Árbol Negro?"

"Are you Guarasquil?"

He ignored the question. "Do you want to know about El Árbol Negro?"

Ainsley stood up. They were the same height. "Yes. How do you know?"

"It's the only reason anybody ever visits us."

Ainsley cleared her throat. He was direct, so she would act likewise. "I would like to buy it from you. Name your price."

He didn't seem to care. "You're too late. El Árbol was sold last week at a *remate* in Montevideo."

"I know. I was there."

That took him aback, but he quickly regained his composure. "So you were told that the real Árbol Negro is here."

"Yes."

"It isn't."

"Why?"

"It was destroyed many years ago."

"I never heard that."

"Very few people knew. It was our secret."

"What happened to it?"

He waved off the question. "I have much to do," he said.

"But I need to know," Ainsley protested. "A collector in the United States would like to purchase it."

"So what?"

"A collector *with a lot of money* is willing to pay for it."

Guarasquil ruffled the back of his hair with his hand. He

paced alone for a moment, then turned. "Do you want me to show you where it was destroyed?" He glanced at Ainsley's clothing. "I see you have come a long way. It's the least I can do."

She felt that sinking feeling that this was the end of the line, the place where her journey stopped. "Absolutely," she said.

"Then come."

He turned and walked away. He was headed out along the riverbank, away from the settlement.

Ainsley shook Sofia by the shoulder. "Wake yourself, stupid. We have to walk. Guarasquil is going to show us where we can find the pieces of El Árbol Negro."

The stylist rubbed her eyes. "The pieces?"

"He says it was destroyed."

"Oh, *pobrecita*." She touched Ainsley's arm sadly.

Ainsley huffed. "Don't *pobrecita* anybody until we verify this. Then, if it's true, you can get *me* drunk tonight." She pulled the sheaf of papers from her bag and removed the carefully folded photo of El Árbol Negro. She stuffed it into her pocket.

She would need this soon.

CHAPTER THIRTY-SIX

With his head start and quick pace, Guarasquil was quickly lost from view. Ainsley and Sofia followed at double time, puffing as they speed-walked alongside the small creek, the grass sinking beneath their shoes and springing up again after they passed.

"Look!" shouted Ainsley. An armadillo was digging furiously in a patch of nearby dirt.

Sofia smiled. "The country people eat them. That little armored one is digging for its life."

Ten minutes later, Guarasquil abruptly turned right and squeezed through some shrubbery. Ainsley and Sofia followed, the branches raking across their faces and clothing.

"Don't worry about us," Ainsley shouted at him, "we're fine. Really."

Guarasquil didn't look back. Maybe he didn't care. Or maybe he actually believed her words, and her intended meaning—that she *wasn't* okay, that the scratches on her face and arms in fact *sucked*—had been lost. Ainsley knew that irony often didn't play well with rural people.

Ainsley followed the trail around a set of boulders, past a

small nest of *nandú* eggs, and snaking up a steep set of switchbacks. She was sweating freely now, her hair was plastered against the side of her face. Sofia was looking even worse: she staggered left and right, her head bowed. She looked like an *indigeno* trudging up to the silver mines at Potosi.

Guarasquil was a different story. He moved lightly and swiftly through the landscape. Ainsley felt jealous. She wanted to feel that comfortable in this place.

At last they arrived on a small plateau, with a stunning view of the green, rolling landscape below. They'd hiked halfway up the *cuesta* and were now hugging its side.

Sofia collapsed and sprawled on the ground. "Ainsley," she said, gasping, "I take back my friendship. This is torture."

Ainsley mopped her forehead with a handkerchief. Their leader was standing nearby, casually inspecting the toe of his boot. Behind him was the dark mouth of a large cave.

"Is it in there?" she said.

"We mostly use it for storage, sometimes for other things," Guarasquil said. "Here. Use this and look around." He tossed her a heavy flashlight.

She caught it and stepped inside. Gravel crunched under her shoes. She shone the light onto the roof. It looked at least twenty feet high.

"This is the last resting place of El Árbol Negro," said Guarasquil. He wore a practiced look of sadness on his face, as if he had given this tour many times before.

"What happened?" said Ainsley.

"We were storing it several meters back," he said, pointing into the darkness. "It was well protected. But part of the cave collapsed. The amethyst tree was crushed."

Ainsley pointed the flashlight around. There was a dusty table with a couple of broken chairs. A set of wooden crates containing cans of food, matches, blankets.

Sofia had propped herself up on one arm. "Where is El Árbol Negro today?"

"I just told you," Guarasquil said, "it was destroyed."

"Yes, but where are the pieces?"

He looked annoyed but answered the question. "My villagers and their children took many of them." He became defensive. "And why not? The value of El Árbol Negro was not in the stones, it was in Tarasconi. The genius who identified the shape and protected it."

Sofia pressed on: "So your village has collected all of El Árbol Negro?"

"Not all. There are still some scattered around." He waved around the floor of the cave.

That's all it took. Ainsley heard this and plunged deeper into the cave. She swept the flashlight across the floor, hoping for the impossible.

There: a telltale gleam. She was at least twenty meters deep now. The cave opening was a small obloid ring of gray light.

Guarasquil cupped his hands around his mouth and yelled. "It is not safe to explore too far. You should come back."

Deep in the darkness, Ainsley ignored the distant warning. She crouched down. Her shaking fingers reached forward and pulled the amethyst from the dirt. It was about the size of a walnut. She wiped it clean on the hem of her shirt. Then she held it up to the flashlight.

The amethyst was shaped just like the hundreds that'd made up the synthetic El Árbol Negro that she'd studied in Bernabé's laboratory. There was one difference, though.

This stone was a very light purple, almost lavender.

El Árbol Negro was supposed to be very dark, almost black.

"*Americana*," shouted Sofia, "are you okay?"

Ainsley slipped the gemstone into her pocket and picked

her way across the uneven rock floor, back towards the ring of light. She shielded her eyes and squinted as she stepped out of the sunshine.

"Did you have a good time?" said Guarasquil.

"Kind of."

He eyed the gemstone. "You found a piece of El Árbol Negro."

"No I didn't."

"You did," he replied coolly. "It's in your hand. You can treasure that for all your life."

"This isn't from El Árbol Negro." She unrolled the photo that Gugina had given her. "Look. It's not even close."

"This photograph changes the color," explained Guarasquil. "It was actually much lighter than people think."

"Then why was it called El Árbol Negro?" said Sofia. "According to you, the name is a lie."

Guarasquil backed away from his two guests. "I have shown you the location that you wanted. I cannot spend any more time here." He paused. "Please know that El Árbol Negro has been destroyed for years. And now you have seen it."

He pivoted on his heel and disappeared down the trail. The two girls watched him descend to the plain and disappear into the *bosque galleria* along the river.

"I think he's lying," said Ainsley.

"I think so too," agreed Sofia.

"But he was very polite to bring us here."

Her friend scoffed. "He wasn't being polite. He was giving us propaganda. I think El Árbol Negro is intact. And I think he is trying to hide it."

That made sense, Ainsley thought. The practiced way in which he brought them up the trail, the routine lines—it definitely felt like he'd shown this cave to other visitors. It's possible that he'd even scattered some cheap pieces of synthetic amethyst on the cave floor.

In fact, the more she thought about it, the more insulted she felt. How stupid did he think they were?

"What now?" said Sofia. "Do we talk to the villagers? See who will tell us the real story?"

"Let's walk and think about it."

CHAPTER THIRTY-SEVEN

Ainsley followed Sofia down the switchbacks, around the boulders, and through the forest along the river.

Neither girl said much. They both felt deflated. Even Sofia seemed to have lost some of her usual pep. The pursuit of El Árbol Negro had been the glue of their new friendship, but if the amethyst tree had truly been shattered, then so might their friendship.

As she traipsed through the grass, Ainsley moodily kicked the head off an innocent mushroom. She'd run smack into another dead end. The hope of gaining the amethyst treasure had already been snatched from her twice—once at the *remate*, again at Bernabé's lab. This was the third time.

She'd be stupid to carry on any further.

Maybe it really was time to consider, once again, the possibility of giving up. She'd already felt this way, that horrible afternoon that she'd fallen into the pit. That had been only two days ago. It felt like eons had passed since then. But she was experiencing that same sense of hopelessness.

She made the decision. She was going to end the search.

She would tell Sofia as soon as they got back to the settlement. Only a fool would keep banging her head against a brick wall. In her mind, she began to rehearse the announcement. A light touch would be best.

Of course, Sofia had nothing to gain from the amethyst tree. She had only wanted adventure. But it would hurt her feelings nonetheless.

They were drawing near to the settlement when a sharp crack echoed through the air. Sofia froze.

"That was a rifle," Ainsley said.

"I know."

Another crack sounded, this one closer. They both dropped to the ground and crawled behind a fallen log in the muddy bank. Was somebody firing at them?

There was a third crack, followed by shouts. The girls peered over the log. One of the residents, the one who'd asked Ainsley why she had no male accompaniment, was hightailing it across the grass, his long hair flying behind him.

Presumably towards the cave they'd just returned from.

Behind him, an open-top jeep followed slowly, bouncing over the exposed roots of the trees. The vehicle was packed with four men, one of whom occasionally fired a rifle into the air. The men were taking pleasure in their quarry's panic. They didn't seem to be in a rush to capture him.

"Do you have any idea what is happening?" asked Ainsley.

"No," said Sofia. "This is a mystery."

When the runner and the jeep had passed, the girls stood up and prowled along the banks of the creek, staying in the shadows.

"There is the settlement," said Sofia. "Look, something is happening."

She pointed straight ahead. Ainsley squinted. There were a new group of trucks in the middle of the settlement. The residents, men, women, and children, had been grouped in the middle of the dirt. A rope had been drawn around them, so that they looked like a herd of cattle.

Standing around the residents was a gang of men holding guns.

In the center of the group, Ainsley saw, with his head high and jaw firm, stood Guarasquil. They'd gotten him too.

Ainsley cocked her head to one side. Nobody was being hurt. They were just being *held*. What was going on?

"I am completely confused," she said. "Who are these people? Why would anyone want to attack this sleepy little place?"

"Maybe for the same reason we came here," said Sofia.

Then a distant motion caught Ainsley's eye. On the hill above the settlement, at the cemetery, there were men working.

"Let's move over there," Ainsley said. "Something is happening on the hill."

"You can go," said Sofia. "I'm not going near those fools."

"They won't see us."

Sofia crossed her arms. "It's not an activity I want to pursue at this moment."

"Fine," Ainsley said. "I'll be right back."

Ainsley crept down the creek even further. The group of hostage residents was no more than twenty meters above her. Staying low, she monkey-walked along the river until she emerged from the creekbed on the other side of the settlement.

The hilltop cemetery was right above her. She was close enough to see what was happening.

They were digging up graves.

Hiding behind a tree, Ainsley felt her breath catch in her throat. A pair of laborers were chest deep in an excavated grave, using spades and shovels to fling clumps of black dirt into the air. She could see that they'd already dug up two others. This was the third.

At the entrance to the cemetery, two vehicles idled, waiting. One was a passenger van, the vehicle the diggers had probably arrived in. The other was a moving truck with an empty cargo area. It had been backed into the cemetery, as if they expected to load something and drive off.

Ainsley felt a sinking feeling in her stomach. She knew what they were looking for.

As if on cue, the dirt stopped flying. The dusty laborers crawled out of the hole. Another man, a wiry rascal with a long crowbar, pushed his tool down into the grave, and began furiously cranking the handle. He was probably working the lid.

Within seconds, he stopped and whistled for the others. They approached warily, peering into the grave, rags held tightly over their faces, their legs braced and ready to run. Ainsley guessed that the thieves had already faced the noxious consequences of opening the wrong coffin.

Not this time. The laborers dropped the rags from their faces and stared, their mouths hanging open stupidly. One whistled loudly, and a man in a white dress shirt and pressed gray slacks came jogging over from the cargo truck. That was probably the boss. He looked down, clapped his hands vigorously, and motioned to several other men nearby.

Ainsley dropped her head into her elbow and closed her eyes. She tasted the salty tang of her own sweat.

Her intuition had been right. Guarasquil had been lying. El Árbol Negro was here.

But these men had just found it.

Now the question: *Who were they?*

The gravediggers had threaded several straps down into the grave and around the coffin. The straps were connected to a set of thick ropes, which met at the winch mounted on the front of the moving truck. Ainsley watched a pair of the burly diggers begin to turn the winch. These guys were basically draft horses.

As the men strained and heaved, the rope slowly began to move. The laborers threw their heads back. Ainsley knew that El Árbol Negro weighed exactly one hundred and thirteen pounds. That, plus the weight of the coffin, plus the friction presented by the sides of the grave, would be a hell of a load for two men to crank up.

Soon the men hit the safety lock and walked away, shaking their arms out. Two other diggers replaced them, released the safety, and continued cranking.

They took turns like this until the coffin appeared at the top of the grave. All the available men threw straps around the dusty box and hauled it to a standing position. This was no average-sized coffin. It was more like an enormous cube, six feet at each edge.

Ainsley felt her heart skip a beat as they swung the lid open.

Inside was El Árbol Negro. It was beautiful.

And it was real.

There was no doubt this time. Even from a distance, its branches flashed darkly in the sun, like crystalware filled with the richest possible port. She remembered hearing that some had nicknamed it The Dark Prince. That was a good description. There really was something regal about it.

A small commotion at the settlement behind her caught her attention. She looked back. Two men with guns were bringing a new person into the circle of hostages.

It was Sofia.

CHAPTER THIRTY-EIGHT

Ainsley's first emotion was anger. Sofia had an unbelievable ability to get herself noticed, for better or worse.

At this moment, it was definitely for the worse.

Suddenly she could see nothing but her companion's faults. Sofia was an adorable stylist, but not at all dependable as a travelling companion or adventurer. Bringing an entire steamer trunk of clothing. Getting wasted in a bar of goatish rural laborers. And now she had been captured by vigilantes, or thieves, or whoever they were.

This journey was taking on yet another dimension.

Ainsley could see discussion happening between Sofia, Guarasquil, and some of their captors. Her friend was vigorously shaking her head no. But Guarasquil was gesturing to the trail where they'd just been hiking.

The men with guns broke away from the hostages and began to fan out across the area.

Ainsley felt her heart begin to race as she realized what was happening.

They were looking for her.

Quietly, she slipped away from her tree and down towards

the creek. She had never seen these people before, hadn't crossed them in any way .... and now they were hunting her.

She stepped into the creek, the water soaking her up to her shins. It was bracingly cold. Then, with three quick steps she bounded across the water, clambered up the bank, and found herself at the edge of a huge field.

El campo, it was called in Spanish. She scanned the area. Everything was exposed, not a tree or a shrub in sight. Where was she supposed to hide?

Ahead, about a quarter of a mile, she spotted a field of high sunflowers. She might be able to hide there. She took off running at top speed across the field.

For the first minute, Ainsley's long legs served her well. She took pleasure in her legs pumping, her heart thumping, her lungs inflating, the feeling of wind on her face.

And then a sharp crack, one that definitely wasn't the wind, echoing across the green landscape. She looked back over her shoulder.

The damned jeep. They had found her. The same four men packed inside. One was pointing a rifle into the sky.

Now *she* was the quarry.

Ainsley raced across the grass like an antelope across the savannah. There was no way on this little blue marble that she was going to be roped and tossed into a group of sad hostages. And it sure as hell wasn't going to happen while her captors stole the very item that she wanted to legitimately buy.

She glanced back again. The jeep was roaring up behind her at an ungodly speed. Her legs carried her closer to the straight edge of the sunflower field, towards the shroud of their tall green stalks and yellow-and-brown heads.

Then she saw it.

A firepit, the remnants of some recent *fiesta*, loomed beneath her legs. She had a split second to decide whether to jump it. She remembered her last pathetic attempt at the long jump, with David watching, when she'd tripped on flat ground.

She would succeed this time.

Ainsley pushed off with her good left foot, executed a double-arm takeoff, and landed nearly perfectly on the other side. She popped to her feet and kept running.

A huge smile lit up Ainsley's face. High school was long gone, had been for more than a decade, but she'd proven herself.

And then she saw the snake.

It was a huge bastard, with a tubular torso, and it was reared up. And she was about two strides away from stepping on it.

Ainsley twisted herself sideways in midair in a desperate attempt to avoid the reptile. As her foot hit the ground, her left ankle twisted and she crashed spectacularly, sprawling facefirst into the earth.

Spitting dirt out of her mouth, she lifted her head. Immediately she held in her breath.

The snake was less than three meters away. It was looking at her. Ainsley didn't know much about reptiles, but she sensed that this was no sweetheart.

She slowly pulled herself back into a crouching child's pose. She was starting to get her feet underneath her when the snake flicked his tongue and inched forward. Since when did a snake advance on a human? She felt panic wriggling through her body like a red-hot knitting needle.

Ainsley quickly rolled in a backwards somersault and leapt to her feet. It was one of her favorite moves. At that moment the snake leapt, fangs out—

There was another loud crack, and a dark cloud of soil exploded between them. When the mist of dirt cleared, the snake had slithered off.

To her left, the jeep was idling. A man was standing up in the back, holding the rifle.

"That was a *crucera*," he said. "They like to chase beautiful women."

"Then it must have changed its tastes," she answered, wiping dirt from her face. "Or maybe it mistook me for Medusa."

He shook his head. "No, you have been the best part of our day." The other men grinned.

"I appreciate that," Ainsley said.

"Now, please come with us."

"Thank you for the offer, but no."

The man pointed the gun directly at her.

There was nothing more to say. Ainsley folded quickly. After all, he *had* saved her from the snake. And now there was the heavy logic of his pointed firearm.

Bowing her head, she held her bag close against her torso, and climbed into the jeep.

CHAPTER THIRTY-NINE

The ride back to the settlement took less than a minute. The men helped her out of the jeep and escorted her into the circle of hostages. No sooner had Ainsley been shoved underneath the rope when Sofia threw her small arms around her shoulders.

"I didn't betray you," she said. "I swear by my grandmother's name."

"I believe you," said Ainsley.

"I would never do that to you. Please. I feel now that you are like a sister to me. Do you understand?"

Ainsley was touched. "Please don't cry, or we'll have a problem."

"I can't help it." Sofia wiped her eyes. Then she lowered her voice. "Was that El Árbol Negro?"

Ainsley nodded.

"Did you see it?"

Ainsley nodded again.

Sofia punched her fist into her palm. She glanced at Guarasquil on the other side of the circle. "He is a bastard."

"No, he was just looking out for his own interest."

Sofia caught Ainsley's eyes. "I think I know who our captors are."

"Tell me."

"They are from the Ferreyra family."

Ainsley remembered hearing that name. "Who is that? I heard someone say that name last night at the bar."

Sofia's eyes widened. "You don't know them? The Ferreyras own three-quarters of Treinta y Tres."

"I can't do that kind of math."

Sofia smacked her on the shoulder. "This is no time for humor. Treinta y Tres is a department. And the Ferreyras are the kings of cattle. They are gigantic. They export beef everywhere."

"What could they want with El Árbol Negro?"

Sofia couldn't answer, because the men in the jeep suddenly swung their rifles at the group. They began issuing orders. Ainsley couldn't understand all the words.

She did, however, understand the fact that everyone began to lay themselves facedown on the dirt.

"Oh no," said Sofia. "No no no no no..." She murmured it all the way down to the ground.

Ainsley obediently followed suit. First knees, then hands, then torso, then face. She inhaled the dust. She'd become way too intimate with Uruguayan soil on this trip.

Nearby, she heard a little girl crying. On other side of the group, she heard Guarasquil barking directions. What were their hostage-takers planning? A group massacre? Ainsley grew more nervous. This was feeling potentially violent.

Sofia turned her head. "I'm ready to finish Lie Detector now."

"You've got to be kidding," said Ainsley.

"I'm not. Are you scared?"

"No."

"That's a lie. Do you think we'll get out of this alive?"

"Yes."

"That's truth. Last one. Do you still have my grandmother's pink agate? For the hair?"

Ainsley paused while she thought about that one. "Yes."

"You lie."

Ainsley couldn't help laughing. "I lost it, I'm sorry."

The girls clasped hands. Then she heard one of the men say, "Not you. Or you. You two, get up."

Ainsley raised her head. His two fingers were pointing at her and Sofia.

Shocker. A gang of outlaws had chosen the two most attractive women for special treatment. Ainsley thought about her options. She couldn't pretend that she hadn't seen him, since they'd made eye contact. But she really shouldn't stand up either.

This day was feeling more and more catastrophic.

Sofia was still whimpering into the ground. Ainsley elbowed her swiftly. She looked up. "Us?"

"Yes. Don't cry."

They helped each other up, then dusted each other off. The man with the gun beckoned.

Slowly they picked their way across the prone villagers. Ainsley stepped on a man's hand and upset himself. She could feel the men with guns watching their every move.

At last the two adventurers stood face-to-face with their captors. Ainsley was surprised to see that the men's eyes stayed focused upon her face. Not a single lascivious comment.

Their boss, the man she'd spotted at the cemetery wearing gray slacks, came to the front. He carried a clipboard, as though this were a perfectly normal workday.

"With your permission," the boss said, "I will need you to come with us when we leave. We have some questions to ask you."

"Ask them here," said Ainsley.

"I give you my word that we will not hurt you," he said.

"I give you my word that I will tell the same answers."

"Please," he said, "I would prefer to keep our relationship civil." His manner indicated that all of this was merely a small inconvenience. He gestured to the passenger van. It was the one that had been in the cemetery. "It's only a few hours' ride."

She pretended to be suspicious. However, truth be told, Ainsley didn't need much convincing. She and Sofia were stranded here, since Cesáreo had undoubtedly left them. And these men now also possessed the very treasure that she was hunting for.

It was a no-brainer, but a cautious one. First, however, there were two things she needed to dispose of.

"I accept your offer," she said. "But if you mean what you say about respect, I demand to use the toilet before we leave."

"Of course," he replied. Then he nodded to the guards.

The men watched Ainsley walk towards the concrete-block privy, her bag held tightly under her armpit. Her legs were trembling with nervousness.

She took a deep breath, covered her nose with her shirt, and pulled open the outhouse door. She entered and quickly locked it behind her.

God, the stink was unbelievable. It was literally making her eyes water.

She unzipped the inner pocket of her bag and removed the brick of pesos. She unpeeled a few thousand, stuffed them into her brassiere, then resealed the package firmly. It was wrapped in plastic. Recovering it would be disgusting, but possible.

This was merely a loan.

She hesitated, then dropped the plastic cash-brick into the toilet. She winced when she heard the splash.

The second item, however, would be more difficult to release. She fumbled around inside her coat until she found it.

Her passport.

She looked at it sadly. She couldn't afford to be identified by the Ferreyras. The reason was simple: There was a dead man in Montevideo whose murder she could easily be associated with. Of course, the Ferreyras could always find her identity in other ways, but she figured that the more frustration for her captors, the better.

Plus, she had another identity she was planning to assume.

Ainsley held the U.S. passport over the pit toilet. Her fingers wouldn't obey their orders, remaining firmly clamped onto the booklet. She furrowed her eyebrows and willed them to unclench.

Finally they released it. The passport fell into soupy brown muck below. Ainsley felt herself starting to panic. She'd just lost a major connection with her past, with her personality.

She felt as though she'd lost a piece of her identity. And she gained the sense that, with no provable nationality, she could do anything, become anyone.

Ainsley closed the lid and exited the bathroom. Two men were stationed outside the door with weapons drawn. She smiled. Had they really thought that she'd burst out with guns blazing? A modern-day Butch Cassidy?

Not a chance. She was smoother than that. Ainsley strutted past the men in an unnaturally good mood. She climbed into the middle seat of the van. Sofia was already there, the sole passenger so far. She was staring daggers at Ainsley.

"What?"

Her friend crossed her arms and said nothing. Ainsley had the distinct feeling that she'd just somehow messed up.

"If you won't talk, then I have a secret to tell you," Ainsley said.

"What?"

"My name is Karin, and I am actually from Germany."

Sofia looked shocked, so Ainsley repeated it: "My name is Karin. I am from Germany." She held eye contact with stylist.

Then understanding dawned upon Sofia's face. She nodded.

The men climbed into the van, and the engine roared to life.

CHAPTER FORTY

The boss with the clipboard climbed into the front seat, next to the driver. Three other men filled in the seats behind them. One touched Ainsley on the shoulder. "Excuse me, but we have to cover your eyes now," he said.

"Impossible," she shot back.

On a look from the boss, the man kept his temper in check: "I respectfully request. Please."

Ainsley rolled her eyes. She didn't possess even a fraction of an ounce of power in this situation. But a woman could maintain her safety by bossing the men around, by bluffing authority.

"Then start with my friend. You put that blindfold on her the same way you kiss your mother goodbye," she said, "or else I'll cook your *huevos* in tonight's *puchero*."

The men chuckled at the mention of their favorite Uruguayan stew. "I will tie it even more gently than that," her captor said.

"Like you would on your *grandmother*," she said. "No, never mind. I would trust a snake before I trust any of you. Give me the blindfold. I will cover her myself."

She stuck her hand out impatiently and waved her fingers. The men behind her were laughing openly now. The man placed a large square of grey wool in her hand. Ainsley wrapped it around Sofia's face and tied around the back of her head.

"They are listening to you," Sofia whispered.

"Of course they are," Ainsley whispered back. "Are you thirsty?"

Sofia nodded. Ainsley turned to the men: "Some water for your parched hostages, please, before we wither up smaller than your little *pingas*."

The men were laughing now. One offered her a new water bottle from his own backpack. She twisted it open and gave it to Sofia first. The men watched the girls.

"Are you ready?" one finally said.

"Not yet," she said. "Stop rushing me."

She brushed her hair, pulled it back with a hair tie. Then she reapplied her lipstick. In the mirror, she could see the man smirking behind her.

"Now," she announced, "I am ready to complete my outfit. Bring it to me." The man dropped an identical piece of wool around her head, then tied it with the utmost care at the back of her hair. It felt scratchy on her cheeks.

Behind them, she could hear the jeep start up. "It may surprise you to know that I have another demand before we go," she said.

"Yes, please, by all means tell us," replied the boss.

"You need to leave the people in this settlement alone. Let them go."

"Of course," he replied. "We didn't come here to be terrorists. These people are our people too."

Ainsley had to bite her tongue. Countrymen don't herd up "their people" into a circle at gunpoint and steal their most valuable gemstone treasures. Furthermore, what kind of fate awaited the American who witnessed such an act? All sorts of grisly scenarios were criss-crossing her mind. How many ways were there to die in Uruguay? Grilled on a *parrilla*? Trampled by cattle?

Or getting your neck sliced on the couch?

She decided to shut out the grim possibilities and focus instead on the here and now. And that was feeling like a sensory-deprivation chamber. Without sight, her four other senses were becoming heightened. She felt every bounce in the road. Heard every grunt behind her. Smelled the eucalyptus in the wool cloth around her face. Felt Sofia's arm, soft and quivery, pressed against her own.

The van began moving, and soon the hours were passing as rapidly as the invisible landscape. Nobody spoke. Ainsley faced forward, listening to the shush of asphalt beneath the tires. One of the men behind her was snoring lightly.

Suddenly she jerked awake. She'd fallen into a microsleep. Losing control frightened her. She needed some light, some air, pronto. Most of all, she needed to figure out where she was.

"My idiot captors," she announced, "I am wearing plastic in my eye. And I need to change it."

One of the men cleared his throat. "It's a *lente de contacto*."

She twisted around. "Are you making fun of my Spanish?"

"No. With your permission."

"You can't make fun of your captives. Our feelings are easily hurt. Look at her." Ainsley pointed at Sofia. "She hasn't said a word since we climbed into this hideous van."

"I'm sorry," the captor said.

"No, sorry is not enough. Untie my blindfold so I can take care of this nuisance."

There was a delay in his answer. Ainsley suspected there were some glances exchanged with the boss up front. Then he must've been given the go-ahead, because there were suddenly fingers fumbling in her hair, and then the woolen mask fell from her face. The sunlight blinded her, and she lifted her forearm to block the light.

"Sofia," said Ainsley, "you look beautiful."

"Like a Saudi woman," said Sofia. "Get this thing off me."

The man behind them leaned forward. "No," he said, "she keeps the face covered."

She knew why. One, Sofia hadn't intimidated the men. Two, they probably figured that the *extranjera* knew nothing about the interior.

It was true. They were travelling across more of the same anonymous rolling *campo*. But Ainsley did notice that the afternoon sun was behind the van, so they were moving eastwards. And she did glimpse a toll booth, a *peaje*, in the distance. Above it read a sign: *Bienvenidos a Treinta y Tres*.

The department of Thirty-Three. Sofia's guess had been right: Their captors were probably part of the powerful Ferreyra family. They had muscled into Guarasquil's settlement and stolen El Árbol Negro.

And then they had kidnapped the only two outsiders who'd witnessed the act.

Ainsley fished inside her bag for her mirror. She opened it up and pretended to remove the offending lens, but really she was studying the faces of the men in the back. Behind them, through the rear windshield, she saw the open-top jeep following, the men's hair blowing wildly in the wind.

Glanced ahead, she could see the moving truck about a hundred meters ahead, passing through the *peaje*.

The truck that was carrying El Árbol Negro.

She closed the mirror, and the man behind her leaned forward to tie the woolen blindfold again. But the image of the amethyst had already been burned into her mind's eye.

TREINTA Y TRES

•

CHAPTER FORTY-ONE

The van drove on for another two hours, then turned abruptly onto a dirt road. Sofia clutched Ainsley's hand. They bounced and rattled for another twenty minutes until the vehicle slowed, turned around in a wide circle, and stopped. The men removed their blindfolds and helped them out.

Ainsley spun around, dazed. She was standing in the middle of a vast green plain. The cold *pampero* wind whipped against her cheeks. Thousands of cattle dotted the landscape in every direction. One, grazing less than twenty meters away, had been branded with a scripted F on its left hindquarter.

Ferreyra.

The men who'd pointed rifles so carefully at Ainsley a few hours earlier now tossed the weapons into a large canvas bag. There was no need for coercion here. There was nothing to run towards, except one thing.

A single stooped structure, brown and weathered, spread out behind her. It was an old ranch with a low ramshackle roof, like the furrowed brow of a field hand. Several wings branched out.

A strong, matronly woman was striding towards her across

the mud. She wore a pair of muddy Wellington boots, straight-leg jeans, a white collared shirt, and a red lariat. She looked like any ranch wife in Wyoming or Idaho.

"Your purse, please," she said in Spanish. "We will hold it for you during the questioning."

"I would like to hold it myself."

"Do you think I am asking?"

The ranch woman drew in her breath and pulled herself up to her full height. They stood eye-to-eye. Ainsley had never felt more thankful for her height.

"The purse," the woman said.

Her stare was made of titanium. Ainsley couldn't bluff any longer. She handed over the bag and was grateful for her private minute with the pit toilet.

"Your stay will be comfortable," said the van boss.

Ainsley whirled on him. "Maybe you should worry more about making cows feel comfortable," she spat. "We women can take care of ourselves."

A tiny smile cracked the ranch woman's stone face. "That is fine advice," the boss said diplomatically. He thrust out a hand. "I am called Atilio. And how you are called?"

"Karin," she lied.

Atilio paused. He gestured to the woman. "This is Señora Nasazzi. She will take you to your room. But not you." He pointed to Sofia. "You will sleep in another place."

Sofia blanched. Ainsley tried not to read too much into that, but she knew it could mean anything.

Ainsley whispered in her ear, "Remember my name."

"It's Karin. And you are from Germany." The stylist managed to grin, but her heart was somewhere else.

They separated. Señora Nasazzi led Ainsley across the dirt, around one wing of the structure, past a work shed, through a circular horse corral, across a patio with a heavy clay oven, and alongside a row of six-foot-high adjustable metal racks. Below was an enormous firepit. It looked like medieval torture equipment, but Ainsley knew it was just the *parrilla*.

Señora Nasazzi walked up to a modest door on the outside of the ranch, opened it, and gestured for Ainsley to enter. She wasted no movements: the telltale sign of a life spent on a ranch. She seemed a *gaucha* to the bone.

Ainsley reluctantly entered. She found herself in a small bedroom with an even smaller adjoining living room. A bathroom decorated with floral curtains opened off the living space. A single high window above the bed cast an orange rectangle onto the bedspread.

It was a pleasant surprise. This wasn't a torture facility, not by a long stretch. In fact, it was nicer than her freakish room in the hotel in Montevideo. And definitely better than the whore's quarters in Artigas.

Then she heard the door shut behind her, followed by an ominous click.

Ainsley raced back. There was no inside knob, no inside handle. Her fingers ran over the smooth wood. It aligned perfectly with the plaster of the wall.

Her lovely room had just become a prison cell.

Ainsley stood on her tiptoes to look out the window. Nobody was in sight. Just the *parilla* and, beyond it, the green hills. Señora Nasazzi had left for some other part of the hacienda. She would be back. They wouldn't ignore Ainsley for long.

She just hoped that they were treating Sofia with the same respect.

She sat down on the dusty couch. Before her, on the coffee table, lay a book titled *The History of the Gauchos*.

Ainsley turned through its pages, translating the Spanish as best she could, enjoying the illustrations of the wild cowboys, the rowdy taverns, the long knives, the weapons made of stones and leather straps.

Soon the book slipped from her fingers and onto the floor. The sound of gentle snoring emitted from Ainsley's open mouth.

CHAPTER FORTY-TWO

Two hours later, the door flew open. Footsteps sounded on the floorboards. A rough hand seized Ainsley's shoulder and shook her sleeping body.

"It's time to talk," said Señora Nasazzi.

Ainsley didn't stir. She was dead asleep.

The *gaucha* filled a cup of water in the bathroom sink, then dumped it onto Ainsley's face. She woke up instantly, spluttering.

"Asshole," she said.

"That will teach you to always stay awake in the interior. Where are you from?"

Ainsley caught herself and remembered her fake identity. "Germany."

Señora Nasazzi bought it. "When did you come to Uruguay?"

"A few days ago."

"What day?"

"Wednesday."

"Why?"

"Vacation."

"I think you're lying."

Ainsley felt her tongue loosen. "And I think *you* locked me in this stupid room and waited for me to fall asleep so you could throw water on me."

She stood up, but Señora Nasazzi motioned for her to sit down. "We aren't finished talking."

"I don't even know why I am here."

Señora Nasazzi stood up and lifted the edge of her shirt. A long, thin leather sheath was hooked onto her belt. From it she pulled an equally long, thin knife.

"This is why you are here," she said.

Ainsley had seen illustrations of it in the coffee table book. It was called a *facón*, and it was the favorite weapon of the *gaucho*. Its presence suddenly made her feel more cooperative.

She sat down on the bed. Señora Nasazzi returned the knife to its sheath, then dragged a wooden chair across the floor and parked herself on it.

That felt too close, so Ainsley scooted backwards on the bed until the twin points of her shoulder blades were up against the concrete block wall. Señora Nasazzi scooted forwards on the chair. She placed her hands on the bedspread and looked at her directly in the eye.

"Tell me what you know about amethyst," she said.

"It's a gemstone."

"Why do you want the amethyst tree?"

Ainsley kept a straight face. "What amethyst tree?"

"The one you stole."

"I didn't steal anything."

"Yes, you did. From José Ignacio Tabarez."

"Who is he?"

"The man you saw at the *remate*."

Shit. This woman had the whole timeline down. Somebody had been doing some heavy investigation of Ainsley's whereabouts. She felt more and more grateful for having chucked her passport into the toilet.

Still, she stayed in character. "I really don't know anything about this."

The *gaucha* harrumphed. Then she leaned in even further, less than two feet away. "We know why you went to see Guarasquil," she said.

Ainsley raised an eyebrow. "Really."

"For the same reason anybody would look for Guarasquil. To find El Árbol Negro."

Now the name was out. Ainsley could finally drop part of the charade. "True," she said. "I thought it was on display. That's what they told me in Montevideo."

The name of the city caused the *gaucha* to make disgusted waving motions in the air. "That little pile of egotists," she said. "They think so much of themselves."

"It's a nice place," said Ainsley.

"My sister lives there. She says everything is different."

"It is."

Then Señora Nasazzi fixed her with a suspicious look. "What did you see when you were watching the men in the cemetery?"

"I saw them digging up, how do you say it, a box."

"Did you see inside the box?"

"No."

"Not even one little peek?"

"No. I don't know what was in the box."

"But you can probably guess."

"No," Ainsley sighed, "I can't *begin* to *imagine* what was inside that box." She was feeling exhausted by this charade.

"Can I tell you?"

"Please."

The *gaucha* drew in a deep breath. She broke eye contact for the first time in the entire conversation.

"It was the body of one of our people."

"Really?"

"The residents of Guarasquil had not known his identity when they found his corpse seven years ago, and they buried him. So we reclaimed the body."

Ainsley tried to keep a straight face. Señora Nasazzi expected her to believe that the Ferreyra empire had invaded Guarasquil's peaceful settlement, with three vehicles and over twenty men, and that the villagers were held at gunpoint in a tight circle in the center of their own village—all to steal a corpse?

This was the flimsiest of fairy tales, the crappiest of crocks. And yet Ainsley had also launched a couple of her own whoppers in this conversation.

So here they were, two grown women, alone in a room, lying at each other like a couple of opposing witnesses in a jury trial. And now they had nothing more to say. They sat quietly in silence for a moment, waiting for more words to materialize.

At last, Señora Nasazzi cleared her throat. "I am not good at indirectness."

"Me neither."

The *gaucha* captured her. "Do you know where El Árbol Negro is?"

"No," said Ainsley. "Do you?"

"I wish that I did."

"Why?"

"There is a large insurance policy on it."

This was interesting. Ainsley perked up. "Really? Who bought the policy?"

"The previous owners of El Árbol Negro."

"Who was that?"

The woman's finger pointed down. "The owners of this

estancia. The Ferreyras." Her mouth constricted itself into a sneer. "They are my bosses."

The *gaucha*'s gaze was level and direct. Meanwhile, Ainsley's brain was twisting itself into knots trying to understand their motivation. Why the hell had these people been stealing something if it had already belonged to them? It didn't make a lick of sense.

Unless Guarasquil had stolen it from the Ferreyras first.

She rolled this scenario around her mind a few times. Maybe the Ferreyras had been duped by Guarasquil? Maybe he'd crept onto their gazillion hectares of land and hauled it away in the dark of night?

In the end, however, the history of the gemstone didn't matter. El Árbol Negro was somewhere on this *estancia*, and Ainsley wanted it.

Ainsley said, "I would love to hear the story."

Señora Nasazzi suddenly shook off the thought. She abruptly stood up. "This tongue is my fate. I have used it too much."

"Let's talk again later," said Ainsley.

"No," she said. "Not like this." The *gaucha* left the room.

Ainsley listened to the door click shut. She had just learned something very important.

Gugina had been lying to her.

CHAPTER FORTY-THREE

True to her word, Señora Nasazzi didn't come back that night. And even if she had, she would've found her captive slumbering once more.

After the initial jitters about being held prisoner by a Uruguayan beef empire had worn off, Ainsley passed out cold. She'd felt it coming too. She staved off sleep just long enough to unpeel her clothing from her sticky body and wash the makeup off her face.

Swaddled in coarse sheets, she dreamed of large purple geodes of amethyst, refracting and reforming. Of miners' bars and the unfamiliar faces of people she'd met on this strange journey.

Ten hours later she woke up, used the toilet, drank a glass of water, and returned to bed just as dawn was rising.

Then she slept another eight hours.

When Ainsley's eyes finally fluttered open again, the sun had sunk low on the horizon, and the same orange rectangle had appeared on the bedspread on her chest. She'd been asleep for an entire night and most of the next day.

A short, bleary-eyed stumble, and she was in the shower. It was a basic home job, like much of the construction in this part of the country, with uneven tiles and a low ceiling. The water that burst from the shower head was inconsistent in pressure and even less in temperature.

No matter. At this moment, Ainsley was grateful for anything remotely hygienic.

She was toweling off when she felt her stomach begin to stir. Within a minute it had made its presence more than known. Back home, Ainsley was famous for suffering under the boot of her appetite. Her older brother had known exactly when to feed her.

Then she noticed a tray on the coffee table. On the tray were a can, a plate, and a fork.

While she was sleeping, somebody had entered and left her food.

She lifted the can. There was a picture of a pouty-looking sheep on the label. There was even an English translation: *Guycan corned mutton with juices*. Ainsley scrunched up her face.

Canned sheep. With extra sheep juice.

Puke.

Still, she peeled off the pop top and slid the contents onto the plate. It looked like regurgitated dog food in oil. But her stomach needed some appeasement. Ainsley tentatively picked up the fork. Was it worth whatever pain might follow?

She was saved from this decision when the door opened. Though, in retrospect, she would rather have swallowed a thousand cans of corned mutton than see the person who walked in.

It was Wait Bitch.

Ainsley's mouth dropped open. The utensil clattered on the plate.

Shit shit *shit*.

That lunatic waitress had ratted Ainsley out. Probably told a pack of lies, now pinning Ainsley to a crime she hadn't even committed. Now the Ferreyras had trucked her all the way up here.

For what reason?

Ainsley immediately shot to her feet. Behind her followed both Señora Nasazzi and Atilio.

Everyone stood regarding each other for a long moment. Wait Bitch was dressed for a nightclub. She wore a silvery cocktail blouse and a lime green miniskirt with annoying fringe. On her feet was a pair of ferociously hideous black flats. Her lipstick and eyeshadow were as garish as a carnival sideshow.

Ainsley didn't feel guilty about her cattiness. She had a feeling that Wait Bitch was going to deserve it for whatever horrendous betrayal she was about commit.

Wait Bitch, in the meantime, was looking the captive up and down. She cocked her head to the side, as if sizing up a new outfit. Ainsley wanted to kiss Sofia right here, for having chopped and dyed her hair. And standing there, wrapped in a towel, with no makeup, she was nearly unrecognizable.

"Shit Pig?" she said in English.

It was time for the real playacting to begin. As a child, Ainsley had learned the basics of the German language from an old disciplinarian down the street who babysat her after school. The old woman smelled like sauerkraut and *spaetzel*, and she'd allowed no English.

This had paid off, though, because Ainsley had a basic proficiency with the grammar and vocabulary. Once she'd even spoken in an exaggerated Bavarian accent for an entire three-hour blind date. By the end she had the guy sitting across from her convinced that she was an exchange student.

"*Schlagen sie?*" said Ainsley. "*Wer sind sie?*" (Do you knock? Who are you?)

"I think we meet the other night?" said Wait Bitch in English.

"*Sprechen de Deutsch?*" she replied. (*Do you speak German?*)

Wait Bitch looked confused. She looked towards Señora Nasazzi, who said, "She speaks Spanish. Talk to her."

Wait Bitch switched to her native language. "Shit Pig? Do you remember me? I helped you find Tabarez?"

"No, I don't know you," Ainsley said in Spanish.

Ainsley realized that she needed to take control of the situation. So she flipped into her best angry German woman.

She pointed at the door, at the bathroom, at the plate of corned mutton, all while barking out a stream of furious German syllables. The words didn't make any sense. They didn't have to. She yammered on about rabbits (*hosenfeffer*, courtesy of Bugs Bunny), jelly doughnuts (*Ich bin ein Berliner*, courtesy of John F. Kennedy), robots (courtesy of Kraftwerk), and whatever other junk came to her head. She stamped her feet. She kicked over a chair.

Wait Bitch and her captors were slackjawed. They listened to the throaty glottal stops, the spat consonants, the controlled changes in pitch. She had them totally fooled.

When Ainsley had stopped for breath, Wait Bitch turned to the others. "This isn't her," she said.

"Are you sure?" said Atilio.

"Yes, I'm sure," said Wait Bitch. "Shit Pig was an American. This one should be wearing a Nazi uniform."

She left the room, Atilio following. But Señora Nasazzi paused at the doorway and looked back. There was a suspicious squint in her eyes.

"What is the problem?" said Ainsley. "I am German. And I'm tired of being held here."

The *gaucha* picked up the tray with the uneaten corned mutton and left the room. The door locked behind her again.

That was mean. But if Wait Bitch was the worst the Ferreyras could throw at her for the murder of José Ignacio, Ainsley knew that she would be in the clear.

They couldn't detain her for much longer.

CHAPTER FORTY-FOUR

Ainsley occupied herself for the next hour by scrubbing her filthy clothes with a bar of soap in the shower. Then she hung them to dry on a makeshift drying line strung across her room.

While they dried, she hunted around the room. She found a folded pair of red gaucho pants on a shelf in the closet. How appropriate. Underneath them was a white collared shirt. She guessed that these items had been left for more voluntary guests.

Still, Ainsley tried on both pieces of clothing and studied herself in the mirror above the sink. Not bad for a hostage. She looked clean, well-rested, and locally fashionable.

And skinny. She spun around a few times. The stress of the journey, the constant running, had dropped another couple of pounds from her hips. She wasn't going to complain.

Ainsley passed more time by doing some pointless cleaning. She straightened the sheets on her bed. Wiped down the coffee table. Scrubbed the grout in the bathroom. Flipped through the book on the history of gauchos again.

Her eyes couldn't make sense of the words. She was starting to lose it.

Finally, Ainsley just sat on the couch, staring blankly at the wall.

She wondered how Sofia was faring. Atilio had covered his bases by taking both of them. Maybe he would offer them a cash settlement to be quiet about El Árbol Negro. Maybe he would offer them jobs at the estancia.

Or maybe he would just kill them.

There went her imagination again. She reminded herself that Atilio had personally guaranteed her safety. And he and his men hadn't touched a single hair on any member of Guarasquil's village. Yes, she was safe in these hands.

Still, Ainsley tapped her feet together and pointed them towards the wall, as if she could push through it, towards something else.

She sat back and tried to remember her previous life. At one time, she'd had a husband, a job, a home. She could've kept those things. She could've tried to accept an ordinary life. Lots of people did.

Then she remembered that old French thinker who said that man's biggest problem is his inability to sit in a room and just *not move*.

That described Ainsley perfectly. Her expectations were higher, bigger, grander. And she had to admit that being paid to travel to Uruguay to find a gorgeous amethyst treasure pretty much topped everything else. Even if the journey was turning out to be a wild goose chase.

The aroma of cooking meat wafted beneath Ainsley's nostrils. She turned her head. It had drifted in through the window. Her stomach started barking like an angry guard dog.

She stood up on tiptoes and peered outside.

There, on either side of the firepit, stood two laborers using long rakes to stoke an enormous fire. Above the pit, the metal racks had been tilted and lowered to a horizontal position, about a foot above the flames.

Across the grill stretched a disemboweled cow. Its stumpy limbs were splayed wide, and the juices from its meat sizzled as they dripped into the flames below. The whole scene resembled medieval torture.

It also reminded her stomach of what it was lacking. She suddenly doubled over. Hunger pains were nothing to be laughed at. She felt as though she was being stabbed.

Gradually, workers from the *estancia* started wandering over. They had taken off their hats and held red plastic cups in their hands. Ainsley guessed what those meant. The same as in America: party.

This must be the Saturday-night *asado*. And they were holding it right outside her room.

She slumped on the bed miserably. Ainsley could handle confrontation. She could handle passive-aggressive types. But she could *not* handle being excluded. From anything.

The aromas grew stronger and more delicious, and the men's conversation started to grow louder and bolder. She peeked through the window again. The grill had been flipped over, to better roast the other side, and the men were passing bottles of red wine around to each other.

Ainsley sighed. She loved beef almost as much as she loved wine. And if anybody knew meat, it was these *gauchos*.

Locked in this room, she felt like she'd been grounded.

She would have to content herself with eavesdropping. She cupped an ear and listened to the men talking. She couldn't understand all the slang, but she could tell that the men were boasting about the usual stuff, their sexual prowess, their roping prowess, their drinking prowess.

Then she heard a woman's voice loudly demand to know where the liquor was. She recognized the person: Señora Nasazzi.

One of the men answered that they had no liquor because she, Señora Nasizzi, had already drunk all of it. She told him to go fuck a goat with a popsicle. The men cackled with laughter.

She soon became the life of the *asado*. For the next half hour, Ainsley listened to the *gaucha* challenge every man around the fire to a drinking contest. As each one turned her down, she insulted his mother in an original way. One mother, she said, was so short that she had tried to commit suicide by jumping off a cow. Another mother was so old that she still owed General San Martín himself forty pesos.

The men howled with every insult. Ainsley smiled. This was proof that Señora Nasizzi was more than she had seemed.

The drunker she became, the more Señora Nasazzi began complaining. She complained that Atilio was too controlling. That men never asked her out. That her children didn't write her anymore. That the cows were getting stupider, if that was even possible.

Then she was complaining about the Ferreyra family. That they'd been shorting her paycheck every week. That they'd promised her promotions to the main office, which Ainsley guessed was several miles away. That they'd been sneaking animal protein into the feed, which was forbidden by national law.

And then the conversation took a very interesting turn.

"This poor Guarasquil," she said. "It's a shame that we took it from him yesterday. God will judge us."

"Took what?" said a man.

"You must know already."

"No," said the man.

"El Árbol Negro."

He gasped. "The real one?"

"Of course."

"What happened to the other one?"

"You didn't hear about Tabarez?"

Another voice interrupted. "This is not our business, *señora*."

Señora Nasazzi made a disgusted sound. "It doesn't matter. Nobody in this stupid family listens to me anyways."

Ainsley was fascinated. She was trying to think of ways to use this information when another voice captured her attention.

A man's voice said, "Hey guys, guess I'm late to the party, huh?"

The language was English. With a flat Great Plains accent.

He was an American.

CHAPTER FORTY-FIVE

Ainsley immediately leaped to her feet and peeked through the window again.

She saw a fortyish man with thinning blond hair approaching the *asado*. He wore an expensive business shirt and silk tie, a brand-new pair of Levi's jeans, and new boots. A goofy smile hung on his face, a red cup from his hand.

What was this American guy doing on a cattle ranch in the interior of Uruguay? He looked like he should be making the afternoon schedule at a Cinnabon somewhere.

But he must have been somebody important, because Atilio was standing at his side. In halting English, the ranch manager said, "So here we have the party every week, the *asado*. Always it is very much fun."

"Oh, yeah, it looks great," the American said.

"And here is the beef. It is the best we have."

The American gaped at the splayed-out cow carcass roasting over the embers. "Wow, that is really something else. Holy cow." He laughed at his own joke. "Get it? Holy cow?"

He looked to the *gauchos*. Ainsley wasn't sure if he understood that they didn't speak English.

But eventually the *gauchos* began to serve up slabs of beef and piles of *papas fritas*, and soon the American's mouth was stuffed full of food. More bottles of wine were passed around, emptied, and thrown into the fire. The laughter grew raucous.

In her room, Ainsley held her stomach and slumped on the floor. This guy was a fellow countryman, a red-blooded, flag-waving citizen of the good old U.S. of A. The kind of guy she would've needed three glasses of wine just to endure a date with.

And yet she felt strangely reassured knowing that he was nearby.

She went back the window. The American was wandering through the party, but now there were two red cups, one from each hand. His face was flushed. He was laughing too hard at jokes that he didn't seem to understand.

Eventually he ran out of *gauchos* to annoy, and he wandered near Ainsley's door.

"Excuse me," she said, in a German accent.

He whirled. "Who's that?"

"Could you please come here? Just for a moment?"

The man spotted the door handle. He pushed it open and entered the room.

There stood the first fellow citizen that she had seen in a week. His American aura was unmistakable, dumb yet cunning, friendly yet arrogant. In a flash, she finally understood how people had tagged her nationality so quickly.

And she understood why the world loved, envied, and mocked the United States, all at the same time.

She dropped down onto her bed and tried to contain her excitement.

The American quickly stepped backwards, sloshing the drinks across his hands. "Jesus Christ, what are you doing in here? The party's out there."

"My name is Karin, and I am from Germany," said Ainsley.

She put her hand out firmly, and he put down a red cup to shake it.

"Sorry my hands are sticky, pleasure meeting you. I'm Tim."

"So, Tim, there is a good party occurring around the fire, yeah?"

"Oh you bet," he said. "These guys are real pros. Why don't you come outside and have a bite?"

"No, I am not feeling well." She made a convincing cough. "But they do not remember that I am still hungry. Do you think you could assemble for me a plate of food?" Her hands shaped an imaginary pile of beef.

Tim seemed thrilled to be asked for help. "Oh, absolutely." He set down his cups and turned towards the door.

Ainsley reached for his arm. "Excuse me, but I do have one request. Please, don't say anything about me to the men. I have already eaten tonight and I do not want them to hold a bad opinion of me."

He tilted his head quizzically.

"I am a woman," she begged. "Please, nobody must know I eat so much."

"It's our secret," he said.

She closed the door after him, then watched him navigate the party. Tim found a plastic plate, and the *gaucho* at the grill used his *facón* to slice off a thick piece of meat. Ainsley felt saliva flooding her mouth.

Tim returned with a plate heaped with food. She accepted the plate and crammed the hunks of beef into her mouth, barely chewing before swallowing. Handfuls of *papas fritas* followed. Then she wolfed down a slab of *torta de pascualina*, a beautiful puff pastry pie with egg, cheese, and chard filling.

She became aware that the American was staring at her. "You can really put it away," Tim said.

"Put it avay?" she said, between bites. "Do you mean in a storage facility?"

He rolled his eyes. "I mean you eat a lot."

Ainsley pretended to finally get it. "Ah, yes. It has alvays been a joke to my friends. Ha ha."

When she'd finished, she slid the plate under the bed and washed her hands. Tim had drained both of his red cups.

He surprised her by saying, "Is it okay if we talk?"

"Yes, that vould be acceptable."

"You're the only person who speaks English here. I mean, Atilio tries, but it's just embarrassing." He shook his head.

"Vat vould you like to talk about?"

"Where in Germany are you from?"

She thought quickly. "I am living in a small town near Munich."

"Which one?"

"It's very small, so small nobody has ever heard of it. Not even other Germans."

He brightened up. "I studied economics in Munich for a semester in college."

Shit. But she pretended excitement. "Really? That's vonderful that you know my country."

"What was the name?"

"Of vat?"

"Of your village."

She thought of the first German word that came to mind. "Gerwürtztraminer," she said.

He thought for a moment. "Isn't that a wine?"

"Yes, of course, that is vat we are known for in my village. Ve vere the first people to grow such a grape."

Tim's eyes focused on her. "And yet nobody has heard of your town?"

Christ, he was smarter than he seemed. She had to backpedal. "My country is a complicated place," she said.

That seemed to satisfy him. He nodded and stretched. "So, Kate—"

"Excuse me, but my name is Karin."

"—Karin, what brings you to the middle of nowhere in Uruguay?"

She'd anticipated this question and had the same lie ready. "My sister is marrying, excuse me, *has married*, a Uruguayan man. So I am here on holiday."

He looked around. "She's not here?"

"No, she is in Montevideo. I vas travelling through the interior alone ven my automobile stopped functioning. The Ferreyras found me and helped me. So I am here until my vehicle is becoming repaired." She hoped the excuse didn't smell too much like bovine scatology.

He nodded. "Yeah, the Ferreyras are a real nice bunch of people."

Ainsley swallowed her laughter. "Vat about you?" she said. "Vat do you do?"

"I'm an analyst," he said.

"And vat do you analyze?"

"I work for a big group called Blackstone. They are looking to invest in some of the *campo* out here. They contracted me to fly out and, you know, evaluate."

"Your job is very professional," said Ainsley. "Vat have you found? Compared to the American ranches?"

Tim pointed at the fields. "These cattle? They blow ours out of the goddamn water. No question. No question."

"Is that so? Vhy is that?"

Tim spread his arms out. "In the U.S., we feed 'em crap. Candy, potato chips, chocolate scraps, chicken feces. Even other euthanized animals. It's disgusting. Here, these lucky babies eat nothing but pure grass. And national Uruguayan law mandates each animal gets chipped, which guarantees one hundred percent traceability. Just try demanding that on the floor of U.S. Congress and see how quick you lose your reelection funding."

Tim shook his head, then pulled a flask from his back pocket and poured it into a cup. Ainsley felt a little sad for him. But that feeling evaporated as she watched his expression change.

"You know," he said, "I don't think I've heard you mention a boyfriend."

His eyes were resting on the bare flesh of her leg, the place where her *gaucho* pants had hiked up above her knee.

Ainsley's stomach dropped. Like every other woman on earth, she had squared off against her share of men, in every seemingly possible situation—bars, restaurants, banks, coffee shops, workplaces, sporting events, elliptical trainers, movie theaters, laundry rooms.

But she'd never had to fend one off while being held hostage and pretending to be German.

"I have a boyfriend," she said. "He is back in Munich. He is amazing. There is nobody like him."

"No doubt," he said. "Is he faithful to you?"

"Yes, of course."

"We can't always be sure," he said. "I was cheated on."

"That's very unfortunate," she said coldly.

"Yes, it made me see faithfulness in a different light."

She didn't respond to that. He suddenly stood up from the couch and fake-yawned. He had her beat by at least six inches and fifty pounds.

"So I guess I'll leave you alone now," he said.

"Please, I am quite tired this evening. But thank you for the food." Ainsley wasn't sure how much longer she could keep up the accent.

His roving eyes landed upon the door. While he'd gone out for food, Ainsley had placed a shoe on the floor under the lintel so that it wouldn't close totally.

"Hey, where's your door handle?" he said.

"I don't know," she replied truthfully. "It vasn't there ven I arrived."

"So you can't get out of your room?"

She shrugged. She'd been hoping that he wouldn't notice. There were too many dangerous ideas that could be hatched.

"That really sucks," he said. "Listen, if you need anything else, you got my name."

"That is very nice of you," she lied.

Tim clapped her on the shoulder, letting his meaty hand rest there for a second too long. Ainsley thought that maybe her friendliness had been a mistake.

"Please, there is something you should know about Germans," she said, removing his hand.

"What's that?"

"Ve do not like to be touched."

He looked at her with some meanness in his eyes. Then he left the room.

Ainsley swiftly closed the door after him. Even though she was just as vulnerable to the whims of the Ferreyra *estancia* as ever, a small part of her felt reassured when she heard the small click of the lock.

CHAPTER FORTY-SIX

The *asado* carried on into the wee hours of the night, the gauchos howling and whooping and challenging each other to equestrian contests, roping contests, spur-throwing contests, drinking contests.

Every now and then, Ainsley heard Tim's voice awkwardly shout with the others, always followed by a roar of laughter. He may have been smart, but he wasn't smart enough to keep himself from seeming like the village idiot.

There would be no sleep like this. Ainsley had already slept too much anyways. Instead, she laid on her bed and drummed her fingers on her belly, half-listening to the commotion. The rest of her brain was busy running over the possible schemes that Atilio could be cooking up.

He'd found Wait Bitch, which meant that the Ferreyras were possibly trying to pin Tabarez's murder on her, which meant the case was possibly getting attention back in Montevideo. But Atilio couldn't call the police, because he'd have to answer uncomfortable questions about how he came to "possess" Ainsley in the first place. Plus, he knew that she would definitely squawk about the theft of El Árbol Negro from Guarasquil.

But why did the Ferreyras care about José Ignacio Tabarez's murder? Why did they care about the fake El Árbol Negro? After all, they now possessed the real one. This was the most perplexing question of the day.

In the end, the Ferreyras had a tiger by the tail. They couldn't hang onto Ainsley, but they couldn't let her go either.

Evidently they'd chosen to keep her on ice.

She thought about Oswaldo, the driver. God willing, he had understood her large donation for what it was: a plea to keep his mouth shut about her presence in Tabarez's mansion, as well as about her theft of the package in the front hall. By her calculation, he was the one wild card that could blow up her carefully constructed anonymity. Then again, keeping silent hadn't seemed like too much of a problem for him.

It would be much more difficult, on the other hand, for Sofia. She loved, loved, *loved* to talk. Just how long could Sofia be quiet? After all, though they were friendly with each other, Sofia had pretty much treated the trip to the interior like a game, a fun ride. And the worrisome part was that she knew Ainsley's name, citizenship, intensity of mission, and depth of cash reserves. That was a lot of leverage.

Now they were both hostages of the weirdest sort. Anything could be happening on the other side of the hacienda.

The noises were finally dying down outside. The *gauchos* were calling good night, you cow-loving bastard, to one another. She turned out her light and decided to try to get some shuteye. To bring her body back into natural rhythms of day and night.

That's when she heard heavy footsteps in front of her

room. She barely had time to sit up in bed when the door slowly cracked open.

"Karin?" said a voice.

It was Tim.

Back to the German role. "Yes?" Ainsley said. "Vat is your concern?"

He pushed his way into the room. In two quick steps, he had fallen upon her in her bed. Wordlessly, he clamped his hands around her wrists and pinned her arms to the mattress. A sour blast of liquor plumed from his open mouth. His face snuffled around her face and neck, his lips greedily trying to slurp up her skin, mouthful by mouthful.

Christ. She should've seen this coming. Ainsley willed herself to stay calm. This drunk bastard may be big, but his beer muscles weren't as strong as they seemed.

She began to squirm. Ainsley was a world-class squirmer, a tube of twisty muscle. Her brothers had been unable to pin her down for anything, at any time, at any age.

Tim was no stronger than they'd been. Hissing his breath through clenched teeth, he struggled to keep his control of her. He pressed even harder upon her hands.

So Ainsley started to gnash her teeth, one in particular. She'd been born with an extra-sharp incisor. It'd sliced the inside of her own mouth innumerable times. A teenage boyfriend had lived in mocking fear of The Fang, as he'd named it.

Now she unleashed the Fang. She snapped at Tim's face, his neck, his beefy forearms. She writhed, squirmed, twisted, thrashed, struggled. She was a vicious rat, cornered by a bullying cat.

Her efforts slowly worked. She managed to get her right hand loose, and quickly smacked him square across the cheek.

He snorted and reared back. It wasn't much of an opening, but enough for Ainsley to loosen her right leg, plant her foot on his shoulder, and push. Her thighs had always been the strongest part of her body.

The force of her kick pushed him off the bed onto the floor. "What the fuck," he muttered.

What the fuck indeed. Ainsley leaped off the bed, hit the light. He grabbed her shoulder.

Ainsley clenched her teeth, tightened her fist, and delivered a full roundhouse directly into the asshole's mailbox. Given her long arms, it connected high, into the side of his neck.

She expected his eyes to roll back in his skull, his knees to give, and his body to crumple to the ground. They didn't. He just stood there, rubbing his neck. She realized that she'd watched George McFly wallop Biff one too many times. Life wasn't like the movies.

In fact, life was often much more painful.

With unusual speed, her drunken rapist hauled back his arm and threw his meaty fist directly into her face.

Ainsley didn't stand a chance. Nobody would've. This was a brutal punch, one from close to the body, with ferocious intensity.

She stumbled backwards on her heels and fell down against the door. She tried to scramble up again but fell again. She couldn't see straight. It'd happened so fast.

Ainsley touched her jaw. She couldn't feel her own fingertips. She guessed that meant that the pain would be arriving soon.

Tim was standing over her, snorting like a bull in a ring. His own jaw was thrust forward. Tough guy.

"What the fuck is your problem?" Ainsley screamed.

"You shouldn't've hit me," he said.

"You shouldn't've tried to *rape* me."

He was staring at her. "You—"

"Shut up," she shouted, "just shut *up*, you drunken *assmonkey*. Get the *hell* out of my room!"

He was staring at her, agape.

"But—"

"*Go.*"

"But I—"

"Just *go. Leave.*"

He was totally incredulous. "Are you *American*?"

Ainsley stopped. That floored her even harder. Oh God. In her pain, she'd forgotten her accent. How could she have been so careless? She felt a wave of embarrassment.

"Of course," she said, recovering the accent, "but ven I begin to feel angry, I vill often choose to curse in English. It is feeling more natural to me at such moments."

He shook his head. "Liar. I heard you. You're American."

Ainsley tried to shake the confusion out of her skull. How did *she* suddenly get put on the defensive? *He* was the would-be rapist scumbag. She didn't need to defend *anything*.

"God," he said. "I wouldn't have touched you if I'd known you were an American."

Ainsley imagined women all over the world shuddering at that comment. She decided it would be easiest just to drop the charade. "Look," she said, "I don't care what you think. Just leave."

"I can't."

Ainsley realized that her back was leaning against the door, and it was closed.

CHAPTER FORTY-SEVEN

She buried her face in her hands. She couldn't swallow the irony. It was big enough to choke a steer.

After all her struggles in Uruguay, she'd nearly been raped by a plain vanilla American. Now she'd just locked herself in a bedroom with him.

Ainsley scooted herself against the wall and pulled her knees up to her chin. Her eyes peered at him over her kneecaps, full of fire.

With nowhere else to go, Tim sat down on the couch, as though he were paying an innocent visit to his grandmother. He drummed his fingers on the armrest, his eyes looking anywhere but at Ainsley. He picked up a throw pillow and inspected the tasseled fringe.

Watching him, Ainsley felt a mixture of pity and loathing. "What would you like to do?" she finally said.

"I'd like to bust down the door," he said, "but it looks too solid."

"And the Ferreyras wouldn't like it either."

He shrugged. "Doesn't matter. I can do what I want here."

"Speak for yourself," she muttered.

"What do you mean?"

God, was he ever dense. She pointed at the door. "How many times will it take your little reptile brain to notice that *I don't have a doorknob?*"

He finally looked at her. His eyes were pouched and reddened, but he was sobering up. He chewed on his lip. "Are you, like, a prisoner?"

"Sort of."

"What do they want with you?"

Ainsley could feel her jaw starting to throb. She sighed. "It's a really long story. But basically we were searching for the same gemstone. I saw them steal it. So they kidnapped me."

"Why?"

"I don't know. Maybe to keep me quiet. To watch me. To figure out how to neutralize me. But nobody ever tried to rape me."

She sent an eyeful of cutlery hurtling towards his head, but Tim didn't notice any of it. She'd known lots of tall guys like him. He would be a real treat as a husband.

"Gosh, that's too bad," he said.

"I have a question," she said. "Were you serious when you said that you wouldn't have tried to rape me if you'd known I was an American?"

He rubbed his eyes and yawned. "I don't know."

"Answer the question."

He shrugged and looked at the ceiling. "I don't know what the hell I was doing."

"This wasn't the first time, was it?"

He shook his head. His eyelids fluttered. The alcoholic stupor was threatening to transform into actual slumber.

"You can't fall asleep here," she said.

He mumbled something.

"You pass out here," Ainsley said, "and I'll beat you in your sleep."

But her threat didn't faze her visitor. He slumped over on the couch. Soft snores floated from his mouth.

That putz. No way that Ainsley would let herself fall asleep. What was she supposed to do? Stay on point and watch him all night?

She walked over to the couch and smacked him in the face with the pillow. "Hey, caveman. Once you finish raping a girl, you can't sleep over. You have to go back to your own hut."

He didn't move. Tim had completely zonked out. Ainsley kicked him in the shin, hard. No response. She tried to roll his unconscious body off the couch, but he was too firmly sunk in the cushions.

Like it or not, Ainsley Walker was stuck with this cretin for the night.

Now she was even more pissed off. She tore the sheets off her bed in a fit of anger, balled them up, and hurled them into the corner. This was a totally sick situation. She flopped onto the bare mattress and looked at the ceiling.

How should she deal with this? How should she deal with El Árbol Negro? How should she deal with her future?

She had no answers. To anything.

She tried mightily to stay awake. But when her eyes closed against her will, and her consciousness slunk away into the dark fields, it was an absolute blessing.

CHAPTER FORTY-EIGHT

The sunlight from the window struck Ainsley in the face.

She woke with a start. She was still laying on the bare mattress. Still wearing the borrowed gaucho pants.

Alarmed, she quickly rolled over and looked at her rapist sleepover visitor.

He was gone.

The sheets had been folded and stacked neatly on the couch. He'd even straightened the cushions and arranged the pillows.

She cocked an eyebrow. That was suspicious. She looked down at her pants. No rips, no tears, no stains. No signs of a struggle. Of course, the pantlegs were flared enough that maybe he could've gotten through that way. She did a quick inspection of her plumbing. Nothing seemed unusual.

He hadn't tried to violate her.

Ainsley smiled to herself. She knew why. He must have woken up feeling like absolute shit. Emotionally and physically. It warmed her heart to know that she'd shamed him. Maybe she'd even done some good for women in the future.

Then she wondered how he'd escaped the room. She hadn't heard anything.

Her door banged open, and Señora Nasazzi entered the room. She was in her crispest ranch garb.

"Dress yourself," she ordered.

"Why?" asked Ainsley.

"You're going to the bus stop." She didn't betray even the smallest trace of emotion.

"I'm released?"

The gaucha nodded. Ainsley's breath caught in her throat. "I need to shower first."

"We leave when you are ready," replied Señora Nasazzi. She paused. "You don't want to ask why?"

Ainsley bit. "Why?"

"The American requested it."

She exited, leaving the door wide open. A cold spring breeze wafted through the stuffy room, carrying the fresh scents of pollen, grass, earth.

But Ainsley still stared at the space where Señora Nasazzi had been standing.

In shock.

An hour later, Ainsley stepped out of the room, showered and refreshed. She'd changed into her own clothing, which was clean but weirdly flat from the unorthodox scrubbing and air drying.

She was a free woman. It felt good.

She strolled across the *hacienda*, feeling the constant ache on the left side of her jaw. Overnight, the punch had swollen and turned purplish black. A gaucho leading a horse had openly stared as he passed her.

There was an aluminum urn on a picnic table. A tray of ceramic mugs had been set out. Ainsley gladly filled a mug. The bitter liquid spread through her mouth and down her throat.

She skirted the trash bags left over from last night's *asado* and moseyed up to the fence. This country was gorgeously empty. Nothing but green hills and blue sky. In the distance was a herd of grazing Herefords. The coffee, the cows, the grass between her toes—Ainsley suddenly felt happy to be alive. She'd never felt such a sense of freedom.

A soft, rhythmic sound drew her attention. Señora Nasazzi was sitting on a bench nearby, stropping a razor on a piece of worn leather.

Ainsley approached her. "You are ready now?" the *gaucha* said without looking up.

"Yes."

"You American girls," she said.

"I told you," Ainsley said, "that I am German."

Señora Nasazzi reached behind her for something. It was Ainsley's white bag.

The *gaucha* held it out. "Everything here is in English. Makeup, laundry tags. Even the names in your telephone."

Whoops. Ainsley had overlooked all that. She grabbed her bag and rummaged inside. Everything seemed intact.

"We didn't take anything," said Señora Nasazzi.

Embarrassed, Ainsley muttered a quick thank you. Then she remembered Sofia. "Where is my friend?"

Señora Nasazzi fixed her with an emotionless stare. "In her room." There was a significant pause. "She is not going with you."

"Yes, she is."

"No, the American told Atilio to release *you*."

"But I'm not leaving without her."

Señora Nasazzi made a hocking sound with her throat. A huge yellow lugey landed on the grass between her feet. Then she squinted at the green hills.

The fun *gaucha* that Ainsley had heard making ribald jokes

around the fire had been stowed away. That squint would be Ainsley's only answer.

"Let me talk to Atilio," said Ainsley.

The *gaucha* rose wordlessly and lumbered across the yard. Ainsley supposed that she was going to find him. Or she could have just decided to have a cigar and shoot some pigeons. She was as readable as a Sumerian tablet.

Surprisingly, she returned a moment later with Atilio, who was talking on a cell phone. He hung up as he approached.

"You are free to go," he said to Ainsley. "Thank you for your patience."

"I'm not leaving without my friend," said Ainsley.

Atilio shared a glance with Señora Nasazzi. A laborer hovered behind him, his hand resting on his *facón*.

"It would be better if you just left," he said.

"I disagree," she replied. "It would be much worse."

"Why is that?"

"Because I have witnessed something."

His eyes narrowed. "Go on."

"Personally," Ainsley continued, "I do not care about those events. This is the truth. But if my friend is not released, those events will become known to the public. Tim will not like it."

She held Atilio's eyes. A moment passed. She was sure that he'd already thought of this angle. He'd most likely just been waiting for her to play the card.

He finally blinked. "Fine," Atilio said. He barked something in very rapid Spanish at the men behind him. "She will need a few minutes to get ready."

"Of course," said Ainsley.

The meeting broke up. Ainsley felt her knees quivering. She was feisty, but blackmailing her former captor only an hour after release was way beyond even her standards.

Still, it'd been a calculated move. She'd gambled that the

Ferreyras had more interest in keeping Tim happy, and the money he represented, than in preserving their homeland reputation. Megacorporations were the same everywhere.

For the next hour, Ainsley sat on the fence, staring at the hills, waiting for Sofia to be ready. A young girl brought her a tray of *bizcochos*, or cookies. She chose one that had been dusted with sugar, but her jaw hurt with every chew. She'd need to stick to a liquid diet for a couple days, which would mean even more weight loss.

Finally she heard a *gaucho* whistle at her. He was pointing to the other side of the building, towards the driveway. "They are waiting for you," he said.

She walked around the house. In the dirt, the passenger van was idling. Señora Nasazzi sat behind the wheel. Several *gauchos* were gathered around the rear door, which was open. Ainsley could see a dark figure silhouetted inside.

That was Sofia.

"Get in," said Señora Nasazzi. "We have to get to the bus station before eleven-thirty."

Ainsley walked around the van and climbed inside. The *gauchos* shut the door, and the van roared off.

Only then did Ainsley get a good look at Sofia.

She was almost unrecognizable. Her face was a purple-and-red bouquet of bruises, cuts, and scrapes. Somebody had beaten her like a gong.

"Hi," she said simply. Her voice was defeated but still had a note of good humor.

Ainsley felt fury rising from the depths of her soul. "Stop the car," she said.

"You don't want to return," said Señora Nasazzi from the driver's seat.

"She is right," said Sofia.

"The Ferreyras can't do this—"

"But they did," said Sofia. "It was just some men. Just

some men. It's okay. Señora Nasazzi looked out for me. It would've been much worse. Let's just go."

Ainsley couldn't calm the fury inside of her. She tried to open the door, but the handle wouldn't budge. The Ferreyras had locked her inside again. She punched the back of the seat.

When she'd calmed down, Sofia took her arm. "They were afraid to touch you. They didn't know what country you belonged to."

"So you got all the attention," said Ainsley.

Sofia nodded. "She told me what you did for me. Standing up to Atilio just now." She clasped Ainsley's arm even more tightly. "You are my light in the darkness."

Ainsley was taken aback by the sudden poetry from her friend's bruised mouth. She didn't know what to say, so she just held onto Sofia's hand.

They looked straight ahead as the van drove off the Ferreyras' property.

CHAPTER FORTY-NINE

Half an hour later, the van pulled up to a lonely bench. It was shaded by a makeshift shelter formed by two concrete poles and a piece of dirty canvas.

Señora Nasazzi stopped the van and opened the door for her two passengers. Ainsley helped Sofia climb out, then seated her on the bench.

The gaucha shoved a small wad of pesos into Ainsley's hand. "This is for bus fare," Señora Nasazzi said. "The bus to Montevideo should arrive in an hour."

"I don't want the Ferreyras' money," Ainsley said.

"It's my money."

She was touched. "Thank you."

The woman's face betrayed nothing, as usual. But after Ainsley had pocketed the money, she didn't leave either. She just stood there like a statue. The moment felt weird, as though the rural woman was trying to say something more, something that wouldn't quite come out.

Ainsley felt the same way. She wanted to ask for updates on El Árbol Negro. Maybe Señora Nasazzi could provide inside assistance.

But the moment ended. Señora Nasazzi spun around and marched back to the van. Ainsley noticed that she slammed her door with extra strength.

She circled the van around and sped off down the road, back towards the Ferreyra empire. Ainsley listened to the sound of its engine climb higher and higher, until it became a high whine, and then disappeared entirely.

Ainsley wiped her nose and looked around. They stood on a strip of black asphalt surrounded by green hills, studded with brown rocks, and blue sky overhead.

Nothing else. Silence.

Sofia was unusually quiet. "What are you thinking?" she said.

"That you missed a really good *asado*."

She pointed to her face. "I would never accept anything from those men." Then she softened. "I couldn't chew it anyways."

Then she looked at Ainsley's jaw. "They said they wouldn't touch you."

"They didn't. This was a gift from another guest. He's also the one who forced them to release me." She paused, then said, "He was an American."

Sofia nodded. "That is a blood relationship. No hiding emotions. We are cruelest to the ones we know best." She thought for a moment. "Did they take the pesos?"

"No. I dumped them in the toilet at Guarasquil. With my passport."

Sofia burst out laughing. "Oh my God! You are so *stupid*. And yet you cut the hair in the air!"

Ainsley had no clue what that meant. But she did know that Sofia was suddenly hugging her, and together they were crying and laughing at the same time.

When their outburst had subsided, Sofia pulled back and

wiped her eyes. "I wish you had told me it would be so hard to travel with you."

"I wouldn't travel with me either," said Ainsley. Then she saw Sofia staring at her queerly. "What?"

"I need to go home."

Ainsley nodded. "That would be best for you."

"What about you?"

Ainsley dropped her head into her hands. What *about* her? She was out of leads. She spotted a vibrant red ladybug crawling slowly along the shoulder of the road, headed for an unknown destination.

"I am going to call Gugina." Sofia looked puzzled, so she explained. "She is my sponsor. Maybe she can help. I have no more leads."

Ainsley fumbled in her bag until she found her phone. She turned it on. The start-up tones made her smile. They were the familiar sounds of home, half a world away.

She opened the contacts list and dialed the number. A moment later, she heard Martina's voice saying, "Associated Industries."

"It's Ainsley."

There was silence. "We have been waiting for your phone call."

"It's been a crazy few days."

"Are you in trouble?"

"Sort of."

Ainsley walked the empty road, heel to toe, the wind whipping her hair, as she told Martina the story of her adventure, the *remate*, Tabarez, the interior, the goats, Cesáreo, Guarasquil, the kidnapping, and the Ferreyras.

When she had finished, Martina didn't say anything. Then she had one question: "So you don't have El Árbol Negro?"

"No. But I know that the Ferreyras have it."

"Oh." She didn't sound too enthused by that news.

"The bigger problem is money. I don't have any of that either."

More silence. When she spoke, Martina's voice radiated professional indifference. "Now you understand the difficulty of the assignment, Ainsley. And you also understand how much we will appreciate El Árbol Negro when you finally recover it."

"Can you send more money?"

With sadness: "No, we cannot."

Ainsley felt the fury rising. "I have suffered *so much* for your company—"

"That is undoubtedly true."

"Witness to murder, physical injury, damage to personal property, severe exhaustion, near rape—"

"Your commitment is extraordinary. But we clearly stated in the contract the potential for much danger."

Ainsley lost her temper. "This isn't about personal danger! This is about being *broke*! All my personal credit cards are maxed out. I have enough *efectivo* to buy a single bus ticket. And I don't have a clue where to go, or what to do when I get there. Do you understand? *I need help*."

She heard Martina sigh. There was a battle of conscience occurring on the other end of the line.

When she spoke, Martina's voice had lowered, as though she were hiding the conversation from someone else. "Did you know that Viviana just arrived in Uruguay?"

Ainsley had forgotten about that. "Really."

"Yes," Martina said, "she decided to go. She is in Punta del Este."

"Oh."

Silence hung between them until Ainsley finally understood the subtext.

Then Martina's voice returned to normal volume. "Thank

you for calling. Let us know when you have found El Árbol
Negro."

The connection ended. Ainsley looked at her phone in
her hand, then powered it down.

Punta del Este.

Playground of the rich, the famous, the elite of South
America.

On cue, a bus came roaring down the road, slowing to a
halt. The electronic display above the windshield read "Tres
Cruces – Montevideo".

Their bus. Now was decision time. She saw Sofia stand up
shakily and hold her hand towards the driver. Ainsley
sprinted back down the road. She arrived at her friend's side
just in time to help her climb the stairs into the bus.

"To where?" said the driver.

"Montevideo," said Ainsley.

"Two?"

She bit her lip and glanced at Sofia. "Is there a bus to
Punta del Este coming?"

"Yes, it should arrive in about two hours."

"Then only one."

In the aisle, Sofia heard this and spun around. "You're not
coming?"

Ainsley shook her head as she paid the driver. "I'm going
to Punta de Este. Someone is there who might help me."

Sofia stood there in the aisle, a crushed look on her face.
Ainsley felt truly guilty.

"I must do this. It's this important to me."

Sofia switched to her adorably accented English. "You are
my friend now. You can't escape it. Promise that you won't
forget about me."

"I won't forget you," Ainsley replied. "And I know where
to find you."

The two women embraced once again, and Sofia found a seat. Ainsley stepped off the bus and watched it pull away.

Then there was nothing but the sound of the wind whistling across the grass. Ainsley sat down on the bench, alone.

Waiting.

PUNTA DEL ESTE

CHAPTER FIFTY

For most of her life, Ainsley Walker had enjoyed a recurring dream of time travel. In her sleep, she always tunneled backwards in time to different famous eras—Restoration-era England, Bourbon France, the Wild West—and enjoyed exciting swashbuckling historical adventures.

She always woke up to a surprise. A home with central heating and sturdy construction. Clean clothing hanging in her closet. Electronics in the living room. A fueled vehicle in the driveway. A life of modern ease.

Now she felt the same shock upon arriving in Punta del Este.

Stepping off the bus, Ainsley found herself in a contemporary urban beach paradise. And after four days in the interior, the contrast seemed especially strong. She felt like a farm girl fresh to the city.

Around her rose high-rise condominiums and hotels. On the street corners were modern cafes, wifi stickers on their windows. Men in casual suits thumbed their phones. Women wearing obscene amounts of lip gloss made air kisses to each other over Cobb salads. Every other car was a luxury model.

She glanced towards the water. Even in the cool weather, people were strolling in sweatshirts and clamdiggers along the golden sand of the *playa*. A young boy was skipping rocks in the calm blue waters of the Atlantic, so different from the murky brown chop of the estuary in Montevideo, a few hundred kilometers down the coast.

She remembered learning a few things about Punta del Este during her crash course with Marco. Situated on a long curving bay, this city swelled to a population of half a million during the height of the summer, during which time wealthy people all over South America flew here for the Christmas holidays. Rich Argentines took particular pride in owning a second home on the beach. Paparazzi flocked here for the photos of Latin celebrities sunning themselves.

Unlike them, Ainsley wasn't famous or wealthy. She was here to find a single person.

Viviana.

The girl had mentioned that she would be getting a rental. Ainsley spun around. There must be literally a hundred condo towers in the city. She would have to start asking around.

No, that would take too long. She needed to get someone to make those calls for her. Someone who knew the place.

She spotted the entrance to an expensive resort, El Melio Sol, on the next block. A large water fountain and circular drive exaggerated the baronial experience.

She hiked up the driveway, feeling like a pauper, worried that she looked even worse. Who should she approach? Ainsley knew from several girls' trips to Las Vegas that bell-hops were the sleaziest workers in any hotel, the grease that turned the wheels of the city. You could count on them for everything and nothing.

She found a target. A middle-aged bellman behind a podium. He looked bored, occasionally texting.

"Señor," she said.

"I'm busy," he replied, his fingers moving.

"Trying to get a date tonight?" she answered. "What's his name?"

A smile crinkled his mouth, and he glanced up and down at Ainsley. "I only accept insults from guests when they have money."

He was a comedian too. "You should know," she said, "that only wealthy people can afford to look this poor."

He never stopped texting. "In that case, what can I do for you?"

"I need to find a specific guest staying in this town. Can you help me?"

"Of course I can," he said, "but I won't. You need to talk to the front desk." His eyes never left his phone.

Ainsley felt her temper break. She snatched the phone from him and stuffed it into her bag. "No, I need *you* to ask."

His eyes were on her Marc Jacobs now. "Why?"

"Because I am asking you."

He raised an eyebrow. Ainsley reached into her pocket and pulled out her last two hundred pesos, left over from the bus fares. She pushed it into his hands.

"This is my last money," she whispered. "And I really need to find this person. Otherwise I am sleeping on the beach tonight, and it will be an even bigger problem for you later when I die from the cold and everybody finds out that you didn't help me."

The bellman paused. "Now you are being honest. Exaggerating, but honest." They locked gazes. He finally gave in. "What is the family name?"

"Carlotti. First name, Viviana. She is on some kind of a list."

He held up a dramatic finger. "A list?"

"Yes."

"Forget the front desk. I know who to call."

His fingers picked up the podium phone and flew across the keypad. He waited with the receiver tucked under his ear. Then a rapid stream of slangy Rioplatense issued from his mouth. Ainsley felt too frazzled to follow closely.

The bellhop hung up. "It's good that you didn't try to find her. You would have wasted many hours."

"What do you mean?"

"She's on the del Vecchio list."

"What is that?"

He looked at her unbelievingly. "Patricia del Vecchio's list? You don't know it?"

She shrugged.

"All the world wants to be on her list," he said. "She controls the best properties in Punta del Este. She keeps a group of three thousand very wealthy clients waiting to vacation here."

The bellhop scrawled something on a piece of hotel stationery. "Here is her address. It's in a gated community in Piriapolis. Do you have a car?"

"No."

"Moped?"

"No."

"Horse?"

Ainsley laughed. "Look at me," she said.

He glanced at her up and down. "It's possible. You look like you slept in a stable."

"You're not too far off," she said.

"See, I know women." Then he pressed her two hundred pesos back into her hand. "This is for your taxi. You can bring the money back once you are feeling better." He paused. "Maybe I will use it to take you out. If you are lucky."

Ainsley folded the pesos back into her pocket. "I promise."

"Don't promise. I know you won't. Just give me my phone back and leave."

She did just that. Then, as Ainsley walked towards the taxi stand, she glanced backwards. He had disappeared.

Bellhops. You could count on them for everything and nothing.

CHAPTER FIFTY-ONE

Ainsley pressed the belly button of a stone cherub and waited. She was standing on the front porch of Viviana's rental house.

The taxi had carried her along the intracoastal road, past more rolling sand dunes, over an oddly undulating bridge, then inland for a while, until it'd stopped before a pair of tall gates and a guardhouse.

Beyond the guardhouse Ainsley had seen the street, lined with small mansions, that stretched to the sea. A quick call from the gate, and now she was standing here on Viviana's front porch.

The door was yanked open. Before her stood a short young buck with scraggly facial hair and a shirt whose v-shaped crew neck dipped stylishly to his sternum. His blood-shot eyes focused on Ainsley. He tipped his chin up. "*Que paso, vó?*"

Whatever that last word meant, the way he spit it out didn't sound friendly.

"Is Viviana here?" she asked.

"Yes I am," shouted a girl's voice.

And suddenly there she was. Viviana. Dressed in an off-the-shoulder, paper-thin white t-shirt, the type that cost three hundred dollars in a boutique. Her black bra peeked through underneath. Green leggings and bangles on each wrist finished off the ensemble.

She slapped the guy in the shoulder and shoved him away from the door. "*Déjate en paz!*"

Then she turned. "Oh my God, I totally forgot to give you my address. How did you find me?"

Ainsley couldn't tell if she was excited or angry. So she took the safe approach. "Martina said you were coming."

The girl huffed. "She *would*."

Ainsley didn't know what that meant. "I'm really sorry for just showing up," she said, "but chasing this amethyst has almost killed me. Can I come in?"

"If you want." She whispered something rapidly to her man, who stalked away into another room in the house.

Ainsley followed her inside. It was unimpressive, nothing but a small living room and decent kitchen. The best characteristic was the patio, with its broad view of the Atlantic Ocean at the end of the dunes.

"How did you find us?"

Ainsley thought back to what the bellhop had told her. "Patricia del Vecchio."

The boyfriend snorted. "*Puta*."

Ainsley tried to hide the look of disgust on her face. In fact, her flesh crawled just being in the same room with this guy.

"He hates Patricia," said Viviana. "She gave us October."

"October?"

"Nobody comes to Punta del Este in October. This place is fucking empty. We could only find two parties last night. In December there will be at least forty."

"Then why are you here?"

"Because my grandmother said we would lose our place on the list if no one represented the family." She pouted again. "So unfair."

Ainsley tried to sympathize, but she couldn't quite summon any pity for someone forced to spend a week in the top beach resort in South America.

Meanwhile, the boyfriend was standing moodily by the window. His fingers were fidgeting with his belt buckle.

"Does he speak English?" asked Ainsley.

"He hates English. He doesn't like Uruguay either. He wants to go back to Medellín."

In his heavily accented English, Nolo announced slowly, "Colombia ... is ... the ... best." Then he looked proudly at the two of them.

Viviana threw him an exasperated look. "Please *don't* speak English, you sound like a complete fucking *idiot*."

Nolo looked crestfallen. Then he slammed a palm into the wall and left the room.

"So what do you think of my grandmother?" said Viviana. The musicality in her voice told Ainsley that the question was loaded with trap answers.

"She's a bitch," Ainsley replied.

That was the right one. "Oh my God, I *know*, right? You should've seen her when she was younger."

"I bet she was trouble," Ainsley agreed.

Viviana's eyes narrowed. "Are they helping you?"

"I called Martina to ask for more money this morning."

"I bet she said no."

Ainsley nodded. "I'm broke."

Viviana shrugged. "It's no surprise. She never helps any of the girls once they're on assignment."

"Girls?" said Ainsley. "What do you mean by that?"

But Viviana was studying Ainsley's outfit. "Those clothes don't look so good. I thought you had better taste than that."

"I do. I left my luggage back in Montevideo four days ago."

"Oh my God. You have no clothes?"

Ainsley shook her head, and Viviana's eyes lit up. "We have to go shopping."

"I can't afford anything," said Ainsley.

"Don't worry, it's on my grandmother. Where are my shoes?"

CHAPTER FIFTY-TWO

They drove back to downtown Punta del Este in Viviana's rented Mercedes. Ainsley listened as the girl talked.

She was twenty-four, Nolo was twenty-nine. They'd been dating for two years. She lived sometimes in California, sometimes in Colombia, and sometimes wherever she wanted, but always in the Spanish-speaking world. She didn't bother to explain how she paid for her existence.

Such was the life of the global elite, Ainsley thought. She tried not to think about her pitiful rental apartment, or shabby car, back in the States.

Viviana also talked about Uruguay, how it was full of old people, how nobody really partied here, how Punta del Este was the only fun place in the entire creaky old country, how she didn't feel like her DNA could've ever come from such a dump, blah blah blah.

Ainsley stifled a yawn. The girl could talk a blue streak.

Her narration continued as they strolled down the trendy Avenida Gorlero. The storefronts offered all the usual suspects: Prada, Hermés, Ermenegildo Zegna. Viviana offered her opinion of every designer, and soon Ainsley stopped listening.

A pair of models passed by, wearing gold tube tops, booty shorts, and matching cowboy hats. Ainsley felt her stomach sink a little. These women were intimidatingly beautiful and smelled of money.

Then they came upon the Givenchy store. "Oh my God," said Viviana, "there is one top that's to *die* for. You *have* to try it on." She darted inside.

Ainsley paused. Normally a shopping spree with someone else's credit card in a luxury boutique would've felt like a dream come true. But today was different. She hadn't washed herself after her long trip, hadn't bothered to change her makeup, and hadn't particularly felt like doing something as frivolous as shopping for designer clothes.

But Viviana was her only lifeline at the moment, so she went along with it.

Inside, the girl had already waved off the help and pounced upon a display rack. She was rifling through the items. She pulled out a red tunic with silver piping and held it up to Ainsley's torso.

"Try this on," she said. "Tall chicks like you can totally own tunics."

Ainsley did as instructed. She took the top and went to the dressing room. As she peeled her own shirt off her torso, she saw her ribs protruding through her skin. Then she looked at her face. It seemed drawn and haggard. This journey was aging her quickly.

Nonetheless, she exited the dressing room with a big smile plastered on her face and modeled the top for Viviana. "That is *super* cute," the girl said. "I would totally wear it."

Ainsley decided that this would be a good time to ask more about her employers. "Do you mind if I ask you a question?"

"Yeah, sure." The girl smiled winningly.

Ainsley smiled back. "When you said 'girls' earlier, did you mean that your grandma has more than one person working for her?"

Viviana looked at her as though she were an idiot. "Of course."

"How many?"

"A lot." Viviana was pawing through another rack.

"So is there is another girl looking for El Árbol Negro?"

"Two. You're the third."

Ainsley suddenly felt dizzy. She leaned into a clothes rack for support.

Viviana inspected an asymmetrical top. "But not anymore. One went home after the first day. The other one disappeared." She put the item back on the rack. "That's why grandma always sends three."

So it had been survival of the wiliest, and Ainsley had won. That gave her a boost of confidence.

But she had more questions. "Does your grandmother usually do this? Pay girls like me to chase foreign treasures?"

"Yeah."

"How many treasures is she chasing?"

The girl shrugged. "I don't know, maybe seven, eight? They're going to train girls for Thailand and Namibia soon." Then she squealed. "Those boots are *so* fabulous. I bet you would look amazing in them."

Ainsley grabbed her arm. "Listen to me for a minute. I couldn't find Associated Industries listed anywhere on the Internet. What does your grandmother do? What *is* she?"

"Do I have to say it?"

"Yes. Pretend I'm an idiot."

Viviana looked into Ainsley's face. "She's a fence."

"What's that?"

The girl shuffled through a rack. "People give her art or jewelry and she sells it for a percentage."

"*Stolen* art and jewelry?"

The girl didn't say anything. That meant yes.

Ainsley thought for a moment. "But I'm not *stealing* El Árbol Negro. I'm supposed to be *buying* it." She lowered herself onto a leather banquette. "I'm confused."

Viviana held a gold cocktail dress to her body and spun in front of a mirror. "It's easy. Just remember that you are part of her new business model."

"Which is?"

"The last recession hurt the international gemstone trade. Especially in the middle range in the U.S., which is what my grandmother worked in. She doesn't believe me, but she's out of touch. Plus I travel more than she does."

"So she started a new business."

"Yeah."

"She decided to find her own treasures."

"Yeah."

"And that's why she's hired a fleet of girls."

"Yeah."

"But no boys?"

Viviana shook her head. "Single guys seem threatening. Single girls seem vulnerable, which helps them get access. It's the same everywhere."

"Is the business working?"

Viviana frowned at the dress and replaced it on the rack. "No. Most of the girls fail. Some disappear with the money. Others go and never come home. Maybe they find husbands. Maybe they get hurt."

Ainsley felt a chill run through her body. Her worst fear had just been realized. Associated Industries *didn't* have her back. They viewed her as expendable. She started to feel upset. All of her personal sacrifices, her injuries, her struggles, had meant nothing to them.

"Are you okay?" Viviana said.

Ainsley realized that she'd been staring at the floor, her fists balled up.

"I just feel…. used."

Viviana was blunt. "They *are* using you. All they need is one success to break even. You seem pretty tough, like you might be that success. Maybe that's why Martina told you I was here."

"Because your grandmother forbade her from sending me any more direct help."

Viviana shrugged. "She's a businesswoman."

Ainsley knew that she'd stumbled into the truth. Gugina and Martina had guessed that she was just competent enough to find the *remate* and make the bid. But once they'd learned that it'd been a fake, they'd withdrawn their support. They'd probably judged the chances of her actually finding El Árbol Negro, on her own, without explicit instructions, to be almost zero.

That made Ainsley feel even worse. She hated being underestimated. "Why did Martina tell me that you were here?"

Viviana shrugged again. She shrugged a lot. "Maybe Martina likes you." Then the girl looked around, frowning. "I'm so over this place. Do you want that shirt or not?"

Ainsley looked at the red tunic with the silver piping. She felt her anger rising against Gugina.

"Absolutely," she said. "And if it's on your grandmother's card, I say we keep shopping."

CHAPTER FIFTY-THREE

Five hours and nearly seven thousand dollars later, they stopped for lunch.

There had been facials at L'Auberge, a total makeover in a department store. Mani-pedis at a faux Tahitian hut. The purchase of beautiful white pants with a drawstring (a classy beach look) at Armani, plus a delicious pair of Ferragamo heels.

This city was lighting up every one of Ainsley's pleasure centers. She'd felt like a crackhead inhaling her smoke, or a smack addict breaking the tip of the syringe through the artery wall. She hadn't been able to splurge like this in years, not since she'd started supporting the Legal Weasel. Now she regretted all the dollars she poured into rent and health insurance for him. That was cash that she could've spent on herself. Or someone else.

Now she and Viviana were sitting on the patio of a swishy restaurant at the marina.

Before them was a harbor full of white yachts. This was truly the playground of the rich. She watched men cleaning the windows of a two-hundred-foot yacht. She noticed the snowy-white egrets eating minnows out of the water. Fishermen stood on the rocks, casting their lines into the waves. Beyond them, green tufts of palms fringed Gorritti Island.

A pair of rum drinks materialized on the table before them. The glasses were wet with condensation. Ainsley felt the plastic shopping bags leaning against her calf.

This was the life of privilege.

Ainsley came down from the clouds long enough to realize that a waiter was standing beside her. He was asking what she wanted.

"What's a *chivito?*" asked Ainsley, pointing at the menu.

"Oh my God, it's *so* big," answered Viviana. "Just order a salad."

She looked at the waiter. "I'll have a *chivito* and a salad."

Viviana was staring at her with her mouth open.

"What?" said Ainsley. "I haven't eaten in almost twenty-four hours."

"Seriously, women don't order those things. You're going to be laughed at."

"Let them."

A short while later, the biggest sandwich Ainsley had ever seen was delivered before her, taller than a pint glass, layered with steak, eggs, olives, tomatoes, onions. Mayonnaise dripped down the edges.

"People are watching you," Viviana said. "I want them to be watching *me*."

"Then order one of your own," Ainsley replied. "This sandwich looks like heaven."

Ainsley had joyfully lifted the meal in both hands, had stretched her mouth out and wrapped it around one edge, like a snake swallowing its prey, when her eyes fell upon the television over the bar.

On the screen was a picture of José Ignacio Tabarez.

She lowered the sandwich back down to the plate. Viviana

was texting, her back to the television, and was blissfully unaware.

The bartender had muted the volume, so there was no use leaning forward. But when the picture changed, Ainsley didn't need the audio to know what was going on.

On the television was a charcoal sketch of herself.

At least that what she assumed. They'd gotten her old hair right, the long tresses, and did a decent job on her lips. But her nose was way too large, and her face was too elongated.

Then a caption to the sketch appeared, confirming her suspicions.

It read, in quotation marks, "Shit Pig".

Ainsley's jaw dropped open. No question about it now: After she'd gotten what she could from the Ferreyras, Wait Bitch had gone to the media.

But what was more unbelievable was that the Uruguayan media had reported this ridiculous moniker as if Ainsley were a criminal with a world-famous nickname.

Then the picture changed again. Now Wait Bitch herself was onscreen. Her hair was brushed neatly and she wore a demure top. She was describing something. A single tear rolled down her face.

Ainsley squinted her eyes to read the closed captioning subtitles. Wait Bitch was saying that the American girl had been obsessed with Tabarez, that she wanted him to herself. That she had promised to murder him if she couldn't get her way.

At that moment, Ainsley completely lost her appetite.

She faked a coughing fit and covered herself with a napkin. She didn't want anybody seeing her face right now.

"I told you don't order that sandwich," said Viviana.

"It's so big I don't even know how to eat it," Ainsley replied. "Can we just keep shopping?"

"For what?"

"If I'm going to be here for a week, I need a beach hat."

Viviana lit up. "Oh my God, I was thinking about buying the exact same thing. There's this *amazing* one at Burberry. You want to go right now?"

Ainsley nodded. Viviana dropped fifteen hundred pesos on the table and stood up.

The shopping spree continued.

CHAPTER FIFTY-FOUR

Later that night, back at the rental home, Ainsley couldn't recognize herself in the mirror.

The new floppy hat enfolded her face. Stylish yet anonymous. Nobody would recognize her under this.

The other girl had gone into their bedroom with Nolo, and Ainsley could hear their two voices rising. They were arguing over something. A heavy object pitched over and crashed.

She ignored them. Instead, Ainsley went to the glass doorwall and looked out at the darkness. She could feel her sense of mission starting to tickle the back of her neck again. The truth was that she'd never been good at shirking responsibility. But she wanted one more day of brainless pleasure. *Needed* it.

She also needed another drink. Pronto.

Ainsley dug around the small wet bar. It was decently stocked: six basic alcohols, a few mixers, plus garnishes and a small refrigerator with an ice tray. She spent a minute assembling a vodka-and-tonic. Extra strong. She needed to get two of these tucked under her belt. Then she could face things.

The bedroom door was flung open at the other end of the house. Nolo came storming out in a cloud of entitlement and simmering rage. His nose was twitching.

He saw Ainsley and stopped. "You ... has ... a ... cocktail."

Viviana had been right; he did sound like an idiot in English. Still, it would pay for her to play it careful right now. Some men took the theft of booze very seriously.

In Spanish Ainsley said, "Would you like me to make a drink for you? I'm a good bartender."

He tipped his chin up. His legs splayed out in a comically wide stance, which cut a few more inches off his height. "I didn't think you could speak Spanish," he said.

She shrugged diplomatically. "Vodka or whiskey?"

"Vodka. With some fruit juice. Yes, you will make that. It will be best for me."

"Excellent," she lied.

Ainsley went about preparing his drink. Nolo watched her for a moment, then he got bored and flopped backwards onto the couch. He balled up his fists and ground his knuckles into his eye sockets.

Then he suddenly screamed. A loud, blood-curdling shriek. It stopped as suddenly as it had started.

The outburst had startled Ainsley so much that she dropped the metal cobbler onto the floor. As she knelt down to pick it up, she sneaked a glance at him. He was sitting up now, combing his hair. Calm, relaxed.

Ainsley realized that this man was completely *mental*. Monitoring this little tyrant was like riding a bicycle across a high wire. And yet here Ainsley was, making him an alcoholic beverage. She dumped out the drink and started over again with half the vodka.

She brought the cocktail out. His jaw was manically working an invisible piece of gum. His eyes had a murderous sheen to them. She placed the highball glass on the coffee table before him.

His blackened pupils followed her every move. "How are you called?"

She shuffled through the list of pseudonyms she'd been using, and decided to make up a new one. "Ilyana," she said.

"Of the United States?"

"Of Russia. I work for Viviana's grandmother."

His nostrils flared. "I am going to give you a different job now."

"What's that?"

His fingers unzipped his pants. A second later, a little piece of pink flesh was lolling outside his pants.

Oh God. There it was.

Ainsley feigned politeness. "I'm proud that you give me such an important job."

He nodded. "Go to it. Make it happy." His eyes were still watching her murderously.

There were many ways to play this. She decided that lightly conspiratorial would work best. "It is a very important job," she agreed, "but I need some time to prepare for it. Maybe later tonight. When Viviana is asleep." She threw a wink at him. There was no harm in this.

"But she's asleep now," he said.

"No, we need to really knock her out. So she won't catch us. We need prescription medication."

He nodded. Of course he would. Drugging his girlfriend so that he could get a blowjob safely from someone else made perfect sense to him.

Ainsley tried to resuscitate the scene. "Viviana said you're going to a party tonight?"

He blinked, then returned the pony to the barn and zipped up the door. "Tonight we go to a *boliche*. Like every night."

Ainsley guessed that meant party. "Where is it?"

"At the home of Gustavo Arenas."

"I don't know him."

"He is an actor on the *telenovelas*. Everybody knows him."

"Not me."

Nolo rubbed his knuckles into his eye sockets again. Ainsley prepared for another scream. But instead he answered calmly. "The women love him. They want to take him to bed. Viviana too." He sipped his drink. "She thinks I don't know."

"It sounds like this man is not pleasing to you."

"Nobody is pleasing to me."

He was utterly sincere as he said this. Then he swallowed the remaining half the cocktail and set it back down on the coffee table. Ainsley watched his watery eyes slowly close.

Nolo had passed out.

She took the glass away and dumped it in the kitchen sink. Looked out the window into the blackness. The day had been blissful, not counting Viviana's obvious need for attention. But why, precisely, was she here with this operatic duo?

Desperation. She'd run towards the only other familiar face. What had she been hoping to get from Viviana? A slap on the back? A wad of cash? A connection to the Ferreyras?

None of that was happening. Viviana just liked having a shopping buddy. She was indifferent at best to Ainsley's true plight. Ainsley suspected that she'd be cast aside any second. That was just how rich girls rolled. You could always count on getting expelled from their lives, sooner or later.

Meanwhile, El Árbol Negro wasn't recovering itself. And despite the impossibility of taking on an enormously powerful beef empire, she couldn't think of giving up. She'd come too far now. She had bills to pay back in the States. She needed that seventy-five hundred dollars.

This was a real dead end. She perched on a stool in the kitchen, pondering her dilemma.

Ainsley knew her decision. She would leave. It would be better than spending the week trying to get this nutjob to stuff his jockey back in his shorts. She would wander penniless around South America like those smelly backpackers she'd always so despised.

She rinsed the empty glasses and set them in the dishwasher. Nolo was still unconscious on the couch. All she needed to do was don her jacket, pick up her beloved Marc Jacobs bag, and walk out the door.

Ainsley was about to reach for her bag when Viviana came out from the bedroom.

An off-the-shoulder t-shirt had slipped off her shoulder and down her arm so far that the upper half of her left breast was exposed. Her hair had become a tangled mess. Her eyes were bulging and reddened.

"I am so fucked up," she moaned. "Oh my God. What time is it?"

"Nine thirty," said Ainsley.

"I want to go out."

"Right now? Nothing is open."

"I don't care." Viviana staggered into the living room and saw her boyfriend passed out on the couch. "Hey, asshole. You're a failure."

She lifted her bare foot and planted it on the side of his face. Nolo woke up mumbling curses. He caught her by the leg and pulled her down to the floor.

This was the perfect time to escape. Ainsley glided as quietly as possible towards the front door.

She wasn't quiet enough. Viviana noticed her tiptoeing away. "Where are you going? We have to leave soon."

"I was thinking I might just stay home tonight."

"No fucking way. You and me, we're going *out*." She

pushed Nolo away. "This mommy's boy can stay here and wet his pants. You and I are going to Gustavo's *boliche*. Do you know Gustavo?"

"No," Ainsley said.

"He's the most gorgeous man ever. Trust me."

"Sure," Ainsley said.

"I'm going to find him this time. For sure. First I need a shower. Go get ready." She stumbled back to her bedroom, stripping off her shirt on the way.

Ainsley looked at Nolo. He'd passed out on the floor.

She *really* needed to get away from these two.

CHAPTER FIFTY-FIVE

That evening, Ainsley continued plotting her escape. But on the outside, she'd played the party girl.

First, she'd helped Viviana pick out an outfit. There'd been literally eighty different pieces of clothing in her closet brought for a one-week vacation. All paper-thin, all pricey, and all trashy.

Then Ainsley had donned a white cocktail dress she'd picked up that afternoon. She'd slipped on a pair of purple Christian Dior heels, another new purchase, and looked at herself in the mirror. Her legs were unmistakably long and slinky. Cover the bruised jaw with makeup, and she looked better than she had in months, even years.

Their first stop had been for cocktails at a swanky hotel bar. To their surprise, it'd been shuttered. Viviana'd said it happened all the time in Punta del Este, that nightclubs had the lifespan of a fruit fly, that word-of-mouth was the only way to party.

So they'd gone instead to a café on the wide sidewalk of Avenida Gorlero, where coffee drinks had magically appeared on their table. A suave man dressed in white linen slid them oily winks before two passing models distracted him.

"This is humiliating," Ainsley'd said. "It's like we're being kept on ice for when the others reject him."

"Don't worry about it."

"But I do worry. We're obviously not hot enough."

Viviana scowled. "Maybe you. But I can have any of these men whenever I want."

Ainsley danced around the subject. "You don't seem to like your boyfriend very much."

The girl sipped her drink. "Nolo wouldn't know what to do without me. But tonight I'm waiting for Gustavo."

She'd clinked glasses, then they'd taken off to a rip-roaring dinner of *langostinos* and grilled vegetables underneath the heat lamps at a beachside shack, where they'd shared a bottle and a half of white wine, after which Viviana had exchanged saliva with the maître d' behind a stack of glassware.

Then there was a white-knuckled drive along the coast with Viviana at the wheel. Halfway there, she'd pulled over, spilled out onto the beach, and dry heaved under the full moon and the highbeams of the passing cars.

Now, as Ainsley crouched in the dark sand, holding the girl's hair back, she stared out to the Atlantic. Somehow, she couldn't quite summon the patience necessary for this drunken escapade. It seemed so frivolous, so unnecessary, after the real life-or-death struggles she'd experienced this last week.

Maybe, she thought, people who go on drinking binges were trying to fill a need for real danger in their lives. Or maybe Ainsley had just matured.

She helped Viviana back into the passenger seat. "Let me drive," said the girl, "I have to get to Gustavo."

"No way," said Ainsley, "just show me this party."

Viviana pointed straight ahead.

Ainsley drove the Mercedes another two miles, up to a makeshift valet stand that had been erected at the edge of a field. She could see at least a hundred luxury cars already parked on the grass.

On the other side of the road was an enormous metal gate. There was a line of partygoers waiting to be inspected by men with earpieces and flashlights. Beyond the men was another guard with a wand and gloves. The security looked nearly presidential.

"It looks like they're checking a list," said Ainsley.

"Oh, who cares about lists," snapped Viviana, reapplying her lipstick in the mirror of the sun visor. "They won't turn us away. Here." She handed the tube to Ainsley, who dutifully brushed a high gloss upon her lips.

It was almost two o'clock in the morning, but here in Punta del Este the night was just getting started. Ainsley worried about Viviana. If they were denied admission, there was no saying what the girl would do.

Ainsley threw the keys to the valet, and they teetered in five-inch heels towards the security line. A guard welcomed them.

Viviana said, "I'm with Patricia del Vecchio."

"That's good," said the security guard, "but so is everybody else. What is your name?"

"Viviana Carlotti."

He scanned the list. "I don't see you."

"I was added this afternoon."

She giggled and preened, twirled her hair, and bit her lip girlishly. The guard exchanged nods with another.

"Okay. ID?"

She showed them her American driver's license. "This is real?" the guard said.

"I think so."

"But you have such good Spanish. No accent."

Viviana giggled and mooned in response. Ainsley watched her with a mixture of loathing and admiration. She'd never learned how to play that girly character. She was too tall, too intimidating.

Then the guard looked at her. "Identification."

Crap. It was currently sitting at the bottom of an outdoor privy on the other side of Uruguay. Along with fifteen thousand dollars.

"This is my friend Ainsley," said Viviana.

"Identification," he said.

"I don't have it." She tossed her hair.

The security man didn't react. But there were some angry shouts from the people standing in line behind them. A man wearing a blinged-out watch and sunglasses threw his arms into the air.

She was holding up the line. The partiers were restless.

The security man pulled a pen from his pocket. "How are you called?"

"Ainsley Walker," she said.

He wrote it down. "Go on."

As she held her arms out for wanding, she realized that she'd given her real name again. Goddamn it. Then she found herself thinking about El Árbol Negro, how she was neglecting her mission by going to a silly party.

But as the security guard held open the gate so she could enter, Ainsley forgot all about these problems.

Because what she saw took her breath away.

CHAPTER FIFTY-SIX

She was looking at an enormous ship, drydocked in the middle of a green lawn.

It was an English schooner, at least a century and a half old. She'd yawned at photos of these things in her high school history textbooks. Seeing one in front of her, however, propped up on blocks in a sea of grass, beautifully lit, crawling with laughing and drinking and dancing people—this was a different story.

This was totally gorgeous.

The ship boasted three masts, a white triangular sail hanging from each. The decks seemed to glow under the bright stage lights that illuminated them from the rigging.

Around the ship, in the field, were nearly a hundred tables, each covered in an immaculate white tablecloth and a small globe light centerpiece. It looked like the ship was bobbing in a constellation of stars.

This wasn't any ordinary beach bonfire. It was a total showstopper.

A waiter floated by carrying a tray of full champagne flutes. Viviana lurched over to help herself but drunkenly knocked three of the glasses off the tray. The waiter wheeled away before Viviana could try again.

"That asshole," she said.

"You're already pretty drunk."

"So what if I am?" she snapped. "I thought you were supposed to be on *my* side, Ainsley."

The two girls glided through the tables. Elegant partygoers, many dressed in white, stared at Ainsley as she passed, drawn by her long legs and mysterious hat that shrouded her face.

At an open bar, a tuxedoed waiter stood at attention with his hands behind his back. Ainsley picked up a glass of chardonnay.

"Where's mine?" said Viviana.

"I can get you a soda," Ainsley replied.

Viviana whirled on her, fury in her eyes. "I want a real *drink*. Don't forget who brought you here."

Ainsley was feeling impatient again. Viviana had taken a hard left turn into bitchiness. What was spurring it? Jealousy? Competition? The only leg up that Ainsley had, so to speak, was her height.

Viviana snatched a glass of wine from a passing man's hand, drained it, then tossed it backwards over her shoulders. "I'm so ready for this!" she shouted. "I bet Eduardo's in the captain's quarters. That's where he likes to hang out."

"You've been here before?"

"Yeah, but I got kicked out last year before I could find him."

Viviana whooped and plunged onwards, the honeybee in her hive. The thumping of the music grew louder as they approached the ship. As they circled its attractive exterior, Ainsley ran her fingers along the hull. It felt smooth and inviting.

On the far side of the schooner they found the staircase.

A pair of beefy security guards were screening people. This was an adult theme park, after all, and Ainsley could imagine the hundreds of ways people could hurt themselves onboard. Falling over the edge onto the grass, just for starters.

A security guard shone a flashlight into Ainsley's eyes. Then she walked along a chalk line, heel to toe, eyes straight ahead. She did so, feeling more like a fashion model than a suspected drunkard. She passed the test. The guards waved her up the stairs.

Halfway up, she turned around to watch Viviana. She fell onto the grass, picked herself up again, then fell again. She yelled at the security guards. They let her try again. She fell down a third time.

She gestured up towards Ainsley. The guard shook his head sadly.

They weren't letting her onto the party ship.

She could hear Viviana screaming now. She flung her wine into the security guard's face and ranted at the air.

Ainsley felt torn. Maybe she should go back and keep the girl company. She'd always felt that loyalty, dancing with the one who brought you, was an admirable trait. On the other hand, she had been trying to ditch the girl anyways. And Ainsley always loved an adventure.

She waved sweetly at Viviana, then turned around and marched up the stairs. Below her, the girl was shouting furiously, but the voice grew smaller and smaller until the sounds of the party drowned her out completely.

Ainsley felt a tiny twinge of remorse, but that was erased when she peeked over the top of the steps.

CHAPTER FIFTY-SEVEN

Before her was an enormous dance party. A quick glance told her that there were close to three hundred people bouncing to the loud samba that blasted from the speakers hanging from the rigging.

There was serious electricity in the air. It gave her goosebumps.

This party felt a lot like the episodes of *Soul Train* that she used to watch when she was a little girl. The difference was that every single reveler onboard was young and Latin. Gyrating, bumping, bouncing, grinding, shaking—the women were a blur of hips, ass, breasts, and lip gloss. The men were nearly perfect caricatures of masculinity, snapshots of broad shoulders, slim hips, dark hair, and white teeth.

A young couple passed by her, laughing in a weird language. The pronunciation sounded vaguely similar to Spanish. Then she recognized it.

Portuguese.

Then it hit Ainsley: These people were Brazilians.

Of *course* they were. Over the years, Punta del Este had

become overrun by rich vacationers from Rio de Janeiro. And nobody on earth could party like Brazilians on holiday.

The problem was that she was alone, couldn't speak Portuguese, and couldn't dance. Much less samba with real Brazilians.

No, she would explore the schooner instead. Ainsley placed one of her Diors onto the wooden deck, which had been polished to a warm chestnut brown gloss.

She glided past the captain's wheel and avoided an open hatchway. Her fingers touched rope stanchions, brass fixtures, and a hundred other nautical items that she couldn't name. She was really putting on her best catwalk stride. If she couldn't dance, she needed something.

After all, there was lust everywhere. A man dressed in a *guayabera* leered at Ainsley even as he romanced another woman in sequined miniskirt. A couple was making out in the rigging overhead. A heavy woman had passed out over the barrel of an antique cannon, her breasts falling halfway out of her dress.

Ainsley couldn't fit in. Her face hidden by the floppy hat, she moved through the revelry like the ghost of an elegant model.

And then a hand touched her on the shoulder. It belonged to a trim, middle-aged man in an expensive suit. He wasn't drunk. He wasn't dancing. He seemed perfectly in control.

"Excuse me, señorita," he said. "The captain would like to invite you to his quarters."

She smiled. "Who is the captain?"

"You do not know?"

Of course she knew. The captain was the *telenovela* star. But she wanted to play the innocent.

"My friend brought me here. I thought we were just going to a bar."

"Come find out," he said.

He offered his arm, and Ainsley accepted. He escorted her down a narrow stairway below deck and through an extremely narrow hallway.

He stopped before a low door. "Watch your head," he instructed.

The door swung open. Ainsley ducked and entered a smoke-wreathed room. Judging from the rich wood paneling, blue carpet, and antique globe, this was the captain's quarters.

And sure enough, in a luxurious overstuffed chair, sat the most beautiful older man Ainsley had ever seen in her life.

The captain.

He was immaculately groomed. His skin was flawless, his eyebrows perfectly shaped, his jaw sculpted from marble, his eyes a beautiful green. She guessed he was probably fiftyish, even though he didn't look a day over thirty. He wore a simple white linen suit. When you looked that good, you didn't need much else.

This was Gustavo, the *telenovela* star. That much was obvious.

Around him lolled a crew of four or five thin, obviously homosexual men. They lazed on chaise lounges, their legs thrown across the arms. All smoked casually. None of them looked to have ever lifted anything heavier than a tube of mascara.

"There she is," Gustavo said in Spanish. He was pointing at Ainsley with a pinky finger, the other three still wrapped around his champagne flute. "Who wanted to talk to her?"

A couple of the men slipped out their poses and approached Ainsley. They moved like tigers, silent and predatory.

"Show us," said one.

"Show you what?" she replied.

"How you move," the other said. "We were admiring your walk."

They gestured to a bank of video monitors on the wall of the room. On each monitor was a different angle of the party on the deck above.

Ainsley grinned. She had been doing the high-stepping sexy walk across the deck, the watchers had scoped her on the monitors, and Gustavo had sent out one of his personal retinue to ask her to perform it for them.

It was a weird request, but because Gustavo was the host of this extravagant event, Ainsley would oblige.

"Like this," she said, "one foot before the other. See. Just like mommy taught us. But with more flair." She demonstrated, putting some extra sauce in each downward step.

The men sighed as they watched her move across the quarters.

"Marvelous," one said.

"Like a goddess," said the other. "Such length in the hips."

"Do you want to try?" she said.

The group laughed. "Oh no," one said. "We're not models."

"Neither am I. I don't know how to dance either. Maybe if you could show me how to do that, we would be even."

Gustavo put down his glass. "I can." He stood up. "To dance like people in Brazil, you have to let go of your hips and tighten your stomach."

"How do I do that?" Ainsley said.

"You would need to ask a woman for more specific advice," he said. "None of us here qualify, though some of us try." He glanced at the foppish men behind him. "Please, let me show you."

Gustavo motioned to the man who'd retrieved her. "Music."

The huge sound of drumming filled the captain's quarters. To Ainsley there sounded at least four different pieces of percussion.

"What is this?"

"This is Uruguayan music," he said. "*Candombe*."

"It sounds Brazilian," she replied.

"It's *not*," he said. "This is from Uruguay. Of course, all such music came originally from Africa with the slaves."

The actor was leaning into her ear to be heard. Ainsley smelled leather and spices. She felt her imagination taking her to places that she didn't want to go, and forced herself to pay attention to his words.

"Do you like it?" he was saying.

"Very much," she replied. "It makes me want to dance." She tried to move her hips, but something felt off.

"That's cute," he said, "but let me show you how. First, listen to the music. Do you hear the low drums? Boom-boom?"

"Yes."

"Ignore them. The low ones provide the melody. You can't dance to melody."

"Okay."

"Do you hear the middle ones?"

"Yes."

"That is the *repique*. Do not listen to them either."

"Why?"

"They improvise too much. The best musicians always play *repique*. You can't dance to that."

"Then what do I listen to?"

He smiled. "The high one."

He placed a finger over her lips. Ainsley cocked her head to listen. Above the low and middle ranges, she could make out a small piece of percussion, a high pitch, playing steadily, *tat-a-tat-a-tat-a-tat-a-tat-a-tat*.

"I hear it," she said.

"That is the *chico*. That is what you listen to. It keeps the tempo. Watch me."

Gustavo began to move his midsection with expert grace. The dance looked free yet controlled.

"Try," he commanded.

She couldn't disobey the host at his own party. Her ear zeroed in on the little *chico*, felt the beat, started to move. But her hips wouldn't pop the way that she saw the other women's hips doing. It frustrated her.

"It was a good try," he said.

"I want to learn how to do that."

"Of course you do, and when you are able to dance like this, you will be a real Uruguayan," he replied. "Now, I am wondering if there is a reason you hide your face?"

Her breath caught in her throat. He was trying to peer under the brim of her hat.

"Every man appreciates mystery," she said.

"Can I unveil the mystery?"

She nodded. He gently lifted the hat from her head. As his eyes searched her face, she realized her mistake.

Ainsley had accidentally given the security her real name. Now she'd given the host of the party, a wealthy and influential Uruguayan, a look at her real face. Add to this the fact that a charcoal sketch of her had been played on national television earlier that day in connection with the murder of José Ignacio Tabarez.

If anybody put these three elements together, Ainsley could have a major problem.

"You have a familiar face," Gustavo told her. "Where are you from?"

"Germany," she lied.

"You don't sound German," he said. "You sound like an American."

"I lived in America growing up," she lied again, "but my parents are German."

Gustavo nodded. His homosexual retinue was watching her. She suddenly felt uncomfortable.

"Enjoy the party," he said.

Ainsley saw that his security guard had opened the door. That was her cue. She muttered thank you and left the captain's quarters.

Glancing back, before the door closed, she saw one of the foppish men curl a slender arm around Gustavo's neck and plant a lingering kiss on his forehead. The *telenovela* star smiled, then returned the favor.

That wasn't a typical South American back-slapping man-kiss. That was a soft, slow, lingering kiss.

For a moment, Ainsley wished that she hadn't ditched Viviana. She might want to know that her crush was playing for the other team.

CHAPTER FIFTY-EIGHT

When Ainsley emerged onto the deck, her watch read almost four thirty in the morning, but the party showed no signs of slowing down. In fact, the music was even louder, the dancers even more drunk, the making out sloppier.

She decided to go back down to the grass. She noticed the security men eyeing her as she descended the stairs. Not in an admiring way, or a mystified way, or even a nudge-nudge-who's-that-hottie kind of way.

They were watching her in a professional way.

Gauging her movements.

She casually glided past them and moved into the sea of tables. It was calmer here. The older partygoers had claimed these chairs hours ago and were sitting back with fingers drumming their bellies. Ainsley felt hungry again.

She found a buffet and loaded a plate with pasta. Her appetite had returned with a vengeance, and she needed to make up the calorie deficit she'd suffered during the last week.

Ainsley took a chair at an unoccupied table and busied herself with the simple task of inputting calories. While she chewed, she watched the candle flame dance and flicker inside the globe centerpiece.

Then she noticed another security guard nearby. He was standing about twenty meters away.

Watching her.

There was no doubt. His eyes were fixed on her and not moving. The hair on the back of her neck rose. She hadn't done anything wrong. But she needed to stay calm. She forced herself to lift the fork to her mouth. *Chew. Swallow.*

Everything would be fine.

Her ear picked up a loud ruckus approaching through the tables. It sounded like two people squabbling.

She squinted. The squabbling belonged to Viviana and Nolo. She must've called him when she couldn't get on the ship. His face was sickly gray and drawn. He wasn't the kind of person who was meant to live very long.

Ainsley considered hiding under the table, but that would've drawn more attention.

It was too late anyways. Viviana had spotted her, and now she was streaking through the tables, knocking over chairs. "I knew it," she shouted. "I knew you were a selfish bitch from the moment I saw you."

Ainsley stayed diplomatic. "What? It looked like fun up there."

"Of course it was fun. That's why I wanted to go."

"You would've done the same."

"Did you meet Gustavo?"

"No," she lied.

"Well, that was your last chance."

"Why?"

"Because I just told security that you were a suspect in the murder of José Ignacio Tabarez." She crossed her arms, arched an eyebrow, and tapped a toe. She waited for the reaction.

Ainsley was stunned. "How do you know about that?"

Nolo interrupted in English. "Your picture ... is ... on ... television. I see you."

He still sounded incredibly stupid. But this explained why security had started following her.

Ainsley felt fury clouding her eyes. "Why would you *do* that? I'm not a *murderer*. I'm just a stupid American girl with a stupid empty American life, who took a stupid job to come to this stupid country to look for a stupid amethyst treasure for *your* stupid grandmother."

"You shouldn't have ditched me," said Viviana. "Then this wouldn't have happened."

Ainsley was speechless. *Then this wouldn't have happened?* Couched safely in the third person? Pettiness couldn't even begin to describe this girl. Her heart was a frozen pebble.

In fact, she was acting like her grandmother. Ainsley should've guessed that this apple hadn't fallen too far from the tree.

She started to respond but stopped. There was no use waging this battle. Her relationship with Viviana was finished.

"Have a good night," Ainsley managed to choke out.

"You're going to have an even better one," replied Viviana.

The operatic couple walked away, arguing about something else. They would always be at each other's throats.

Then Ainsley saw that the security guard had moved closer to her. Another had appeared on the other side.

She was the quarry. Again.

She left her plate on the table and began strolling towards the exit gate. Behind her, the security guards followed at a medium distance. A small crowd of people stood between them.

If she tried a little harder, she could probably lose them. The milling crowd near the entrance had grown larger, friends starting their long goodbyes. She could get lost amongst them.

But the security guards would still recognize her clothing. And they'd undoubtedly communicated with their compatriots at the gate, where she'd be nabbed for sure. That would be followed, she guessed, by an off-the-books detention that could go any way the off-the-clock police officers pleased. And she'd already suffered one of those at the Ferreyra ranch. She wasn't eager to repeat the feat.

Ainsley racked her brain. There must be a way out.

Her eyes lighted upon a woman's jacket tossed over a chair. The owner was most likely dancing and humping the night away on the deck of the schooner. In fact, as she glanced around, she noticed that every table offered at least one orphaned article of women's clothing.

That was the answer.

She slipped alongside a group of women. They paid scant attention to her. And when she threw her floppy hat over the bushes, nobody noticed.

She hazarded another backwards glance. The guards couldn't see her for the thirty-odd heads between them.

Now was the moment.

Casually, she dropped to her knees the ground, pretending to look for something that she'd dropped near a table—

—then rolled underneath it. Quick like a rabbit.

Beneath the table, hidden by the full-length tablecloth, Ainsley felt momentarily safe, like she was in a secret world. She could hear the murmur of partiers' voices, the distant samba music on the party schooner.

And then she heard something else. An oddly familiar five-note melody coming from her purse. It took her a moment to recognize it.

It was her ringtone. Someone was calling her.

She'd kept her phone off for so many days since arriving in

Uruguay that she'd forgotten what it sounded like. Those five notes jerked her back to the sounds of her old life, back in the United States, so distant, so gray, so empty.

She fumbled in her purse for the phone. The caller ID read "Unavailable". She took a chance and answered.

"Hello?" she said.

"Ainsley," said a Latin woman's voice. It sounded strong, earthy. Ainsley recognized it instantly.

It was Señora Nasazzi.

Her would-be torturer from the Ferreyra estate. The *gaucha* who had subsequently pulled a one-eighty by handing her money, out of her own pocket, for bus fare.

"No, this is Karin," she lied.

"Ainsley, there is no time for that game," said Señora Nasazzi. "I need to meet you."

"How did you get this number?"

"I had your phone for two days."

Ainsley had forgotten that. Then she realized that Señora Nasazzi was calling at five in the morning. It was natural for her. She'd probably been awake and whipping cattle for hours already.

"Why don't you just tell me now?" said Ainsley.

"I can get you El Árbol Negro."

Ainsley sucked in her breath. Her abdomen became perfectly tense. She didn't dare to move.

She managed to croak out a single word. "How?"

"Come to me. I'm in Punta del Este too."

Ainsley wondered for a moment how this woman knew that she'd come to this resort community. Probably via the bus lines. That *gaucha* had some serious sleuthing skills.

"When do you want to meet?" said Ainsley.

"When can you meet?"

"Right now."

Señora Nasazzi paused. "Meet me at the Fingers in an hour."

"Where are the Fingers?"

"On Playa de Barra. Ask someone."

The line went dead. Ainsley looked at her phone and chewed on her lip.

She didn't have much time.

CHAPTER FIFTY-NINE

First things first. Ainsley would need camouflage to escape the party. She reached under the sham and felt around on the chairs until her hand found a loose piece of fabric. She pulled it under the table.

It was a gold chenille wrap with tasseled fringe. She lifted it to her nose. It smelled like rose hips and camomile. Nobody but an old woman would wear this.

But it would do.

Ainsley worked quickly. First, she stripped off her shirt, then wrapped the piece around her shoulders and upper torso. Then fixed it at the base of her throat with a safety pin from her purse.

She looked like a fusty old lamp. But it would work.

Then Ainsley noticed a half-empty plastic bottle of water on the ground. She poured it over her head, then ran her fingers through her soaked hair. It would look wet, plastered, and glossy.

Finally, the makeup. She pulled out her compact and drew garish blue cat eyes with her eyeliner. She then smoked her eyelids until they looked like the crusted bottom of a blackened pan. Finally she applied a layer of cherry red lipstick.

She looked at herself in the mirror. It would be a miracle if anyone could recognize her behind all the clownishness happening on her face. Add the gold wrap and the androgynous hair, and she looked like a dancer from a New Wave music video.

But this bizarre costume could carry her out of the predicament.

Ainsley rolled out from underneath the table and cautiously peered over the edge of the table. No security anywhere nearby. She'd thrown them off.

There was still, however, a knot of security near the gate. A gang of partiers was milling around there, saying long goodbyes.

That was the final obstacle. Something would need to be done. She invented a two-part plan.

First she sat at the table, took a paper napkin, and held it to her face. To mimic crying.

Second, she needed a group of guys. There were hundreds of those. Within seconds, she saw the perfect candidates, a gang of four young bucks, all testosterone and swagger and shoulder punches. She remembered seeing them on the deck of the ship.

She edged her chair into the aisle, so that she would be directly in their path. Then she hid her face inside the napkin and plucked a nostril hair. It was slightly disgusting, but it had always triggered tears. Actors even used the same trick for the camera.

This would amp up the drama.

She buried her face in the napkin, and within seconds, she felt hands on her shoulders. Voices were talking. She looked up. The gang was crowded around her. They were talking at her in Portuguese.

Ainsley couldn't understand them, which she knew made her look even more pitiful. She hoped that her mascara was running.

The Brazilians were talking louder at her now, trying to make her understand something. A communication strategy that always worked wonders.

There was no point in even trying. Ainsley just pointed towards the exit, then dramatically buried her face in the napkin. Sobbed loudly.

Her thespian powers carried the day. Ainsley felt hands cupping her elbows, then felt herself being lifted to her feet. A man's hand at the back of her head pressed her face into his chest. His shirt smelled like liquor and sweat. His arm wrapped around her shoulders. The group began walking again. She kept the napkin up to her eyes as her feet shuffled along.

They were guiding her out of the party.

While American guys might've walked past her, Ainsley knew that Latin guys could be depended upon to come to the rescue. She could hear the guys joking with each other. She guessed they were joking about what they were going to do with her. That was okay. Let them feel like they got lucky.

When Ainsley heard a security guard ask in Spanish if the girl was okay, her arm squeezed her bag even more tightly. The guys answered loudly in what sounded like a reassuring tone. The guard asked if he could see Ainsley's face. Her adopted protectors talked even more loudly. She caught the word *prima*.

It was the same word in Spanish. *Prima* meant cousin. They were pretending that she was family. Just to get her out of the party.

At last Ainsley felt hard asphalt under her shoes. She cracked an eye open. She was standing on the road, outside the party, near the valet. The security, the metal gate entrance, and the party were all behind her.

She'd made it out.

Ainsley dropped the napkin onto the ground. She disentangled herself from the guy, then wiped her eyes. The Brazilian guys motioned to her to come along. She refused. Then she made a walking motion with her fingers.

The guys cried out, no no no no. They surrounded her, yammering in Portuguese, tried to propel her towards their own automobile. Ainsley resisted. She knew the reputation of young Latin guys—if you gave them an inch, they'd take a thousand miles, and she'd unfortunately already given them all kinds of signals that she was an invertebrate, a piece of human luggage. She needed to assert herself.

Ainsley threw her arms down, like a martial arts fighter, and shouted one word: "No." Her eyes dared any and all to touch her.

The Brazilians finally got the message. Her thighs would be glued shut that evening.

As she turned her back on them, she could hear the tone of their voices turn to mockery and aggression. Grunts, curses, chimp-like whoops. It was the same in every language. That was fine. Let them feel pissed off.

She'd gotten what she needed.

CHAPTER SIXTY

Ainsley held her head high as she walked along the road.

It was about five miles back to downtown Punta del Este. If the average person walked about three miles an hour, given her long legs and brisk pace, Ainsley should be downtown in about the same amount of time. She would find the Fingers from there.

As the headlights from passing cars strafed her legs, she found herself in the midst of undeveloped sand dunes. The first streaks of orange stretched across the sky, through the clouds, illuminating the sand dunes all around her.

It was an earth symphony played by sea, sand, and sky. It was absolutely gorgeous.

She was lost in reverie when a BMW slowed down along-side her. It contained the Brazilian guys. They were leering at her from inside the vehicle. One opened the rear door and patted his lap.

Her nostrils flared. She ignored them and kept walking, head held high.

Then there was a loud electronic squawk. A tiny police car had quietly rolled up behind them. The officer spoke barked something through the roof-mounted PA system. It didn't matter that neither Ainsley nor the Brazilians could understand the garbled Spanish command. Everybody knew what the police wanted.

The driver hit the accelerator, and the BMW disappeared down the road. Ainsley breathed a sigh of relief.

Then the police car pulled alongside her. It was a tiny vehicle, a glorified golf cart, with room enough for two. The word *Maldonado* was printed on the side, and an orange light on the roof blinked intermittently. It looked like a parking enforcement vehicle that had wandered away from the city and gotten lost in the dunes.

The passenger side window rolled down. The driver leaned over. It was a female police officer.

"Where are you going?" she asked.

"The Fingers," said Ainsley.

"I'll give you a ride."

"Thank you, but I prefer to walk."

"Don't say no."

"But I really need the exercise."

The police officer frowned. "What you need is to buy a real shirt and reapply your makeup."

"Thank you for the advice."

Ainsley kept walking. The little vehicle kept rolling alongside her.

"Will I have this motorcade accompaniment all the way back to town?" Ainsley said, a bit more snappishly than she had meant.

The woman grinned. "Get in, or I'll detain you for public drunkenness."

Ainsley couldn't believe her bad luck. This police officer was blackmailing her.

The car stopped, and she reluctantly got inside the vehicle. The driver was five feet nothing, with a pretty face, strong chin, and sleeves rolled up to display her finely cut biceps. Her eyes sparkled with excitement.

Ainsley's heart dropped as she recognized the signs of an incipient lesbian crush. Right now, she had no time to deal with this.

As the vehicle moved slowly through the dunes, the police officer spent more time watching Ainsley than the road. "So why are you going to the Fingers?" she said.

"I'm meeting a friend."

"For breakfast?"

"Probably."

The woman cocked her head and looked at Ainsley. "I feel like I've seen you before."

Ainsley felt her heart try to bolt from her chest. She would have to deny, deny, deny.

"I don't know why you would. It's my first time in Uruguay."

"From where do you come?"

"Germany."

"Really? You sound softer than the Germans."

Ainsley bit the inside of her cheek. People kept seeing through her fake German identity. Maybe she needed to concoct a different persona. But she was stuck with this for now. "I guess I'm just different," she said.

"You sound more American. They have more Spanish too. Like you."

"Yes, they do."

"It's because of all those Mexicans." The woman thought for a moment. "I'm glad I'm not Mexican. I don't like spicy food."

Ainsley shut her eyes and prayed for the ride to finish soon. The small electric vehicle zipped silently through the early dawn. Ahead, over the dunes, she could make out the highrises of Punta del Este.

"I pick up lots of people in the mornings," said the police officer. "All coming come from the *boliches*. Sometimes I see them passed out on the sand. I have to wake them up because they will get sunburned without my help." She looked at Ainsley. "I know all the places to hide in the sand dunes."

Ainsley understood the subtext. She thunked her head wearily against the window. She was trapped in a slow-rolling nightmare.

"Are you sure I don't know you?" the police officer said. As she tried to peer at Ainsley's face, the small vehicle swerved over the center line.

"You should probably watch the road," Ainsley said.

"Didn't I pick you up last month after Eduardo Sanchez's beach party? In Piriapolis?"

"No."

"There was a girl who looked just like you. She was drunk too."

Ainsley dreamed about bullets, large ones, entering her skull. It would be preferable to this slow torture.

"I'm not drunk," she said. "Just tired."

"So where is your boyfriend?" the police officer asked. "You came alone?"

"Not alone. My friend left without me."

The woman made a *tsk-tsk* sound. "We are famous for that."

"Who?"

"Uruguayan women. We abandon each other all the time."

The police officer was quiet for a moment as she drove along the ocean side of the Punta del Este peninsula. Ainsley saw a sign reading Playa de Barra.

Suddenly the officer said, "I'm sorry, but my mind will not leave the subject alone. I know have seen you before."

At that moment, Ainsley spotted the Fingers. They were unmistakable: large, several meters high, formed of sand, reaching up out of the beach. She'd never been happier to see a sand sculpture.

"You can let me out here," she said.

The police officer slowed down, and Ainsley had leaped out before it even came to a stop.

"Have a good morning," she said.

"Equally," the officer replied. Then a dark cloud came across the woman's face. She was looking at Ainsley with new suspicion.

The American recognized that look. But as she ran onto the sand, she couldn't afford to think about what it might bring.

CHAPTER SIXTY-ONE

Carrying her shoes, Ainsley made her way across the *playa* towards the ocean. The sugar sand felt perfect, squeaking under her feet with each step. Seagulls wheeled overhead in the still morning air, while the distant thunder of waves crashed in her ears.

As she drew closer to the Fingers, she was struck by the size of the piece. The sculpture was huge. It could represent almost anything: a drowning swimmer, a giant climbing out of the earth, the eternal grasping for something else.

It made Ainsley think of her own life.

She pushed those thoughts out of her head as she shaded her eyes with her hand and scanned the beach.

The closest person was a shirtless jogger, about two hundred meters away. Nearby, a tractor crossed the sand in slow lines, dragging what looked like a five-meter-wide comb across the beach.

Where could Señora Nasazzi be?

She squinted harder. Five hundred meters farther down the beach was a rock jetty. On the jetty stood a tiny figure. It looked possibly female.

Ainsley swore to herself as she started walking. She was exhausted and dressed bizarrely. Why did this resort town have to be so spread out? She couldn't even verify a person's identity without expending five hundred calories on a bare-foot beach marathon.

She was getting cranky.

Fifteen minutes of sour-faced trudging later, Ainsley had arrived at the rock jetty. The figure was staring out to the open sea.

It was Señora Nasazzi. And she was holding a fishing rod.

"Señora," said Ainsley.

The *gaucha* didn't even turn around. Ainsley would have to go to her. She sighed and began the painful process of picking her way barefoot across the jagged rocks.

Several scrapes and muttered curses later, Ainsley stood wearily beside the woman on the rocks.

"I came to the ocean once, years ago," Señora Nasazzi said. "But then I started to work at the *estancia*. And I couldn't come anymore."

Ainsley didn't know what to say.

"I have always dreamed of fishing again," the woman continued. "Now I am doing it."

She smiled at Ainsley. It was a peasant's grin—broad, simple, heartfelt, an expression of her very soul. Ainsley melted a little inside. Her would-be torturer really was a softie.

"Nice to see you again."

The line jerked, and Señora Nasazzi fought it for a moment. Her lower lip curled over her upper lip. Then the line went slack.

"That little bitch swam away. I would too." The *gaucha* laughed to herself. She seemed in no hurry to talk business.

So Ainsley stood there, waiting for the woman to catch something or give up. She clutched her gold wrap tightly around her torso and watched the waves wash against the rocks. She listened to Señora Nasazzi humming to herself.

Finally the *gaucha* shifted her stance. "I know," she said, "that you have been searching for El Árbol Negro since you arrived here."

"Yes."

"I think we can help each other."

"How?"

"Because I know something important."

"What?"

She reeled in the line, then pulled a shrimp out of a small can at her feet and stabbed it onto the hook.

"I know you didn't kill Tabarez."

She cast the line into the water with a short movement. Ainsley felt an immense relief to hear someone say those words.

"If you know what has been going on, please tell me," she said.

"The Ferreyras killed Tabarez."

The *gaucha* said this calmly, as if she were chatting about last night's vegetable soup. Ainsley's eyes widened. "*They* killed him?"

"You remember the synthetic El Árbol Negro? The one you took from his house?"

Ainsley wouldn't ever forget. "It should've been mine," she said. "The auction was unfair. I was prepared to spend whatever it took."

Señora Nasazzi shook her head. "Tabarez didn't even buy it. The whole auction was fixed ahead of time. He was part of the scheme."

"What scheme?"

The woman smiled mysteriously but said nothing. Ainsley was even more perplexed than before. If Tabarez had known it was fake, then why did he participate in this scheme? He had seemed authentic, a true *aficionado*, someone who wouldn't have lowered himself.

Señora Nasazzi seemed to read her mind. "Tabarez's ex-wife is part of the AgraDulce shipping family. The Ferreyras have supplied them for many years. The two families have a very close relationship."

"So?"

"The Ferreyras asked her to blackmail him."

"With what?"

The *gaucha* shrugged. "I don't know. They were already separated. Maybe something that would hurt him in the divorce. Whatever it was, Tabarez agreed to participate in the scam."

"Then why did they kill him?"

"Now *that* is the real question." Señora Nasazzi reeled in the fishing line again. The shrimp was gone. "You little bastard."

She looked around uselessly for her bait can. It was between her feet, just out of sight. Feeling impatient, Ainsley picked up the can and stuck another shrimp on the hook herself.

The *gaucha* cast the line again. "The answer is that Tabarez wasn't supposed to sell you that synthetic amethyst. He was violating the agreement. Because you could've learned that it was fake. Any experienced gemologist could tell you that."

Ainsley nodded. "Yes, mine did. He recognized it immediately."

"It was made in Japan two months ago."

That was pretty much was Bernabé had been discussing. "If the Ferreyras didn't want me to have the fake one, why was it all wrapped up and waiting for me in the hallway of the house, when Tabarez was already dead?"

"Because his servant, the German, was preparing to hide it."

"Heinrik."

"He was the Ferreyras' watchdog. He conveniently went to the store during the murder. Left the door open too. In fact, he probably stayed a little too long, because when he came home, you had already paid a visit. The tree was gone."

Ainsley eyed the woman. "How do you know all this?"

She smiled. "Everybody at the *estancia* thinks I am stupid. So they speak freely when I am around. I have been listening to people for years." She paused. "Also, I can read upside down. It's a very good skill to have in an office."

Ainsley tried to ignore the fact that a woman who wrangled cows for a living was offering her career advice.

Then Señora Nasazzi spoke again. "The one thing I don't know is the name of your gemologist, the one who identified the synthetic El Árbol Negro."

"That's a secret," Ainsley said. She needed keep something private from this woman who had almost magically monitored her every move.

"He is a very skilled liar," the woman replied. "The Ferreyras have sent their men to interrogate every gemologist in Montevideo. They found nothing."

That wasn't surprising. Ainsley thought of the elderly Bernabé. He knew all the players and would've already hidden the fake amethyst tree. He would be brilliant at playing dumb.

"The one thing I am trying to get around," said Ainsley, "is why. Why did the Ferreyras do all of this?"

"Because they couldn't get the real El Árbol Negro."

"What does that mean?"

"El Árbol Negro had belonged to the Ferreyras once, long ago. When the military junta came to power in the seventies, the family hit some bad years. And it looked like the government would start to confiscate valuable property from Uruguay's leading families. So they sold it to Guarasquil's family, who were friendly with the regime. It was kept secret."

"Guarasquil? That guy has money?"

"He used to. His family was very proper, very influential, all *estancieros*. And his grandfather was the leader of the Blancos." She paused. "That's a political faction."

Ainsley had guessed that. Still, it was hard to imagine that rugged outdoorsman wearing starched shirts and knee-pants as a child, sipping tea from a porcelain cup.

"So in the late eighties, the junta was tossed from power, and the Ferreyras began to recover their fortunes. Uruguay became a much better place. The Ferreyras decided they wanted El Árbol Negro back."

"And Guarasquil wouldn't sell it."

"Sell it? They couldn't even find him. He'd renounced his family, don't ask me why. He was always a little crazy in the head. He took El Árbol Negro and went into hiding."

"So this week—"

"—the Ferreyras finally took back the treasure. They'd always seen El Árbol as rightfully theirs."

"Did they pay him?"

"You were there. Did it look like they paid him?"

Ainsley shook her head. "No."

"That's right. They just stole it. And they killed Tabarez." The woman's eyes were flaming. "Now you know why I am here, talking to you."

"No, I don't understand that yet."

The *gaucha* reeled in the line and picked up the bait can. "Walk with me."

CHAPTER SIXTY-TWO

They returned down the beach, back towards the Fingers. Seagulls wheeled overhead. Señora Nasazzi walked barefoot, fishing rod over her shoulder, plainly enjoying the salty sea air. Ainsley guessed that, after a while, anything smelled better than cattle.

"I am talking to you," said the *gaucha*, "because I have learned something important." She paused for dramatic effect. "The Ferreyras are planning to hide the real El Árbol Negro."

"What do you mean?"

"They want to display the treasure to the public, so they look like friends of the people. But it's too valuable. So they want the fake one to become the real one. I learned this two days ago, while you were being held captive."

"What will they do with the real one?"

Señora Nasazzi shrugged. "Maybe sell it? Maybe admire it? My knowledge doesn't extend that far. But there is something standing in the way of this plan."

"Me."

"Yes."

"What do they know about me?"

"Only what that waitress said on television."

Ainsley rubbed her knuckles into her eyes. "I never should've taken her inside Tabarez's house."

Señora Nasazzi spit on the sand. "I can't believe that she actually thought you were German."

"So far, she's the only person who's believed it."

"That's because she is very stupid," said the *gaucha*. "And believe me, I know stupid. I work with cows."

"True."

"So they are searching for the synthetic El Árbol Negro. And that means they are searching for *you*. You are the one person who could destroy the story they are creating for the public."

Ainsley squeezed sand between her toes. She didn't like the feeling of being pursued, or of being this important. "So what do you propose?"

Señora Nasazzi sighed. "You know, I was not born a *gaucha*. Nobody believes this, but it is true. I only moved to Treinta y Tres because my husband worked for the family. When he died, I just stayed."

Ainsley listened closely but said nothing.

"Lately the Ferreyras have changed. They have no sympathy. I am tired of working for such people."

The woman stopped walking. "That's why I propose we steal El Árbol Negro back."

Deep down, Ainsley had felt this coming, and truth be told, she'd been hoping for it.

"I completely agree. How?"

A cunning look passed across Señora Nasazzi's face. "Years ago, when Guarasquil bought El Árbol Negro, he bought something else to go with it."

"What?"

"An insurance policy."

"From who?

"Someone named Lloyd."

"Who is Lloyd?"

"I don't know. But Lloyd will give reward money for the recapture. I'm sure that Guarasquil has already called him and alerted him of the theft."

"How much is the reward?"

"Ten percent of the value."

Ainsley felt excited. That was a lot, maybe twenty or thirty thousand U.S. dollars. "But you don't know who Lloyd is?"

"All I know is that he is from England."

Ainsley thought about it. Then the answer hit her.

The *gaucha* was talking about Lloyd's of London, the world's most prestigious insurance company. Of course they would've insured something as valuable as El Árbol Negro. And that ten percent sounded exactly like a finder's fee.

"So how much do I get?"

"Two percent. I get the other eight percent."

"That's not fair."

"Listen, I'm quitting my job and leaving the country. You're risking nothing."

Ainsley couldn't argue with that. But she decided to play hardball anyways. "Four percent."

"Three."

"Deal." They shook hands.

Ainsley did the math in her head. Depending on how much it had been insured for, she could probably expect anywhere from six to nine thousand dollars.

That was exactly how much she would lose by cutting out Associated Industries. It was an even trade. Martina and Gugina would be disappointed in her failure.

She didn't feel too bad about that.

"So how will you steal El Árbol Negro?" she asked.

The *gaucha* was ready to answer that. "I am very familiar with one of the men guarding it. He doesn't like the Ferreyras either. So we will disappear. Maybe to Argentina, maybe to Chile, maybe to Paraguay. I would prefer not to tell you."

"No problem."

"And when you get the money from this Lloyd, you will give us our portion."

"Why do you trust me?"

The *gaucha* stared at her coldly. "Because you can be easily associated with the murder of Tabarez."

Ah, the threat of blackmail. It was always a powerful guarantee of good behavior. "That's fine," Ainsley said, "I'm honest anyways. Where is El Árbol Negro right now?"

Señora Nasazzi checked for people in both directions, then lowered her voice. "At this moment, it is in a house in Montevideo. The Ferreyras are cleaning and repairing it. But only for two days. After that, the family will sell or hide it. And Uruguay will never see it again."

"When did it arrive?"

"Last night."

Ainsley felt a shooting panic. "So you only have a day and a half?"

The *gaucha* nodded.

"What do you expect me to do?"

Señora Nasazzi caught her arm. "We need your English."

"Let me guess. You want me to find Lloyd."

"Yes. Bring him to evaluate the treasure. Get that money from him. I already know how good you are with words."

The sun had grown brighter, and people had appeared on the beach now.

"Are you with me?" asked Señora Nasazzi.

Ainsley nodded. "We had better move quickly. Where is your car?"

"My truck is right over there."

They raced across the sand. Ainsley climbed into the passenger seat. As she watched the Fingers disappear in the rearview mirror, she noticed that, far behind them, a series of flashing lights were racing onto the sand.

Those were police. If they were searching for her, she didn't want to find out.

"Drive faster, please," Ainsley said, slinking down in the seat.

MONTEVIDEO

CHAPTER SIXTY-THREE

A few hours later, Ainsley was taking off her makeup, a process that felt as though it was never going to end.

A pile of wadded-up tissues lay at her feet, most colored red, blue, and black. She'd used half a box of tissues to strip the garish makeup from her face. Desperate times, desperate measures.

The drive here had seen her wild-eyed. Señora Nasazzi had plowed down the two-lane road that connected Punta del Este to Montevideo at nearly ninety miles an hour, swearing at slower traffic, zooming across pasture land, weaving between more sand dunes.

They'd arrived at noon, and Ainsley had headed straight for Sofia's hair salon. She'd found the stylist upstairs, in her apartment.

Ainsley looked around the bathroom. The old-fashioned taps in the sink, the built-in cabinets, the clawfoot bathtub, the small black-and-white honeycomb tiles. It had been her grandmother's home, and still felt like one, in the best possible way.

There was a knock on the door. "I have empanadas,"

Sofia's voice said. "Which one do you want? *La chacha? El bosque? El clasica?*"

Ainsley scrubbed the edges of her hairline with a cotton ball. "It doesn't matter. I want all of them."

The door cracked open, and Sofia's arm thrust a bag inside. Ainsley took it, then grabbed her hand and kissed it. "If you were a man, I would marry you."

"I have news," said Sofia.

Ainsley wrapped a towel around herself and opened the door fully. "You've become a man?"

Sofia stood there. Her black eyes had changed from dark eggplant purple and were now a sickly yellow. Her scrapes had scabbed over. "No. I passed your hotel just now."

"Hotel Real?"

"You can't go back there. The police have set up surveillance."

"How do you know that?"

"A man was standing on the corner watching traffic without trying to look conspicuous. I saw him there yesterday too."

Ainsley thought about the belongings she'd left in that room. Clothing, some makeup, a pair of shoes. She wouldn't miss any of it.

"Then I need something else to wear," she said.

"I'll find something. Don't worry."

Fifteen minutes later, when Ainsley stepped out of the shower, she found a pile of clothing at the foot of the door. A simple brown top, gray pants, underwear, and a pair of unremarkable flats.

She put on the clothes and came out into the living room. Sofia was watering her plants.

"The underwear doesn't fit," Ainsley said.

"Nothing fits in Uruguay. We make most of our own clothing."

"It's the right size, but it's uncomfortable."

"That's the way it is."

Ainsley didn't have time to be picky. "Is it okay if I use your phone for a while?"

"Of course. Who are you calling?"

Ainsley explained the situation, and Sofia listened closely. When she was finished, her friend said, "So you are about to find El Árbol Negro?"

"God willing."

She clapped her hands excitedly. "What can I do?"

"You can find the phone number to Lloyd's of London."

Sofia pulled out her laptop, an awful model that looked to be a decade old. The screen was cracked. Ainsley counted four missing keys.

"Pardon my poverty," said Sofia, "but it still functions. We repair a lot in this country."

"Why don't you get a new one?"

She shrugged. "Same as the underwear. That's the way it is."

But the Internet browser worked perfectly, and she called out the international country code, followed by the number.

Soon Ainsley was connected to London, with a representative named Gordon. For the next thirty-five minutes, she engaged in a long conversation, patiently explained everything.

Yes, she was an American. No, she wasn't a Uruguayan.

Yes, she'd found El Árbol Negro. No, it wasn't fake.

Yes, she was sure it was real. No, she wasn't lying.

Yes, she wanted the finder's fee. In cash.

Then she'd listened to hold music for several minutes while he pulled up the records.

"I've found it," Gordon finally said. "El Árbol Negro. Darkest amethyst in the world. Dimensions, specifications, et cetera. Ah, here it is. A man named Jorge Guarasquil took out an insurance policy for two hundred thousand fifty thousand U.S. dollars on the fourth of May, nineteen hundred seventy-four."

"Yes."

"And he called yesterday to report its theft."

"That makes sense."

There was a pause. "We are indeed quite grateful for your call, Miss Walker."

"I bet you are."

"We'll need to begin the verification process, of course," he said. "It's quite lengthy, so I hope that your stay in Uruguay can—"

"Actually, I was hoping to shorten the process."

"By how much?"

"Let's verify it today."

"Heavens, no." He chuckled.

"This is urgent, Gordon," she said. "We're stealing it from the thieves. Do you understand that? And for your company, being on the hook for twenty-five grand is a lot cheaper than being on the hook for two hundred fifty grand."

There was silence. Ainsley knew that she was pushing hard. "I need to talk to my superior," he said.

"By all means."

Several minutes more of hold music. Ainsley walked heel-to-toe across Sofia's living room.

Then Gordon came back. "Good news. My superior has instructed that we indeed can expedite the verification process. I will call our gemologist representative in Montevideo immediately and—"

"May I call him as well?"

"It must be conducted independently."

"We don't have that luxury. We have *one day*."

More silence. Ainsley pressed on. "Twenty-five versus two hundred fifty, Gordon."

The Englishman cleared his throat. "It's not usual, but given the circumstances, I don't see why not."

"What's the name of the gemologist?" she asked.

She could hear him clicking through the file. "I have here a gentleman named... Bernabé Gradin."

Ainsley had to clap her hand over her mouth to keep from squealing with delight. Of course Bernabé would be contracted with the biggest insurance company in the world. He had fingers in every possible pie.

"His phone number?" she said.

While the representative read the number, she danced a little jig.

"One last question," she said. "When Mister Gradin verifies the authenticity of the amethyst, how long will it take for the fee to arrive?"

Gordon sounded breezy. "Oh, typically you will find the reimbursement in four to six weeks."

"That's not possible. See above comment."

"Ah. Hold, please."

Another minute of music, then Gordon returned. "We will guarantee payment in four days, following verification."

"Thank you," she said.

"Please take my mobile number as well should you need, ah, immediate assistance."

"Of course."

She hung up the phone and reached for her coat. There was no time to lose.

CHAPTER SIXTY-FOUR

Under stress, some people fall into bad habits. Some chew their nails. Others shred paper into tiny ribbons. Ainsley craved nicotine, a residual urge from her younger days.

And she was jonesing for a cigarette now. Bad.

She was in the Barrio Sur neighborhood of Montevideo, south of the Centro and bordered by the Rambla. She could peer downhill and see the brown waters of the estuary.

She had come full circle, back to the place where she'd begun her journey only a week earlier. It felt like a lifetime ago.

Ainsley was huddled in the doorway of a building. The façade was a long French colonnade. The entire barrio felt incredibly historic, like a seedy but authentic neighborhood of Paris. She felt a wave of nostalgia, wistfulness, *something* flash across her body.

She was waiting for Bernabé. She was supposed to escort the gemologist to the back door of the nearby colonial house where Señora Nasazzi guaranteed her that El Árbol Negro was being kept. The old man, however, was an hour late. It was the Uruguayan way.

Her knees felt wobbly and weak owing to her near-total lack of sleep for the last forty-eight hours. Sophia had fed her five empanadas, and yet her stomach was still growling.

The wind whistled off the estuary and numbed her nose and ears. She wrapped her coat, borrowed from Sofia, more tightly around her shoulders, and tucked her white bag under her arm. It was the only personal item that had survived this journey.

A taxi pulled to a stop before her. Bernabé emerged from the backseat, wearing a porkpie hat and a long fur-trimmed coat. His sad-faced assistant, Héctor, followed behind, carrying a brown leather satchel.

"Trying to avoid attention?" she said.

"It's cold," he said. "Just wait until you turn eighty-four." He looked around. "Why can't we meet at the house?"

"They said it was more discreet to enter from the back alley, on foot."

He grimaced. "This is a pain in the ass. Did I tell you I'm eighty-four?"

The taxi moved off, and she helped the old man maneuver his way across the rutted sidewalks. Héctor followed behind, mute as usual.

"Aren't you going to congratulate me for finding El Árbol Negro?" said Ainsley.

"No," he said.

"Why not?"

"I told you where it was."

She smacked him in the shoulder. "I was taken *hostage*."

He waved a dismissive hand. "We Uruguayans suffered through twelve years of such abuse. And you're here now, aren't you?"

"I am."

A glint entered his eye. "Meeting El Árbol Negro has been

my lifelong dream. If you are lying to me again, I will be very upset."

He winked at her, and Ainsley knew not to be offended. "Were you surprised to hear from me again?" she said.

"No," he said. "But I was surprised to hear from Lloyd's."

"Why?"

"Those bastards haven't called me in years. They don't like to pay either. Getting money from them is like pulling a tooth from a walrus."

That didn't bode well. Though the chilly barrio streets were mostly empty on this Sunday afternoon, Ainsley spotted a cluster of men straight ahead. They were huddled around a gutter bonfire, pointing the skins of several drums towards the flames.

"What are those men doing?"

"Ah, the *cuerda*," said Bernabé. "They are getting ready to play."

"Where?"

"In the street. Don't worry, you will hear them. When they start, everybody in the neighborhood comes out. It's very special to Uruguay."

"Can I ask you something else?" she said.

"Yes."

"Did the Ferreyras send anyone to talk to you?"

He nodded. "I lied like a cheating husband. They would've learned more from a cow."

"Did you keep the synthetic one in your laboratory?"

He shook his head. "No, it's somewhere else. Don't ask any more questions."

Ainsley agreed. "Are you going to tell Gugina about this? About my cutting her out?"

The old gemologist said nothing.

"Please don't. Tell her I've failed and given up."

Ainsley directed him down a tight alley. Towering above

them, on either side, were the four-story back walls of century-old colonial mansions. She felt a tingly feeling zip down her spine, the same shiver that always struck her near gorgeous old buildings.

It'd been a tough walk in the cold, and the old gemologist was starting to falter. Héctor came from behind and took his other arm.

"We are almost there," Bernabé said, "please say this to me."

"Yes," said Ainsley. "Look there."

Ahead, Señora Nasazzi was waiting for them inside a quiet door. She looked angry.

"You're late," she said.

"It's not my fault," replied Ainsley. "You didn't say English hours."

"Señora," said Bernabé, "I had to digest my lunch. With your permission." He offered her a long, lingering kiss on the cheek. Afterwards, she pulled back. There was a fire in her eyes. Ainsley remembered Señora Nasazzi complaining that men never paid attention to her. It seemed that he'd touched a button.

The *gaucha* recovered herself. "How long will the verification take?"

The gemologist shrugged. "With a laboratory test, two days. But with my eye, five minutes. If it is true." He winked. "That is sixty years of experience talking to you."

"Then hurry," she said. "We only have a short time until the two guards come back from lunch."

Behind her, Ainsley could see a heavyish man pacing the floor, his fingers nervously plucking the air. He wore a security guard's uniform.

Ainsley felt her hair stand on end. She could be walking into a trap. "Who is that behind you?"

"He is with us. He told the other two to go without him."

That was better. Ainsley turned to the old gemologist. "Are you ready?"

Bernabé nodded.

The group ducked their heads and passed through the small door into the mansion.

CHAPTER SIXTY-FIVE

They walked into a dank basement. Stacks of boxes and dusty junk were strewn across the floor.

"The Ferreyras have owned this house for decades," said Señora Nasazzi. "It's their only property in the city. Now it's mostly storage. Follow me."

She began to climb the staircase, which was only slightly wider than a pair of shoulders. Ainsley heard Bernabé puffing behind her and wondered what would happen if he got wedged.

They emerged into the middle of an old-fashioned kitchen. Several copper pans were hanging from hooks above a black-and-white checkered floor. A few dirty dishes lay in the sink.

"This way," said Señora Nasazzi.

They slid down a narrow hallway. Ainsley treaded softly, didn't know why. It was just that type of house.

They emerged from the corridor into a grand old living room. The ceiling was twenty feet overhead, oval mirrors were built into the walls, and ancient chairs with enormous butt dents sat awaiting the return of long-dead owners.

But Ainsley didn't notice any of that.

In the center of the room, stood El Árbol Negro.

This time, there was no doubt. As dark as a nightmare, as majestic as anything the mineral world has ever offered, the amethyst tree glittered inside a cocoon of steel rigging. It felt both alluring and somehow vicious, the stones bursting with black brilliance under the lights.

Everyone gaped. Ainsley clasped her hand to her mouth, feeling tears come to her eyes. A gemstone had never moved her in this way before. Even Héctor was taken aback for a moment.

Bernabé, however, wasn't impressed yet. Just as he had done in his lab, the gemologist began to circle the amethyst, chin cradled in his hand. Then he motioned to Héctor, who opened the satchel and pulled out the loupe and other instruments of analysis.

Together the duo ducked under the rigging, approached the amethyst, and inspected several points on various branches. They murmured in very low voices. Ainsley found her palms sweating.

They conferred for three, four, five minutes. Ainsley shifted her weight nervously.

"What's taking them so long?" said Señora Nasazzi, glancing at the door.

"Be patient. I know Bernabé."

The gemologist put the tools back in the satchel, and Héctor helped him out of the rigging. "Tarasconi was touched by genius," he announced. "But it was a genius of omission. He didn't change the stone. He just removed enough to bring out nature's gift."

"So what is the verdict?" said Señora Nasazzi.

He faced the group. "This is true. This is the real El Árbol Negro."

"Are you *sure*?" said Ainsley.

"I will pay all of you the fee myself if I am wrong," he said. "And I am never wrong."

Señora Nasazzi immediately dialed a number on her phone. "It's good," she said, then hung up. She turned to the security guard. "Go, go. The truck will be here in two minutes."

The guard clutched his head, a man in agony. He was clearly having second thoughts about the size of the shit-storm that the Ferreyra family would be sending his way for taking part in this theft.

She slapped him across the rump as if he were an errant cow. "Work!" she shouted.

Whimpering, he hurried to the rigging and began dismantling it. Señora Nasazzi herself kicked all the rugs against the walls, then flung open the front door.

Bernabé was filling out some paperwork at a table. Ainsley joined him. "Is there anything I can do?"

"Send this document to London as soon as I am finished. The number is at the top."

He signed his name with a flourish to the last of a three-page form, then handed it over to Ainsley. "Is this the entire claim?" she said.

"No, there is a fuller report I will write tonight. But, when they receive this, they are going to release your fee."

Then the gemologist lowered his glasses. "About Gugina." He cleared his throat and looked directly at Ainsley. "You and I see the situation with the same eyes. I am sorry to say this, but she is too greedy. Sending out girls all over the world to find other people's treasures." He shook his head sadly.

Ainsley breathed a sigh of relief. If Gugina were to find out about her betrayal, she could conceivably sue for breach of contract. But Bernabé was on her side.

"And I am tired of her using me." He sighed. "True, I did something very bad many decades ago. But I have been paying for it ever since." He paused. "I think I have paid enough now."

Ainsley had a pretty good idea what that could be. The same thing men have been doing to women since time immemorial.

Another glint of steel came into the gemologist's eyes. "So, I have made up my mind. Tomorrow Héctor and I will ship the synthetic amethyst to her."

A wicked smile crept onto Ainsley's face. "And you'll tell her—"

"—yes, that it's the authentic one. I'll put my report on it. She will never know unless she gets the gemstone independently tested."

"Thank you, Bernabé," Ainsley said.

"No, thank you for your hard work," he said. "It hasn't been easy for you. Now give me a kiss." He tapped his cheek.

Outside, the sound of a heavy door rolling upwards told Ainsley that the movers had arrived. She peeked out the window. An ordinary small moving truck was parked in front of the house. Three burly men were bounding up the steps.

"Later," she said.

"I never forget a promise," he replied. Ainsley stuffed the document into her bag and zipped it shut.

The movers had entered and were conferring with Señora Nasazzi. Ainsley heard someone mention a box, but she nixed the idea, saying there wasn't any time.

One of the men pointed at Ainsley. "*La americana?*"

"Yes," said Señora Nasazzi.

The three movers smiled at her. Ainsley felt the creeping sensation that she'd been the subject of an earlier conversation. She wondered how many other people had been talking about her.

The movers found canvas sheets in the corner and quickly wrapped the amethyst statue, securing it with straps and bungee ropes. Then they slipped an enormous dolly under the platform and wheeled the entire treasure out from the lighting rig.

In the blink of an eye, the room was empty. These guys worked too quickly to be from Uruguay. Ainsley considered asking what their regular jobs were, then realized it would be better not to know.

Now the movers were lowering the package down the front steps, one by one, with the utmost caution. When El Árbol Negro cleared the last step, all three men hoisted the treasure into the back of the truck.

They took turns kissing Señora Nasazzi on the cheek. Two of the men hopped in the back, while the third rolled the loading door down and locked them inside. He looked around the street then climbed behind the wheel and drove off.

Just like that, it was gone. Ainsley was in shock. El Árbol Negro had been rescued. And it was going back to its legal owner, Guarasquil, who had never wanted it sold to begin with.

Mission accomplished.

Ainsley turned around. Looking at the end of the corridor, she could see Bernabé and Héctor had already disappeared down the stairs to the basement. No use sticking around.

Señora Nasazzi had run into the living room, shut off the lights. Her eyes were as agitated as Ainsley had ever seen them.

"They're coming back!"

She meant the two guards who'd been at lunch. Ainsley panicked. "Where is the third? Can't he intercept them?"

"He's already gone. The idiot goat!"

"What do we do?"

Señora Nasazzi thought for a second. Then she said, "I'll

hide upstairs. You run down the street. They can't catch both of us that way."

It made sense. Señora Nasazzi, with her stubby legs, couldn't hope to keep up with Ainsley. But there was no use in both of them being caught huddling together. Splitting up was best.

"I'll call you," said the *gaucha*. "Now go!"

Ainsley walked outside and shut the front door. She slowly descended the front steps, her heart pounding. With her peripheral vision, she saw two youngish men approaching from the right. Those were the guards.

She casually turned left. Then resisted the urge to look back at them as they crossed paths.

One of men yelled something at her. It didn't angry or urgent, just curious. She ignored him and quickened her pace.

When she reached the corner, she hazarded a glance backwards.

Both men were running down the front steps. Both were pointing at her. Both carried billyclubs.

Dammit. They'd been inside the house, seen the theft. A shot of adrenaline surged through Ainsley's body.

She took off running.

CHAPTER SIXTY-SIX

Ainsley bolted like someone had fired a starting gun in her ear. She had no idea where she was going. She only knew that she had to get somewhere else fast.

Her legs flew across the rutted sidewalk. Her arms pulled at the invisible handrails, the technique her high school track coach had taught her. She crossed another block and looked back.

The men were following. They were equally fast.

Goddamnit. She hung a right, sprinted another block, then hung a left and sprinted two more.

That'd been at least four hundred meters. She stopped to catch her breath and glanced backwards again.

The men had stayed on her, easily. Shit shit *shit*. Why did these guards have to be young? A pair of middle-aged fatties would've given up by now. Or been distracted by a *parilla*.

Then she heard it.

Drumming. It sounded about four or five blocks away.

Bernabé had said that when the *cuerda* started playing, she would hear them. And that the entire neighborhood would turn out for the party. That would mean a crowd.

Ainsley wheeled around and raced towards the sound of the drums. Sure enough, the sidewalks were starting to fill up. Families, adults, children, elderly were pouring out of the houses. The sidewalks were filling with excitement.

She dodged through the people, took a right, ran two more blocks, then stopped. She was at the corner of Isla del Flores.

The party was here.

The *cuerda*, all eight men, were in the middle of the street, their drums strapped across their left shoulders and tilted to the right across their bodies. They were walking very, very slowly, an inch at a time, and beating their instruments with passion and precision. The booms of the heavy low drums bounced off the walls. It was a natural amplification.

They were surrounded by several hundred people, hanging out of the French windows, bouncing on stoops, massing on the sidewalks.

On the street before the *cuerda* were the dancers. Nearly fifty women, just ordinary neighborhood girls, a mix of black, white, yellow, brown ... and each one moving in a way that was very, very Latin.

It was the most spontaneous display of community that Ainsley had ever witnessed. And she needed to be a part of it.

Ainsley dashed into the crowd along the sidewalks. There were men grilling sausages already, slapping them between buns and handing them out, as though they'd been waiting for this party to erupt all day. Others were pouring Coca-Cola and red wine together into plastic party cups. She had heard of that concoction: *siete y tres*. The name indicated the proportions.

She beelined for the enormous crowd that encircled the drummers. In awe, she watched the percussionists for a moment. The *candombe* was hypnotic. She could feel the beat in her sternum. The women dancing were equally enraptured.

She glanced uphill. Her pursuers, the two guards, stood at the top of the parade, but hadn't spotted her just yet. She knew that they would. They'd gotten a decent enough look at her back on the steps. This was going to be a problem.

The solution: She needed to disguise herself again.

A small knot of young teenage girls had assembled next to her. One of them was carrying a jacket across her shoulder. It had a Uruguayan flag on the back, nine blue-and-white stripes with a perky yellow sun in the corner.

"Señorita," shouted Ainsley over the drumming, "let me try on your jacket. *Please*."

The girl looked at Ainsley skeptically.

There was no time for hesitation. She needed to offer collateral. Ainsley drew in a deep breath and shoved her purse into the girl's hands. The teen squealed with delight. She took off the jacket and flung it towards Ainsley.

The item was several sizes too small, but that was no matter. Ainsley threw it around her shoulders, then fastened the top two buttons, like an undersized cape.

Judging from the girls' chatter, her purse was as exciting as a bar of gold. They took turns modeling with it, snapping photos.

"Only for ten minutes," she said. "Clear? Oh, I need a hat too."

One of the girls handed Ainsley a red baseball cap. Ainsley marveled at how popular this form of headgear had become over the last few decades, even in countries without baseball.

Now, her face covered in shadow, her torso wrapped in the national flag, Ainsley felt sufficiently hidden. She accepted a *siete y tres* and tossed it down her throat.

Meanwhile, the two guards had descended into the crowd, one on each side of the street. They were easy to spot. They moved like sharks through schools of fish. They were the only two people not smiling.

One was coming her way. He was checking faces. Then she felt hands pushing at her from behind.

She had been unconsciously moving her hips to the music, and the teenage girls had noticed. "Dance," they said, pointing at the women in the middle of the street.

"With them?" Ainsley said.

The girls nodded. She declined. Then the teens pushed her out again, even further. "Dance!" they shouted.

These little teenyboppers had no idea what trouble they were causing. But then Ainsley noticed something: the oncoming guards were ignoring the dancers. They were only interested in the people on the sidewalk.

That was a major oversight. If she could blend in with the dancers, the men might just pass her by.

Public dancing. This was her absolute worst nightmare come true. And the consequences of sticking out here, of not moving well enough to blend in, couldn't be worse.

But Ainsley felt no other choice. She stepped out into the crowd of women dancers. She could remember Gustavo, the *telenovela* star, telling her to follow the high drum. She could remember failing badly.

But this time, she could actually see the players. One of the drummers was playing a tiny *chico*, eight inches in diameter, his stick and left hand tapping an insanely fast *tat-a-tat-a-tat-a-tat*. That was her man.

She locked eyes with the drummer. His eyes stared back. She felt her hips moving. She kept her stomach tense, pulled inwards, towards her center.

Then he nodded at her. Approval.

That was all Ainsley needed to let loose. She felt the excitement explode, the rhythm take over her body. Felt her ass shaking in ways it hadn't ever before. She lifted her arms overhead, hiding the sides of her face from the guards.

She was in the zone.

Sweat trickled down her face. She was lifting off, flying far from the predatory guards, from amethyst trees, from ex-husbands, from purposelessness ...

Minutes passed, but Ainsley, lost in the music, felt nothing. *When you dance like this, you will be a real Uruguayan*, Gustavo had told her.

Was she a Uruguayan now? Was that even the point?

Minutes later, hours later, she couldn't tell, the drumming ended, and Ainsley came back to reality.

The parade had reached the end of the street. Now all eight members of the *cuerda* had unhooked their drums and were sitting on the stone bench along La Rambla, drinking from water bottles. Around her towered the tall condominiums, like sentinels, gazing out across the white-capped waters of the brown estuary.

Best of all, the guards were nowhere to be seen. Her ruse had worked.

Then she froze.

Her purse was gone. Inside was everything she needed, including Bernabé's document. The one that would get her the finder's fee.

The crowd was breaking up now, returning home. Ainsley jumped onto the bench next to the drummers and spun around, scanning for the teenage girls. She spotted a likely group about two hundred yards down La Rambla.

Those little thieves.

Ainsley took off sprinting after them. She wondered if she would ever stop running in this country.

She caught up with them on a side street lined with tall elms and even taller colonial homes. These buildings in the Barrio Sur were benefitting from the solid construction standards of earlier times. This whole neighborhood could be rehabbed with enough investment money.

"You forgot your jacket," she shouted.

When the girls heard her, they giggled. As though they'd been daring each other to walk off. Ainsley didn't blame them. Giving up a cheap jacket and baseball cap for a foreigner's purse would've tempted her, too.

She tossed their clothes at them and yanked her bag back. Then she froze.

The two guards were coming down the street towards her. They were yelling at each other, gesturing wildly.

They hadn't spotted her yet.

Ainsley glanced around. She couldn't blend in with the teenagers, and they were already walking away. The street was empty otherwise. There was nowhere to run, nowhere to hide.

And then she heard a clip-clop, accompanied by the creak of an old axle.

It was the *hurgador*. The horse-drawn trash cart she'd seen and been repulsed by, on her very first night in Montevideo.

The driver sat on a humble box at the front of his cart, holding the reins to his horse. His long hair was flowing from underneath his knitted winter hat. In the bed of the wagon was an enormous heap of overstuffed gray trash bags.

She had a choice to make. It was disgusting, but she knew it was the only way to go.

Ainsley quickly darted into the street and around the far side of the cart. She pulled on the driver's elbow, walking alongside, and handed him her final fifteen pesos.

He accepted the money and looked straight ahead. As though random foreign women chased him down every day to hand him cash.

Ainsley ran to the back of the cart, drew a deep breath, and climbed aboard. Within a few seconds she had completely buried herself under the gray bags. Their weight pressed down upon her body. The plastic stuck to her face.

But she could see a snatch of blue sky above, in the cracks between the bags. And when she thought she couldn't stand the position anymore, the cart stopped.

The bags were flung off her face. Framed against the sky was the toothless face of the *hurgador*, smiling. He offered her his hand.

She accepted and was gently pulled up to a sitting position. He was handing her a clean towel and pointing to her face. She put the towel to her cheek and found a weird brownish liquid. She cleaned herself and thanked him.

Then she peered around. The guards had disappeared.

She looked inside her bag. Document, check. Wallet, check. Phone, check. Those things were all that really mattered right now.

Then Ainsley sat for a moment in shock.

She had succeeded. El Árbol Negro had been recovered. She'd been given a purpose and achieved it. Soon she would receive the reward.

And best of all, despite the difficulty of this journey, she'd enjoyed the adventure.

A lot.

EPILOGUE

From the comfort of a slingback folding chair, Ainsley watched the crowd gather around the outhouse. She sipped a chilled glass of sauvignon blanc and lifted her face to the sun.

Life was good.

After stumbling back to Sophia's apartment, she'd passed out cold for a day and a half. The stylist had sent the document to London for her, brought her food, and let her crash. During her few waking hours, Ainsley had stayed holed up in the apartment. She hadn't wanted to show her face in public for a while.

On the fourth day, she'd received the finder's fee. A courier, a silent man in a suit, had handed her a flat, unmarked envelope. It had contained twenty-five thousand U.S. dollars, in cash, as agreed upon.

First, she'd sent seventeen thousand five hundred dollars to Señora Nasazzi at an unmarked postal box, as they'd agreed. Second, she'd bought some new underwear and clothing. Third, she'd rented a car.

Then she'd driven that vehicle for seven hours to this place, the dirt courtyard of Guarasquil's settlement. It'd been a maddening hassle, driving across the open *campo*, finding her way back down the *cuesta* to this remote place, but now that she was here, her nerves were steadier.

A man exited the outhouse carrying a fifteen-foot-long improvised net. It looked like a pool skimmer, but half of the tool was coated in filthy brown slop. He removed the neckerchief covering his face.

It was Guarasquil. This was his punishment for lying to her.

"I found your passport," he said. "We're almost finished cleaning it. But we can't find the other thing."

"It's a plastic bag," Ainsley said.

"What's inside?"

"You'll see."

"Are you sure you dropped it in there?"

She nodded. He sighed, then replaced the neckerchief around his face and returned to the outhouse.

Ainsley smiled to herself and sipped her wine again. Her demand had been that Guarasquil personally search for the items in the toilet, since she'd gotten El Árbol Negro returned to him, even after he'd flat-out lied to her about its accidental destruction in the cave. And to his credit, he'd accepted this punishment without complaint.

She looked at her phone. Associated Industries had called her twice in the last two days without leaving a message. She had no intention of speaking to those women ever again. Even the prospect of returning to the United States left a bitter taste in her mouth.

Then her phone started to ring in her hand.

Her brow wrinkled. The number was unknown. With a nice buzz brewing in her skull, and absolutely nothing else to do, Ainsley picked up the call.

"Hello," she said.

"Is this Ainsley Walker?" a man's voice said.

"It might be," she replied. "Who's calling?"

"You don't know me," the man said, "but my name is Gabriel, and I live in the country of Argentina. My employer heard about your recent success with the amethyst."

"How did you get this number?"

"It's not important. I am calling because I would like to know if you are available for another assignment."

Ainsley set down her glass of wine and stood up. She felt herself snapping back into performance mode.

"Yes, I am *quite* available."

"And may I ask what you charge?"

She glanced at the outhouse. She'd never in her entire life been asked for a quote. "Usually I work on a percentage basis," she lied.

"This gemstone isn't valuable to anybody except my employer, so I'll advise you to give me a number."

This was feeling unrealistic. So she decided that maybe an unrealistically highball price could work.

She finally replied, "Twenty thousand U.S. dollars." She winced while she waited for the answer.

There was a pause. "I think my employer will agree to that. When can you come to Buenos Aires?"

"I'm in northern Uruguay right now."

"If you can get here by tomorrow, I'll add an extra thousand."

"I'll see if I can do it." She paused. "Who is your boss?"

"He is a very famous public figure. I can't reveal his name until you arrive."

"Let me call you back for more information when I return to Montevideo, okay?"

"Yes, hurry."

The call ended. Ainsley glanced at the crowd of poor rural people crowded around the outhouse. They were watching their leader literally dig through shit for her.

"Guarasquil," she called, "I'm sorry, but I need to go."

He emerged from the outhouse, sweating. "So soon?"

"Do you have my passport?"

He pointed to a small child, who stepped forward holding her passport. "We washed it in a bucket of hot water," he said. "Clean it again, *hijo*." Ainsley watched the child wipe the covers again with a towel.

Then Ainsley flipped through the book. The outsides had been laminated, and the muck hadn't penetrated the covers. Governments made these things nearly indestructible.

She put it into her bag. "I'll be back," she said. "You will definitely want to keep searching for the other object. And remember that I know *exactly* what is inside."

"When will you return?"

She shrugged. "Life is a series of discoveries. Who knows what any of us will find?"

As the people of Guarasquil's settlement watched, Ainsley Walker slipped into her rental car, started the engine, and pulled away down the long road.

Towards Argentina.

PLOTWORKS PUBLISHING

If you enjoyed this novel, please leave a review at the place where you purchased it.

Then visit Plotworks Publishing to follow Ainsley Walker on her next exciting gemstone travel mystery, *The Argentina Rhodochrosite*!

Turn the page for a sneak peek!

THE ARGENTINA RHODOCHROSITE

AN AINSLEY WALKER GEMSTONE TRAVEL MYSTERY

J.A. JERNAY

THE ARGENTINA RHODOCHROSITE

When Ainsley opened the door, she found herself face-to-face with a dark young man, early twenties, dressed in a natty suit. Inside, he'd reached for the door at the same time.

"That's an excellent sign," he said. "We are on the same wavelength. My mother would approve." A couple days' stubble sprouted from his face, and a smile cracked the corners of his mouth. He was short and slight and seemed absolutely harmless.

"I'm already taken," she lied.

"So am I," he replied, "by my mother." He stuck out his hand. "I'm called Gabriel. *Mucho gusto*."

She returned the handshake. "Ainsley Walker. *Igualmente*."

He kissed her cheek in the customary way. "You are the person I was looking for. Please, enter. We have no time to waste."

He strode across the minimalist lobby and beckoned over his shoulder. Ainsley followed him. Several assistants were sitting at chic, colorless workspaces, wearing headsets, typing on laptops.

Gabriel ushered her into a conference room, which was

dominated by a glass-topped table and black Aeron swivel chairs. It made Ainsley think of every conference room she'd ever been bored to death in, back in the States. Every job that'd ever frustrated, infuriated, or dismissed her.

"You can wait here for Nadia," he said. "Can I get you something to drink?"

"Sure," she said.

"What would you like?"

"Get me your favorite."

While he was gone, Ainsley looked around. On one wall were several broadsheets advertising musical theater performances, each featuring a lineup of heavily caricatured actors. On another wall were colorful photos of Argentine singers performing in concert, striking Christ-like poses under dramatic lighting.

Gabriel returned with a Perrier. He noticed Ainsley studying the photos.

"What do you think?"

"These performers all look so confident," she replied.

"Is it your first time to this country?"

"Yes."

"Then you should know our most popular joke. How does an Argentine commit suicide?"

"How?"

"He jumps off his own ego."

Ainsley laughed. "That can't be true."

He suddenly became very serious. "Oh, that is our character. Believe me, you will see." He handed the green bottle. "Nadia said she prefers to meet in her office. Are you ready?"

"Absolutely."

"Then, as my mother says, it's time for us to eat our vegetables."

"I don't quite understand that," she said.

A grimace passed over her face. "Me neither. I also don't understand why I'm twenty-five and still living with her."

Gabriel shook off the thought and led Ainsley further into the office. Ainsley glimpsed executive offices through open doorways, all of them expansive and airy. In one, a male executive chatted on a headset while steepling his fingers. Another had propper his feet on his desk. A third winked at her.

Minus the flirting, these people didn't look too different from the people in most professional, high-stakes offices back in the States.

A single door waited at the end of the hall. It didn't look forbidding as much as neglected.

Gabriel knocked and pressed his ear to the wood. "She's ready," he said. He held the door open.

Inside, this office was as clean, smooth, and colorless as the others. However, it was quite a bit smaller than the others. And there was a woman sitting in it.

This was Nadia.

She was in her mid-forties. She stood up, came around the desk, and shook hands vigorously. Ainsley immediately noted her broad shoulders, thrusting jaw. She was probably a former athlete. Heavy testosterone. The type of woman who could hold her own in a boisterous male environment.

"*Señorita* Walker, thank you for coming on such short notice." Her voice was professional and strong.

"My pleasure."

"I am Nadia, you already met Gabriel."

"Yes."

She offered the only other chair in the room, and Ainsley took it. Nadia closed the door firmly, locking it, and returned to sit behind her desk.

"Our custom is to relax before starting business, to chat a

bit. But unfortunately we don't have that kind of time." She paused. "You were recommended to me by Bernabé Gradin."

Ainsley couldn't help smiling. Her friend, the old gemologist in Montevideo, bless his heart, was giving himself as a reference.

"He's quite a character," she replied.

"That's what I hear," said Nadia, "but I only know his reputation. It's a pity he refuses to come to Argentina."

Ainsley smiled inwardly at this bit of provincial rivalry. "I agree," she said.

"He also tells me that your tenacity in finding lost gemstones was remarkable."

"That's very kind of him."

"He said that you were born to do this job."

Ainsley's heart leaped at that. Until this moment, she had been steeling herself for an eventual return to the States, to a flat and featureless future as a wage slave, maybe an unhappy second marriage someday, a couple of kids dutifully birthed and tended to, followed by another divorce, a decade of aimless wandering and an ugly, impoverished demise. But Bernabé had validated her decision to find another way.

"Finding gemstones is more than a job," said Ainsley, "it's a calling." These words came out more easily in a foreign language than they did in English. It was as though she were opening a new personality.

"Have you ever been to Argentina before?" Nadia said.

"Never."

"What do you know about our country?"

"Only the stereotypes."

"Steak and tango."

"And Evita."

Nadia nodded. "I'm sure you are sophisticated enough to know that we have much more than that."

"I'm sure. What kind of company is this?"

"We are a management company. We control celebrities' careers. In exchange, we get a percentage."

Ainsley felt a little piqued. She wasn't an idiot, she knew what a manager was. "What kind of celebrities do you represent?"

"Mostly performers. Actors, singers, athletes, magicians. Even a couple of writers."

Ainsley noticed a picture on her wall. A soccer player, dark haired and well-muscled, was hanging like a monkey from the crossbar of a soccer goal. His mouth was wide open, his incisors unsheathed, like an ape screaming from a newly-conquered tree in enemy territory. Behind him, a wall of fans were on their feet, arms thrust into the air, screaming with him.

"That guy seems like he has a big personality," Ainsley said.

"Ah, you noticed him," said Nadia. There was a secret behind her smile. "He is a very special individual."

"Who is he?"

"Ovidio Angeletti. He is Argentina's most famous soccer player. And he is my biggest client."

"I've never heard of him."

"That's too bad," said Nadia.

"Why?"

Nadia caught her eyes and held the gaze. Suddenly Ainsley knew what was coming next.

"Because you're working for him."

PLOTWORKS PUBLISHING

Visit Plotworks Publishing to follow Ainsley Walker on her next exciting gemstone travel mystery!

Now explore a new series by J.A. Jernay—the Cosmo Bennett Mapping Thrillers!

Turn the page for a sneak peek!

J.A. JERNAY

BOUNDARY

A COSMO BENNETT MAPPING THRILLER

FROM THE AUTHOR OF THE AINSLEY WALKER GEMSTONE TRAVEL MYSTERY SERIES

BOUNDARY

Cosmo Bennett and his assistant Noah shuffled down the dirt shoulder of the boulevard in the midday heat, sweating and miserable.

Each was lost in his own thoughts. Cosmo dreamed of hitting a heavy punching bag at his gymnasium. Noah dreamed of passing level nineteen of Operation Earlobe, an obscure RPG he'd abandoned last semester.

The morning's meeting had been a complete bust.

"I don't think we should continue this case," said Cosmo finally.

Noah didn't respond. Cosmo took no notice and continued: "I don't think anybody here takes our task seriously. I don't think this propaganda map was as influential as they say. I don't think this map has driven the civil unrest. I think social media and centuries of tribal warfare are more to blame for the unrest than anything else."

He looked over at Noah, waiting for a response. "What about you?"

The graduate assistant came back from his reverie. "Huh?"

"Did you hear anything I said?"

"No."

"I was just saying this is pointless and we should go home."

"I don't have a problem with that."

They arrived at Vida e Caffe. It was a chain café, with hundreds of similar franchises scattered across the southern part of the African continent. The branding was modern and inviting. A hundred people sat beneath umbrellas at small tables on the large outdoor patio.

An arm was waving at them. It was Christopher, their fixer, a cup of tea on a ceramic saucer in front of him. Two other cups awaited them.

"Hello sirs," he said. "I ordered us all a rooibos. It's a vanilla tea that is extraordinary."

Cosmo and Noah pulled out the chairs and sat down. The driver quickly sussed out that something was wrong.

"It was a bad meeting?" he said quietly.

"Yes," said Cosmo, "there was no progress made."

"I'm very sorry."

Cosmo sighed. "I think we have to leave."

The fixer looked confused. "But you just sat down—"

"The country," he clarified. "We have to leave Fabajouti. We can't seem to do any good here."

Christopher looked crestfallen. "I do understand your frustration."

Noah said, "If it's okay with you, we'd probably like to just get in the car and go back to the hotel."

The fixer rediscovered his manners. "Of course, as you wish—"

"But we'd love to try the tea first—" added Cosmo.

"You two enjoy the rooibos," said Christopher, "while I fetch the car. The parking lot is very jammed and it will take quite a while to remove. I've already paid the bill."

Before they could object, the driver had shot to his feet. He clapped Cosmo on the shoulder and left the patio. They watched him cross the boulevard to an off-street parking area that was crammed tightly with vehicles. On his approach, the attendant began shifting other vehicles.

Noah sipped the tea. "This does taste really good. I don't drink enough tea."

"I like tea," said Cosmo. He sipped from the cup. "This one is good."

"What's your favorite?" asked Noah.

"Maybe pu'er."

"That one's bitter, right?"

"Yeah. It's fermented."

"What about Earl Grey?"

"A cliché."

"I think I'm more of a fruity tea guy," said Noah.

Cosmo nodded. "Yeah, they have their charms."

"You ever try chamomile?"

"It's good for sleeping," said Cosmo, "but otherwise it's not—"

His comment was cut short by a massive fireball that erupted from the parking lot across the street.

————

In a split second, Cosmo and Noah instinctively rolled off their chairs and onto the ground beneath their table. Their eyes met. Each was filled with terror.

Then the shock of the overpressure hit. Cosmo felt the force of the blast wave hit the left side of his body. The highly compressed air rattled the left side of his skull. It even sent his lips and cheeks flapping to the right.

The initial sound of the explosion was deafening, but that was soon replaced by a symphony of falling destruction. A thousand pieces of metal, plastic, glass, and upholstery rained down upon the boulevard, the grass, the other cars.

A small shower of tiny shrapnel hit on the patio of the cafe. One hit Noah in the hand and sizzled his flesh. He shook it off.

They waited another few seconds for the shrapnel rain to end. Then Cosmo and Noah lifted their heads.

The patio of the café was transformed into pandemonium. The patrons started to pull themselves up from the ground and flee out to the street and in the opposite direction. The street itself was coming alive with panicked people running in every direction.

"What the actual—" said Noah.

"Christopher!" interrupted Cosmo. "What about Christopher?"

He scrambled up to his feet. Without waiting for Noah, he sprinted out of the café and across the boulevard, weaving through the stopped cars. The air was acrid with chemicals and the heat had somehow intensified even further.

The parking lot was a field of wreckage. The bomb had exploded in the middle of the space, shredding every vehicle and person within twenty meters. Pieces of concrete and metal and glass had been blown across the scene.

"Christopher!" he shouted again. "Christopher! Don't do this!"

He saw a shoe with a foot still in it. He saw a red string of guts entangled in a hubcap. A wave of nausea gripped his stomach. He covered his nose with his t-shirt and backed away.

He tripped backwards over a piece of metal, stumbled, and fell to the ground.

That's when he saw it.

A long strip of shredded fabric. A yellow-and-green printed tropical shirt.

It was bloody and torn.

Cosmo turned his head and retched onto the asphalt. All the tea he'd just drank came out.

He somehow pulled himself to his feet and staggered back to the café. Noah was waiting at the far corner, on the sidewalk, pacing frantically.

"So?"

"I found him," said Cosmo. He forced the next words out. "A little bit."

Noah's face went white. "Oh my God."

Cosmo didn't say anything. He just gripped Noah by the upper arm. "Walk with me. And don't look back."

———

The pair moved briskly down the boulevard, away from the scene. People were running past them, mouths open, eyes full of fear, but Cosmo maintained a steady pace. His face betrayed an intense desire to appear as normal as possible.

"So we're just going to leave the scene?" said Noah.

"Yep."

"Why?"

"Don't make me answer that, Noah."

"I think we should talk to the police, cooperate, tell them everything—"

"In a different country," Cosmo replied, "in a different scenario, you'd be right. But not here, not now."

Noah looked back over his shoulder at the scene.

"Look straight ahead," Cosmo said through his teeth, "and listen to me. Our Mercedes is gone. Christopher is ... gone."

"Shit—"

"And I'm going to suggest something else that could blow your mind."

"What?"

"It's possible that we were the intended target."

"That's insane."

"Is it?"

"How do you know?"

"I don't. But it's a possibility. Here's another one. It's possible that we are going to be used as scapegoats. We were the last people seen eating with Christopher. Do you want to be put in a Fabajouti jail on suspicion of a crime?"

They walked for another half minute in silence. Behind them, the chaos grew distant.

"Where are we going?" Noah said finally.

"Back to the hotel."

"And then?"

"We're leaving, like we planned."

"For home?"

Cosmo's mouth grew hard and his jaw jutted out. He stared straight forward at an invisible point on the horizon. "No, we're going to England."

PLOTWORKS PUBLISHING

Visit Plotworks Publishing *today* to find all these titles—and more!